
★

The shock of it must surely have followed in the instant. Even Roper, who had been looking at mutilated bodies for thirty years, still felt his stomach shrink when he had to crouch down and touch one. That kind of horror swiftly turns to panic. Murder's been done, a life taken. You still the panic. There's a mess. It's got to be cleared up. Wipe everything with blood on it, and a few other things to be sure, but missing a few spots because you are out of breath and not thinking right.

But it wasn't going to work. It rarely did. Murder was like a bad marriage. You did it in haste and sweated over it at leisure; and remembered the old adage of being sure your sins would find you out. Eventually. Somebody somewhere was sweating.

★

ROY HART
ROBBED BLIND

WORLDWIDE®

TORONTO • NEW YORK • LONDON
AMSTERDAM • PARIS • SYDNEY • HAMBURG
STOCKHOLM • ATHENS • TOKYO • MILAN
MADRID • WARSAW • BUDAPEST • AUCKLAND

ROBBED BLIND

A Worldwide Mystery/October 1998

First published by St. Martin's Press, Incorporated.

ISBN 0-373-26289-2

Printed in U.S.A.

ROBBED
BLIND

ONE

Under an Easter full moon and scudding black clouds the village of Little Crow lay in a state of faint fermentation. Murder had been done, a child had been born, an old woman had died. The driving rain had stopped a few minutes before midnight and now there was only the chill wind.

On the southern outskirts of the village, Brian Seymour belched crapulously as he fumbled his door key into the latch of Number 18 Cawnpore Terrace. Dated by its very name, Cawnpore Terrace was a mean narrow lane of run-down labourers' cottages. A motley collection of cars, many of them rust-pocked and of dubious vintage, and several of them the temporary property of Brian Seymour, were parked solidly nose to tail along each side of it under the street-lamps.

Seymour stealthily extricated his key and sidled around the edge of the door and closed it quietly behind him, keeping a tight hold of the plastic carrier bag to stop the cans of lager inside it banging against the wall. She had ears like a bat, that woman. He felt his way along the passage wall, gritting his teeth and briefly freezing as a floorboard rocked under his right foot. The place stank of damp, and mildewed carpet and yesterday's cooking and cheap scent. If his luck held, he would be out of here soon. Another town, another woman. Women had always come easily to Brian Seymour. It was the getting rid of them that was the difficult part.

His fingertips found the frame of the door to the front

room, what *she* called the lounge, then the knob of the door, his fingers curling around it and turning it; but no more than that because the switch on the landing clicked like the crack of doom and a stair creaked and he was screwing up his eyes against the sudden blaze of light.

'I suppose you know it's gone bloody midnight,' she grumbled, leaning over the banister rail.

The light still hurt his eyes and it took him a few moments to bring her into focus. This week she'd gone back to being a blonde. She was wearing her blue see-through baby-doll outfit and her fluffy mules. These days, she roused him little more than a plate of cold stew.

'Yeah, well...' he mumbled thickly, trying to sound drunker than he really was. 'Met a couple of the lads. Did a bit of business.'

'You had a phone call,' she said, still tight-mouthed. 'A bloke rang about the van.'

'Did he leave a number?'

'I told him to ring back tomorrow.'

'Yeah,' he slurred. 'Right.'

Her mood changed ominously. She flashed her tart's smile at him. 'What's in the bag? Something nice?'

'Just a couple of cans.'

'Nice,' she said. 'I could do with one of those, m'self.' She bared her teeth and rocked her behind playfully. 'We could light the gas fire in the lounge, if you like. Make a night of it, eh?'

Seymour felt his stomach lurch. After what had happened tonight, the last thing on his mind was a sweaty bout on the front room sofa with Doris Broadbent.

'I've had a Chinese,' he lied. 'It's upset the old guts a bit.'

Her face turned sour again. 'Yeah,' she said. 'I'll bet. You can bloody well sleep down there, then.'

'Yeah,' he grunted, and finished opening the door to the front room. 'I'll do that.'

He found the light switch and dumped the plastic carrier bag on one of the armchairs. In front of the gas fire, he crouched and felt around his damp pockets for matches. His hands were still trembling. First thing tomorrow, he'd have to find somewhere to ditch those keys. He had used them now just once too often.

AT ROUGHLY THE SAME TIME as Brian Seymour was letting himself into the house in Cawnpore Terrace, so was Clive Hubert, dinner-suited and trenchcoated, arriving home after an evening out. In the double garage he parked his grey Volvo beside his wife's red Metro, and he noticed, in passing, that the nearside of the Metro had a scrape along the paintwork that had not been there earlier in the evening, and that beads of moisture still clung to the roof and bonnet. The actuary in him assessed the cost of filling and respraying the door at about eighty pounds. He swung down the up and over door to the garage and crossed the gravelled drive to the cottage, shut the front door behind him and reset the burglar alarm. Unlike the house in Cawnpore Terrace, Clive and Samantha Hubert's house was a housebreaker's paradise.

The sound of glass clinking on glass greeted him as he turned into the lounge. No word passed between them. She was wearing the green robe she usually put on after a bath. He watched her several and inaccurate attempts to screw the cap back on the vodka bottle.

'Can't get enough of it, can you, old darling?' he sneered.

'Mind your own bloody business,' she retorted. She took a sip of vodka, then she returned to her armchair and stretched her legs to rest her feet on the coffee table.

'See you've bent the car again,' he said, baiting her.

'I scraped a tree,' she said. 'Some bloody dog ran out; I almost hit the bloody thing. But don't worry; I won't be asking you to pay for it.'

'Bloody right,' he said. 'I won't be. So who was it tonight? Bill Pumfrey again…or something a bit more sleazy? Back of the car job, was it?'

Her face set white and tight and hard. 'None of your bloody business,' she said. 'I don't ask where you've been and you don't ask where I've been. Okay?'

'You're a slut,' he said amiably.

'Bog off,' she said, and went back to the cabinet and began to top up her glass again.

WITH HER ABUNDANCE of hair fanned over her pillow, Sharon Moffat twitched in sybaritic dreams. She had scaled yet another rung of the social ladder tonight. There'd been a little bit of heavy breathing in the car on the way back, but she'd expected more and had been a little disappointed that he hadn't been more forthcoming. But afterwards he'd offered her a job, and he was going to pay her at least three times what she was earning at that crummy newsagent's down by the post office. All she would have to do was to put herself about a bit and smile at the customers. And later on, around the summertime, he was going to start divorce proceedings against that cow of a wife he had. The world indeed looked rosy for Sharon Moffat. She had certainly come a very long way since her days with Brian Seymour; and was going to go further yet if Sharon Moffat had anything to do with it.

A COLD AND WET PC Carter tried the stout oak doors of the Crow Hill branch of Barclays Bank, moved on a few paces and peered through the window of the post office, saw that the green light was on over the office behind the counter where the safe was. No problems there. Next door was Johnson's the newsagent's. He rattled the door, peered inside, paused briefly to scan the postcard advertisements beside the front window. PC Carter was in the market for a car, a decent second-hand one, and preferably cheap.

A card near the bottom of the display frame caught his eye. A seven-year-old Ford Escort, only one careful previous lady owner and only twenty-three thousand miles on the clock: £2,400, or nearest offer. Ring Crow Hill 0296 between seven thirty p.m. and midnight. Carter took out his pocket-book, turned to its back page and pumped a millimetre of lead from his propelling pencil. But then, tipping his notebook towards the light of the nearby street-lamp, he saw that Crow Hill 0296 was identical with the telephone number he had written down a few days ago, only the car in question then had been a Vauxhall Cavalier and it had been advertised in another newsagent's window. Also with only one careful previous lady owner and only twenty-odd thousand miles on the clock. Carter had telephoned about that one a few minutes too late. The Cavalier had been sold. Interesting, that. It might be worth looking into Crow Hill 0296. A spot of illegal on-street car-dealing, perhaps; or an even more illicit spot of what, in the jargon of the second-hand car trade, was known as 'clocking'. All was grist to a new young copper with an eye to promotion, preferably into the CID where most of the job was done in the dry.

BERNARD CRESSWELL, a whisky tumbler depending from the thumb and forefinger of each hand, crossed the hearth-rug and held one out to his wife.

She took it wordlessly, and sipped from it. 'Somebody

die again, did they?' she said, not looking at him. Her hair was damp and hung in rat-tails. He wondered if she had been out again on one of her nocturnal rambles.

'As a matter of fact, yes,' he said. He perched himself on the arm of the armchair opposite her. 'Old Mrs Bentley.'

'Convenient,' she said, with a twist to her mouth that made her look ugly.

'Convenient?'

'All your old ladies die on Friday nights,' she said spitefully. 'Or hadn't you noticed?'

'No,' he replied patiently. 'I hadn't.'

They fell to silence. She had averted her eyes again. He sipped at his whisky.

'You let the fire go out,' he said, to make conversation.

'It was getting too hot in here,' she said. 'I didn't need it.'

'It's cold outside.'

She made no reply. He let it pass. Marriage brought most couples closer together. The Cresswells it had only pushed further apart. There was very little space left now for either of them to go.

When the telephone rang she only hugged herself closer in her bagged-out woollen cardigan and stared down into the cold fire. There were times now when he hated her as passionately as he had once loved her.

He crossed the room to the telephone beside the French doors out to the garden. She hadn't even bothered to draw the curtains tonight.

'Dr Cresswell,' he said. '…Hello, Carlos.'

She had half turned and was watching him.

'What…?' he said. She saw his jaw drop, his eyebrows arch. 'Jesus,' he said softly, his eyes swivelling to meet hers across the no-man's land of carpet and furniture.

'No… No. I'll come at once… Have you called the police?… You'd better do that, just in case. I'm on my way.' Stunned, he lowered the receiver shakily back on its cradle. All the blood had drained from his face.

'That was Carlos,' he said, stumbling over the words in his shock. 'It's Stella. She's fallen down the stairs… He thinks she's dead.'

In the silence the wind muttered down the chimney and made the shrubbery stir restlessly in the garden. Then Sarah Cresswell raised her glass and slowly drained it. 'Good,' she said.

And smiled.

TWO

ROPER STUDIED each of the photographs with great care before passing it over to DI Price. They were not the best photographs he had ever seen, since they had been taken with a half-frame pocket camera and been hastily processed, but in the circumstances it was fortunate that they existed at all.

The woman lay on her face on a green rug at the foot of a flight of broad, crimson-carpeted stairs. Under her white silk dressing-robe she was naked. From her profile, even in death, it was obvious that she had been a singularly attractive woman. She was—had been—somewhere in her middle to late thirties. Blonde, perhaps tinted, her face washed of make-up in readiness for bed. At the crown of her head was a mess of blood.

Another photograph showed a gold lighter and a crumpled cigarette lying on the green rug a few feet away. So perhaps, at the head of the stairs, she had momentarily dropped her concentration as she had struck the lighter; because, if she had fallen, she had obviously begun her fall at the head of the stairs and not halfway down them, where there was another landing. Apparent proof was the embroidered white mule, depicted in another flashlit photograph, with its tiny spike of heel still hooked against the edge of the carpet on the upper landing, where she would have turned, perhaps too quickly, to start down the stairs.

The last shot showed the scene as a whole, the woman still on the floor but now with a blanket thrown over her,

the doctor who had attended her talking into a telephone
in the shadows beside the staircase, a man and a woman,
he short and moustached and in his shirt sleeves, she in
a woollen dressing-gown, both with the swarthy complex-
ion of the Mediterranean, standing arm-in-arm a few feet
from the body and looking terrified as they gave a statement to a uniformed sergeant. The light from the miniature flashgun had fallen off rapidly so that most of the
staircase was underexposed and dark, but it was clearly a
staircase of quality, carved newel posts, oak balustrades,
brass stair-rods trapping the crimson, and probably very
expensive, carpet into place. Gilt-framed pictures hung in
the shadows all around the entrance hall.

'And this arrived an hour ago,' said Chief Inspector
Lambert, whose patch this was, sliding a formal post-
mortem report across his blotter.

Body formally identified as that of Stella Elizabeth
Pumfrey, Roper read. Apparent age—the word apparent
had been obliterated with a row of typed 'x's, 37 years.
Height, 170 cms (5 feet 7 inches); weight, 57.3 kilos (126
lbs). Well nourished. White. Estimated time of death:
23.30 hours on April 1…last night; it had been the night
of Good Friday.

Marks of violence or identification: a depressed fracture
of the skull over the parietal area, approximately 3 cms
to the right of the centre line. Initially presumed to have
been caused during the subject's fall. Further examination
showed that the blow had possibly been occasioned by a
sharp and heavy instrument, triangularly prismoidal and
approximately 3.5 cms thick. Penetration had been sufficient to drive fragments of bone into the brain to a depth
of 2 cms.

Thoracic cavity…Mrs Pumfrey had been a smoker…
and a drinker. Her heart had been sound. She had eaten

a chicken sandwich, perhaps an hour before her death…
no signs of recent sexual activity.

And there had been little external evidence of her fall
down the stairs, apart from a small chip in the ulna of her
right forearm, so she must have fallen with all the exper-
tise of a judo exponent.

At the bottom of the page, under Any Further Remarks,
Roper read: Further investigation is deemed necessary in
this matter. It had been countersigned by the County Coroner.

Roper lit a contemplative cheroot and reached for an
ashtray. A lot of time had gone by, or a lot of time in-
vestigatively speaking, because it was now Easter Saturday evening at half past five and seventeen hours since
Mrs Pumfrey's manservant had found her body. Chief Inspector Lambert, in uniform, sat at one side of his desk,
Roper and Price at the other. Detective Constable Mills,
who had accompanied the uniformed sergeant to the incident, and fortuitously taken the photographs, sat
bomber-jacketed, jeaned and T-shirted between two of
Lambert's filing cabinets.

Roper picked slowly through the photographs again.
'Had she been moved, son?' he asked Mills.

'Yes, sir,' said Mills. 'When the doctor got there she
was lying on her back. He turned her over to look at the
injury.'

It would be difficult to blame the doctor in the circumstances. At the time it would have been reasonable for
him to suspect that Mrs Pumfrey had only fallen down
the stairs; especially with that mule still hooked up on the
landing carpet.

'Who called us in?' asked Roper.

'Mr González, sir. He's the one who found her.'

'And who rang for the Coroner's Officer?'

'Dr Cresswell, sir,' said Mills.

'And where did this doctor reckon the lady had struck her head?'

Mills unwound himself from his cubby-hole between the filing cabinets. He took the photographs from Roper, selected one, and with a forefinger circled a point about halfway up the right-hand newel post. 'There was blood, sir. Just there, sir.'

'Any hairs caught up in the woodwork?'

'No, sir.'

'Did you look?'

'Yes, sir. And there weren't any hairs. Just blood.'

Roper held out his hand for the photographs. Mills handed them back. He was a good-looking lad, broad-shouldered and dark-haired, and probably devastated all the girls at the local discos, but as a copper he was too young and too callow and too dangerously sure of himself.

'Mrs Pumfrey's blood?' asked Roper.

'I thought so, sir.'

'But you didn't think to take a scraping?'

Mills flushed under Roper's stare. 'No, sir. She was lying at the foot of the stairs, there was a slipper, like one she was still wearing, on the upstairs landing and blood on the newel post. And there was that lighter and cigarette—'

'Her lighter?' broke in Roper. 'Or somebody else's?'

Mills' flush darkened. He would be quick to anger, would DC Mills. 'I assumed it was hers. It was engraved. And one of the initials was hers—an S—and the other letter was B. And her husband's name is William...Bill.'

'Did anyone in the house *identify* it as hers?'

'I didn't ask. I thought—'

'You're too quick, son,' said Roper. 'You stop, you look, you listen, and you ask a lot of questions. Right?'

Mills didn't answer.

Roper's wrath subsided as quickly as it had surfaced. With any luck, young DC Mills might have learned a lesson. And, in fairness to him, the conclusions he had drawn last night had probably seemed the most logical ones at the time. No sensible copper, faced with an apparent accident that has been confirmed by a doctor, looks much further than the evidence at hand. But he should at least look thoroughly at what was at hand.

'Did you get a statement from the husband?'

'He arrived soon after the ambulance, sir. About one fifteen. He was pissed legless, sir.'

'So he was out when this all happened?'

'Yes, sir,' said Mills.

'So you haven't taken a statement off him yet?'

'No, sir,' said Mills. 'He was reeling about. Even when we left the house, I still don't think what had happened had got through to him.'

'Dave and I'll go along to see the husband this evening, Laurie,' said Roper to Chief Inspector Lambert. 'If that's all right by you.'

'Fine by me,' said Lambert. 'Frankly, the less I have to do with it the better. I've had several dealings with Mr Pumfrey. Can't say I care for the man all that much.'

Roper laid the photographs back on Lambert's desk and took up the several sheets of DC Mills' Occurrence Report.

The call from the Pumfreys' manservant had been logged in at Crow Hill police station at twenty past midnight this morning. Mills and a Sergeant Tatfield had arrived at the Pumfreys' place, Chalk House, Priory Lane, Little Crow, at twenty-five to one. Dr Cresswell, the Pumfreys' GP, had arrived some ten minutes before, at twelve twenty-five. The Coroner's Officer had arrived at a few minutes to one. The immediate conclusion had been that Mrs Pumfrey's death had been occasioned by a fall, probably terminating in her head striking a projection on the newel post. The ambulance had arrived to collect the body at one fifteen, at which time Mr Pumfrey had also arrived—in a state, somewhat rashly described in Mills' report, as one of advanced intoxication.

A verbal statement from the Pumfreys' Spanish manservant revealed little. Both he and his wife had Friday evenings off from six o'clock onward. Because of the rain they had not gone out on Friday night and had instead stayed in their room and watched the television. They had heard nothing untoward throughout the entire evening. So far as they had been aware, since Mrs Pumfrey had not asked Mrs González to prepare a meal, no important caller had been expected. According to Mr González, he had come downstairs, on his nightly duty of securing the house and switching on the burglar alarm, at twelve fifteen. Apart from the hall the remainder of the house was in darkness. He had glimpsed Mrs Pumfrey's mule on the landing, and a fraction of a second later seen her body sprawled on its back on the rug at the foot of the stairs. He had telephoned Dr Cresswell at once. Mrs Pumfrey's body had been taken to the local infirmary mortuary where her husband, by then sober, had formally identified her in company with Chief Inspector Lambert and the Coroner's Officer at half past ten this morning.

'Were there any signs of intruders?' Roper asked Mills. Mills shook his head.

He probably hadn't even looked. Roper would have thought better of him if he'd admitted it. 'Mr Pumfrey hasn't noticed anything missing?'

'He didn't mention anything of the sort to me this morning,' said Lambert.

'What sort of state was he in?' asked Roper.

'He went a bit green about the gills,' said Lambert. 'But he was surprisingly calm, in the circumstances.'

'Glad to see her out of the way, d'you think?'

Lambert shrugged. Like Roper, the Force had nurtured him from his youth to his grey hairs, and, equally with Roper, he had long ago learned never to take anything at face value. 'Who knows?' he said.

'This Little Crow,' said Roper. 'Where is it?'

'About a mile down the hill,' said Lambert. 'DC Mills can show you the way.'

IT WAS A PRECIPITOUS DRIVE from the ramparts of Crow Hill to its satellite village of Little Crow. From time to time, between the trees, Roper caught a dizzying view of mist-scarved Cranborne Chase spread out below them. But, if nothing else, it was warmer down here. Crow Hill had the reputation of being the chilliest, wettest and windiest spot in the county.

Thatched and crooked, and straight out of the tourist brochures, Little Crow appeared where the arcade of trees abruptly thinned. In the summer it would probably be awash with camera-happy visitors; on this cold spring evening it was almost desolate.

Mills turned down beside a crumbling brick wall of a graveyard littered with weather-worn tombstones and scabrous stone angels, then past the old village school; like a miniature prison and much too cramped now for its original purpose. It had been turned into an antiques gallery. Mills slowed as a higher and more purposeful wall appeared on the right-hand side of the lane, and stopped opposite an entrance framed by two massive brick piers from which a pair of tall, wrought-iron gates hung open. On the left-hand pier, incised into a stone plaque set in the brickwork, was the name of the house beyond the wall, Chalk House, which was just visible behind more trees and shrubbery in the middle distance.

'Big place by the looks of it,' said Roper, leaning forward and looking out at it through Mills's side window.

'Yes, sir,' said Mills. 'The Pumfreys aren't short of a few bob, so I've heard.'

'We'll see for ourselves, shall we?'

Mills swung the car across the road and into the driveway. The well-worn tarmacadam was breaking up and stone chippings were flung up noisily into the car's wheelarches. The house was a rambling pile of mellow grey bricks, Portland granite and sashed windows, and a tiled roof that sagged here and there as further evidence of the house's antiquity. The two or three acres of untidy front lawn were dotted with trees and flower-beds, most of the plants in the latter beaten and bedraggled by the rainstorm of last night. A red Scimitar, with current registration plates, stood parked a few yards from the front step. Mills drew in behind it.

Closer to, the house looked criminally neglected. Paint was lifting from the wooden window frames and the oak front door had already begun to split for the lack of a coat of varnish. A dark stain on the brickwork beneath a nearby window looked ominously like damp.

The man who answered Price's double rap on the iron door-knocker was the Spanish manservant Roper had seen in Mills' photograph. Slight, and nervous, he wore a black mourning brassard on the left sleeve of his grey alpaca jacket. His dark anxious eyes swept from one to the other of them before he finally decided that Roper was probably their spokesman.

'Sairs, yes, sairs?' he said.

'Superintendent Roper, sir,' said Roper, proffering his

warrant card in its plastic holder. 'County CID. I rang Mr
Pumfrey for an appointment about half an hour ago... And
this is Inspector Price...and I think you know Detective
Constable Mills.'

'Oh, yes, sair.' Dipping and bobbing, like a marionette
on inexpertly worked strings, the little butler, or whatever
he was, drew the door wider open and ushered them into
the hall. Mills' wide-angle lens had lent it a little more
grandeur than it in fact had. Some twenty feet square, and
panelled, and hung with a dozen or so pictures in baroque
gilt frames. The flight of stairs down which Mrs Pumfrey
might, just might, have fallen last night, rose straight up
some fifteen feet to a balustraded gallery that went off to
left and right, presumably to the first-floor bedrooms.
From a room off to the left of the hall came the rumble
of two male voices.

'Sair, this way.' Still dipping and bobbing, the Spaniard
led the way across the hall to the open doorway whence
the sounds of voices were coming.

Two men sat in capacious leather armchairs either side
of a blazing coal fire in a sitting-room the size of a small
barn. Both had fallen instantly to silence the moment the
butler had knocked on the door. One rose hurriedly, the
other hastily picked up a newspaper and dropped it over
a heap of papers littering one end of the coffee table.

'The policemens, sair,' said the Spaniard.

The man who had risen came forward. 'Thank you,
Carlos,' he said. 'You can shut the door on your way out.'

The manservant flitted soundlessly back to the hall. The
door closed softly behind him. The other man had risen.
A sheepskin driving coat hung over the back of his armchair; so he was probably the owner of the sleek red Scimitar parked outside.

'Pumfrey,' the first man said, advancing a few paces

with his hand extended, but letting it fall back by his side
when Roper affected not to notice. It was Roper's practice
never to shake hands with anyone whose collar he might
be feeling a few days hence. 'You're Inspector Roper, I
take it.'

'Superintendent, sir,' said Roper. He introduced Price
and Mills. If Pumfrey remembered DC Mills from last
night he showed no sign of it. Behind Pumfrey, the visitor
was stuffing a few papers into a document case and col-
lecting the sheepskin coat from the back of the armchair.

'And this is Jack Foyle,' said Pumfrey, turning towards
his departing visitor. 'My wife's solicitor.'

'Sir,' said Roper, with a nod.

'Superintendent,' said Foyle. Then to Pumfrey: 'Better
if I get out of the way, Bill. I'll get a few things sorted
out and commit them to paper. I'll probably give you a
ring tomorrow.'

'I'd be grateful, Jack,' said Pumfrey.

'Perhaps you might leave a business card with me, Mr
Foyle,' said Roper. 'I might need to contact you.'

'Yes, of course,' said Foyle. He was about thirty-five
and wearing a glaring chalk-striped grey suit with a lot of
white cuff and collar on display. Dark and hatchet-faced,
he was the epitome of the eager-beaver young solicitor
who had made the top early. 'My home number's on the
back. And my office is near the war memorial in Crow
Hill High Street.'

Roper nipped the card between two fingers. 'Thank
you, sir,' he said. He watched Foyle and Pumfrey
exchange a parting handshake. If his guess was right,
Pumfrey had been very quick off the mark to ascertain
his expectations, a guess prompted by the pocket calculator lying at the end of the coffee table where Pumfrey

had been sitting. With a nod then, Foyle was gone and
the door to the hall closing behind him.

Roper slipped Foyle's card into his wallet.

'Would you care for a cup of tea?' asked Pumfrey, in
the curt manner of a man who only has to snap his fingers
to make one appear.

'No, sir, thank you,' said Roper. Something else he
never did was to break bread or share a beaker with anybody who was likely to belong to the opposition.

'You said on the phone that you wanted to talk with
me,' said Pumfrey. 'And have a general look around.'

'If you don't mind, sir,' said Roper. 'And perhaps have
a few words afterwards with Mr and Mrs González.'

'Yes, of course,' said Pumfrey. Over the telephone he
had told Roper that there was no need for a warrant; that,
at least, was a point in his favour. He was a tall, florid,
fleshy man with wavy grey hair that looked as if he took
a lot of trouble over it. Probably in his middle fifties.
Under a thin charm he wore an air of impatient authority.

Roper sent Price and Mills off on an exploratory tour
of the house, and to look for possible signs of entry that
might have been left behind by someone last night. When
the door was closed behind them, Pumfrey gestured towards the settee, then lowered himself into the armchair
near the pocket calculator and got quickly to business. Mr
Pumfrey plainly lived his life in a hurry.

'You said that the post-mortem examination had thrown
something up,' he said.

'Yes, sir,' said Roper, as he unbuttoned his raincoat.
'A possibility. It could be nothing.' Even after thirty-odd
years he had still not developed a glib facility for telling
a man that his wife might have been murdered. 'It was
the wound, sir. It was caused by something that penetrated
deeply. Something sharp; and pointed most likely.'

Pumfrey stared back hard at him. 'For Christ's sake, man. She fell down the stairs, didn't she?'

'She might have done, sir,' said Roper. 'Except that her injuries don't quite fit the circumstances.'

'Might?' said Pumfrey, his voice taking on a rising note. 'I thought she *had*. Bernard said—'

'Who's Bernard, sir?' asked Roper, breaking in.

'My wife's sister's husband,' said Pumfrey. 'Dr Cresswell. Carlos called him as soon as he found Stella lying in the hall.'

'I see, sir,' said Roper. A husband who had been out at the time of his wife's accident and the doctor who was a close relative conspired to give him a distinct feeling of unease. Pumfrey leaned forward and plucked a cigarette from a silver casket with lion-claw feet on the coffee table. It looked an Edwardian piece. Pumfrey struck his lighter.

He blew smoke as he snapped the lighter shut again. 'So what are you saying exactly? That she *didn't* fall down the stairs?'

'I think, sir,' said Roper, 'that you ought to prepare yourself for the possibility.'

Pumfrey leaned forward again and stood the lighter on the coffee table beside the silver casket. 'Well,' he said. 'At least that's straight from the shoulder. I can only say I hope you're wrong.'

'So do I, sir,' said Roper.

A ticking wooden clock with brass facings measured the silence on the shelf above the fire. Some nice pieces of porcelain about. And handy, too, like the ornate silver casket. They tended to discount the housebreaking theory.

'When did you last see Mrs Pumfrey alive, sir?'

'Yesterday,' said Pumfrey. 'Two…three o'clock in the afternoon.'

'And you went out yourself when, sir?'

'About five,' said Pumfrey. 'Give or take.'

It was too early yet to ask Pumfrey to account for his movements last evening; at least, to ask him directly.

'Spend the evening in company, did you, sir?'

'Yes,' said Pumfrey. He flicked a cylinder of ash from his cigarette into the fire. 'I was with Lance Wainer.'

'This Mr Wainer...?'

'He runs the antiques gallery. He lives at Lime Cottage. Across the way.'

'All evening, sir?'

'I met him at eight o'clock,' said Pumfrey. 'Roughly. It was Wainer who drove me home last night. I was rather pissed, I'm afraid.'

So, if one were needed, Pumfrey had an alibi till well after the manservant's telephone call had been logged in at Crow Hill police station at twenty past midnight. But it still might be worth having a word with Mr Wainer of Lime Cottage.

'So far as you were aware, your wife was alone in the house last night, sir. Apart from Mr and Mrs González. That right?'

Pumfrey shook his head. 'I've no idea,' he said. 'We didn't make each other privy to our personal arrangements. Hadn't for some time.'

'I see, sir,' said Roper, weightily. So that's how things had stood between the Pumfreys, and why Pumfrey wasn't as distressed as Roper had expected him to be.

Another silence hung. Like the entrance hall, the room might have had an air of grandeur once; now it was faintly tatty. The chairs were well worn, the Chinese carpet threadbare in places and one or two paler rectangles around the wallpaper might have been where pictures had hung once. Foyle the solicitor hadn't quite dropped the

newspaper accurately enough to cover completely the
documents on the coffee table. Peeking out was a corner
of a foolscap-sized photocopy with half a signature and a
bit of an address showing. A copy of Mrs Pumfrey's will,
most likely. It would be interesting to know who the ben-
eficiaries were.

'Have you noticed anything missing about the house,
sir?'

'No, I haven't,' said Pumfrey. 'Perhaps I ought to look.'

'Yes, sir,' agreed Roper. 'I think that's a good idea.'

'Now?' said Pumfrey.

'I think so, don't you, sir?' For the moment there was
little more to say, and Roper needed a look around the
house himself.

Pumfrey rose with what looked like reluctance, leaned
forward and stubbed out his cigarette in a cut-glass ashtray
until the very last red spark was extinguished, and generally put out all the body signals of a man about to impart
a confidence.

'I might as well tell you before someone else does,
Superintendent,' he said, still grinding the cigarette to
fragments in the glass bowl. 'My wife and I heartily detested each other.'

Now why, Roper asked himself, had he chosen to say
that?

'Enough to kill her, sir?' he asked, throwing in the
question in the manner of a lightweight aside, and smiling
a smile sharp enough to cut a throat had Pumfrey realised
it.

Still bent over the coffee table, Pumfrey raised his face
and met Roper's eye.

'Good God, man,' he retorted. 'Of course I bloody
didn't. I wasn't within ten miles of this place last night.
Ask Wainer.'

THREE

ROPER TOOK IN the view from the topmost landing. There
were two flights, each of ten stairs, with a broad landing
between stairs ten and eleven. The stairs were wide, six
feet six inches, according to Price's tape measure. The
balustrades, like the newel posts, were of oak, and polished to the sheen of silk by a couple of centuries of use.
The faded crimson carpet was held down by old-fashioned
brass stair-rods. He dropped to his hunkers, and with a
thumb rucked aside the edge of the carpet where the mule
had been caught up. The floorboards were stained and
polished. There were no scratches; in fact it would have
been difficult to tread on the boards since they were only
visible for about two inches between the edge of the carpet and the spindles of the gallery balustrade.

He rose again. At the head of the stairs, the two pineapple finials had been worn much smoother than the two
downstairs in the hall, perhaps by people swinging around
them to start down. He could hear Pumfrey moving about
in a bedroom over on the left-hand side of the gallery.
Down in the hall Price was taking a close-up photograph
of the right-hand newel post where Mills had seen the
blood splashes in the early hours of this morning.

He moved downward, one stair at a time, checking each
width of carpet for bloodstains even though it was unlikely he would find any. The middle landing was five
feet from back to front edge; so that *if* Mrs Pumfrey had
fallen from the top landing, this one might have brought
her to a stop. It seemed to Roper that she would have

needed a great deal of momentum to overshoot it, to roll on over the edge and down the next flight. Momentum was the mathematical product of mass times velocity; and Mrs Pumfrey had not been a heavy woman, nor would she have been moving all that fast at the point of her turn off the topmost landing. The act of tripping, too, would have *reduced* her speed. And if the carving on the downstairs newel post had not caused her fatal injury, then it was even likely that she hadn't fallen, either. And given that premise, another followed; she may not have *been* upstairs in the first place.

He reached the bottom stair. The green rug that Mrs Pumfrey had been found sprawled on had been removed. The exposed crimson carpet was very nearly threadbare.

'Anything?' he said.

'It's been cleaned,' said Price. He stooped to put the camera back in the equipment case and stood upright again with a magnifying glass and a handlamp. Roper took both and examined each newel post for himself. The only really serious projections, enough to have caused a deep wound, were the square bases under the pineapple finials. They might have cracked a human skull, but they could never have penetrated it sufficiently to drive fragments of bone into the brain to a depth of very nearly an inch. And since Mrs Pumfrey's wound was near the top of her head, and only an inch or so off centre, she would have to have been virtually airborne if she had struck one. And people didn't fall from top to bottom of a flight of stairs without striking them somewhere along the way, from which point they rolled and tumbled from stair to stair—or perhaps slid on their face or back. For Mrs Pumfrey's head to have been anywhere near the top of either newel post it would have to have been some three and a half feet above the line of the stairs.

He handed back the glass and torch to Price.

'Have a good look around, Dave,' he muttered, as a bedroom door closed upstairs and a footfall started along the gallery. And to DC Mills: 'Go back to the car, son. Get patched in to HQ on the radio and tell them I want a Scene of Crime Officer here. A good one. And pronto.'

'ANYTHING MISSING, SIR?' Roper asked, as Pumfrey took the last stair down into the hall and stood between himself and Price.

'Yes,' said Pumfrey. 'Possibly.' He held out a small jeweller's box covered in faded blue leatherette. 'It was on my wife's dressing-table... Empty.'

Roper held out his hand for it and depressed the spring catch to open the lid. The empty box was lined with dark blue velveteen with two shallow depressions in it. The pair of somethings might have been earrings. The box had come originally from Cartier's in Paris; and a very long time ago, eighty, maybe even a hundred years. There was always a smell to things. In this case cedarwood and fish glue and real leather and old age.

'They could be about the house somewhere,' said Pumfrey. 'My wife had a habit of leaving things around for someone else to clear up.'

Roper noted that little hint of bitterness. 'What was in here, sir?'

'Earrings,' said Pumfrey. 'Pendants. Gold, and rose-cut garnets. My wife's grandmother's.'

'Worth?'

'A couple of thousand,' said Pumfrey. 'They were antiques.'

Mills was only gone a couple of minutes. Still bomber-jacketed and jeaned Mills looked thoroughly out of place here. Roper was of the old school who believed, in circumstances like these, in his officers looking like the public servants they were paid to be.

'Mrs Pumfrey wasn't wearing earrings last night, sir,' said Mills. 'She was only wearing a couple of rings. I gave those to Mr Pumfrey before the ambulance took her away.'

'Mrs Pumfrey had a fair bit of jewellery, did she, sir? Where did she keep it exactly?'

'She had a safe…' Roper noticed how easily Pumfrey had slipped into the past tense. 'Upstairs in her room. It's a key and combination safe. Unfortunately, she never made me aware of the combination, so I can't open it. But from the look of it I'd say it hadn't been forced.'

Fortunately, Pumfrey had photographs of all his wife's important jewellery pieces. He would look the particular photograph out; although he was still fairly certain that the earrings would be lying about the house somewhere.

'I'd be obliged, sir,' said Roper, 'if you wouldn't mind, I'd like a word now with Mr and Mrs González.'

'The kitchen,' said Pumfrey. 'You'll find the door immediately under the stairs.'

They were in there together. She was cutting sandwiches, and her husband was brewing a pot of tea and laying out china on a tea-trolley. They both looked anxiously towards the open doorway as Roper tapped lightly on the door and took the single step down into the kitchen. A puff of wind would have blown González over. His wife was slightly shorter, but probably three times his weight. She still bore traces of an earlier handsomeness. The back of the house looked out on to more shrubbery and trees. Dusk was already turning to darkness.

Roper said, 'I'd like a few words with you and your wife, Mr González; if you're not too busy.'

'Sí, yes, sair.' Like a scurrying mouse, González scut-

tled around the table and drew out a chair. 'I take Mr
Pumfrey tea first, sair; yes, sair?'

'Yes, sir, you do that,' said Roper.

With half an eye on Roper as he seated himself at her
table, Mrs González finished quartering her sandwiches
while her husband completed the arrangement of the tea-
trolley.

'Do you speak English, Mrs González?' Roper asked
encouragingly as he took out his pocket-book. So far, she
hadn't uttered a sound.

She glanced questioningly across at her husband.

'Not good,' said González. 'But she understand good.
You speak slowly, she understand very good.'

Roper smiled at her and generally tried to signal good-
will. They might, either or both of them, be murderers;
but somehow he doubted it. They were both too nervous,
and taking no pains to hide it.

'Have you been working for Mr and Mrs Pumfrey very
long, Mrs González?' he said, enunciating each word
carefully. 'One year? Two?'

'T'ree month,' she said, after a moment. Her husband
came around the table and took the plate of cut sandwiches from in front of her. She watched them go with
an expression of loss, still holding the knife as if she no
longer knew what to do with it.

'Why don't you sit down, too, Mrs González.'

Her husband gabbled something at her in Spanish, and
reluctantly she drew a kitchen chair closer and lowered
herself gingerly on to it. She glanced warily at Roper as
he opened his pocket-book on the table and pumped at
his ballpoint.

'Did you make a sandwich for Mrs Pumfrey last night,
Mrs González?' asked Roper.

She shook her head.

'Mrs Pumfrey make her own food on Friday nights,' said González. He was poised to wheel the tea-trolley away. 'Unless she have visitors. Mrs Pumfrey very kind lady.' He spoke to his wife again in Spanish. She nodded at him and looked at last slightly reassured. 'I tell her I come back quickly,' he said to Roper. She watched his every step to the door, much as she had watched the sand-wiches go.

'You liked Mrs Pumfrey, too, Mrs González?' Roper asked her, when González had gone.

She nodded earnestly.

'And Mr Pumfrey?'

Stony silence. It spoke volumes.

'Are there children here?'

She shook her head.

Roper tried the sandwich tack again. 'Last night, Mrs González, Mrs Pumfrey ate a sandwich. Chicken. Did you hear her in the kitchen?'

'Not hear,' she said. 'But on TV…' She pronounced it 'tivvy' and it took Roper a second or two to work out what that was.

'On the television?'

'Sí,' she said. 'Yes.' Her left hand rose and she fluttered her fingers. 'On the tivvy… Lights; you understand? The knife.'

'I'm sorry…' said Roper, still puzzled. But she was on her feet. From a bracket on the wall near the sink, she took down an elderly electric carving knife and mimed depressing the switch on the handle and making down-ward cutting motions. 'Electric knife. Always same. On tivvy. Very old knife.'

In a flash of inspiration, Roper realised that she was trying to tell him that when the knife was being used it interfered with the television picture in her room.

'I understand,' he said. 'It makes spots on your TV. Yes?'

She nodded eagerly, immensely relieved, it seemed, to have arrived so easily at such a complicated phenomenon to which her English would never have stretched.

'Do you know what time that was, Mrs González?'

She couldn't remember. But her husband could, when he came back. 'It was football. On the television. Goal come...then picture go all...' It seemed, as with spiral staircases, that television interference was better described with hands. The little clock on the television screen showed that the goal had been scored in the thirty-first minute of play; which, since the programme had started at nine thirty, would have made it a minute after ten o'clock. Which was about right. The pathologist's report had stated that Mrs Pumfrey had probably died around half past eleven last night, and eaten a chicken sandwich perhaps an hour or so before that. So at least the approximate time of death was whittled closer.

'Did you hear Mrs Pumfrey moving about at all last evening?'

Both shook their heads.

'Did she go out?'

'No,' said González. 'When she go out and Mr Pumfrey not home, she always tell us.'

'But Mr Pumfrey, he *was* out?'

'*Sí*, yes,' said González. To the best of his memory Pumfrey had gone out soon after five o'clock last night. Their room overlooked the double garage at the back of the house. They had heard his car start.

'Mr Pumfrey didn't come back at all; at any time during the evening?'

Both shook their heads, although both admitted that they could not be certain. Their room was in the roof

gables, the tivvy had been switched on all evening, and
of course the rain had made much noise last night, especially on the roof. If Mr Pumfrey had entered the house,
using his key, they would not have heard, nor if Mrs Pumfrey had let anyone in, because they would not have heard
the doorbell or the knocker over the noise of the television. And because they had been off duty, they had had
no need to listen out for anything.

'Would any windows or outside doors have been open
or unlocked last night, Mr González?'

'*Sí*, yes, sair.' González nodded with fervour. 'Mrs
Pumfrey always have window open. Even in winter. Mr
Pumfrey say draught; but Mrs Pumfrey say fresh air.'

'And the alarms were switched off?'

'Yes, sair. With windows open alarm ring.'

'If the alarms had been switched on before Mr Pumfrey
had arrived home; what would have happened then?'

'There is a wait, sair. One minute. And a switch in the
hall.'

'A reset switch?'

'Yes, sair. For coming in and going out late. To stop
bell ringing.'

It was becoming clearer by the minute that practically
anyone could have entered the house last night without
too much trouble. Alternatively, of course, Mrs Pumfrey
could have let someone in, someone she knew.

'Did Mrs Pumfrey have many friends? People who
called here?'

'Yes, sair,' said González.

Mrs Wainer, the wife of the man who had driven Pumfrey home last night; Mrs Hubert, who again lived in this
same lane. These were the most frequent callers. But it
was a small community. Everyone knew each other. When

Mr Pumfrey was working up in London, Mrs Pumfrey kept an open house.

'TELL ME about Mrs Pumfrey.'

It was Mrs González who answered. 'She was very *lonely* lady,' she said. 'Carlos tell you same. Mrs Pumfrey very good to us.'

Roper glanced across at González. He nodded. 'Yes, sair,' he said, sadly and reluctantly. 'Sometimes I go out for whisky for her. So Mr Pumfrey don't know how much she drink.'

Roper's ears pricked. From what Mr and Mrs González had heard, it seemed that Mrs Pumfrey had taken to the bottle seriously just after last Christmas. Before that she had drunk only moderately.

'Did anything in particular happen about then?' asked Roper.

They both shrugged. They didn't know. They had not been working here then. Roper made a note to find out. Someone would know, perhaps Mrs Hubert or Mrs Wainer, or Mrs Pumfrey's sister, or her doctor husband. One of the traits of lonely humankind is that when it does find a willing ear to bend it talks a very great deal.

'There was a green rug at the foot of the stairs,' said Roper.

'*Sí*,' said González. 'Mrs Pumfrey tell me to put it there. She keep catching her shoe in the stair carpet at the bottom. Once she fall over.'

'That rug, Mr González; where is it now?'

'Mr Pumfrey tell me to put it in dustbin,' said González. 'I put it in plastic bag and tie up.'

'When?' asked Roper.

'After policemans had gone last night, sair,' said González. 'Mr Pumfrey say to me to clear up mess.'

'*Bloody* mess,' broke in Mrs González. She showed a

momentary spirited anger. 'Mr Pumfrey say to Carlos: Get rid of that bloody mess, for Chris'sake, it making place untidy. And you better bloody do it now.' The little outburst left her breathless and flushed and embarrassed. 'I am sorry,' she said, dropping her gaze to her lap where her hands were. 'But that is what Mr Pumfrey say to Carlos.'

González nodded unhappily. 'But you do not tell Mr Pumfrey we tell you this. He get very angry very quick.'

Roper had already read that between the lines. 'So you can lay your hands on this rug, Mr González?'

'*Sí*, yes, sair… I fetch now.' He shot to his feet so enthusiastically that his chair all but fell over. He unlocked the outside door and went out into the dark garden. There was a metallic clatter as he took the lid off a dustbin.

'There should have been a new carpet on stairs,' ventured Mrs González, gathering her courage at last. 'Two times I repair. But Mr Pumfrey buy nothing. She have to buy *everything*. When she ask him for things, he say: Your bloody house, you buy bloody things for it. I know. I hear. I do not say much…but I hear.'

Roper's ears had pricked again. 'So this isn't Mr Pumfrey's house?'

She shook her head. 'He marry to it. House is mother's and grandmother's of Mrs Pumfrey. They dead now.'

Which was a motive if ever Roper had heard one. Despite its run-down state, the house, on the open market, would fetch the best part of a million, perhaps more with the several acres of secluded land that surrounded it.

'So Mrs Pumfrey had all the money, did she, Mrs González?'

'*Sí*. And she *keep* it, too. From him. I hear.' She tapped her ear. 'Many times.'

The door to the garden was opened again and González staggered in hugging a black plastic rubbish bag with a roll of sopping wet green rug sticking out of the top of it. He dumped it down by Roper's feet.

It looked a fairly new rug. Thickly piled. Pale green. Probably a mixture of wool and nylon. There were no bloodstains on the wet, rolled end that showed.

'You didn't rinse the blood off?'

González shook his head. 'No, sair. Mr Pumfrey make me too quick to put it outside. I only scrub stair-post to get blood off.'

Well, that was something. Given a little luck, the forensic laboratory might find a pointer or two when they unrolled the rug.

A rap on the door out to the hall preceded the entry of Price. He was holding a small plastic evidence bag.

Roper held out his hand for it. 'What is it?'

'Contact lens,' said Price, as Roper took it from him and held it up to the kitchen light.

Not much larger than a little fingernail, it was easier felt through the plastic than seen. It felt vaguely rubbery, like a jelly.

'Where did you find it?'

'On the bedroom floor, under one of the castors of the dressing-table,' said Price.

'Just the one?'

Price nodded.

'Did Mrs Pumfrey wear contact lenses?' asked Roper, of Mrs González.

'Sí,' she confirmed, nodding. 'Always. She could not see without them. She only take them off to go to bed.'

Which, from her attire when she had been found, Mrs Pumfrey had been on the point of doing. And since the post-mortem report had not mentioned the finding of another contact lens, the other one had to be in the house somewhere. According to Mrs González, both lenses, and a spare set, together with their cleaning materials, had been kept by Mrs Pumfrey in the top left-hand drawer of her dressing-table.

Roper held the plastic envelope up to the light again. There were three ways a contact lens might be removed: by being taken out in the normal course of events, by falling out...

And being dislodged by a fall. Or a violent blow to the skull.

And perhaps not at the foot of the stairs; but upstairs.

In the bedroom, by the dressing-table.

FOUR

WITH AN ARC of white plastic tape on the carpet around him to show where he had already been, the Scene of Crime Officer, with a quartz halogen handlamp and magnifying glass, was quartering Mrs Pumfrey's bedroom floor. Roper watched him, going deeper into the room himself as the arc of white tape grew longer. It was half past seven, still Saturday evening.

Every step of the way so far, thanks to Mrs Pumfrey's doctor and DC Mills, the investigation had been bungled. A trail, if there had ever been one, had grown cold. The only small mercy was that no housework was ever done here at weekends, except in the kitchen. Both Mr and Mrs González had said that they had not been in Mrs Pumfrey's bedroom since Good Friday lunchtime, when Mrs González had gone around with the vacuum cleaner and he had cleaned the insides of the windows and polished the mirror and glass top of the dressing-table.

It was a large airy room, with two small bay windows, one each side of the dressing-table, on the opposite side of the room from the door, and one larger bay window looking out over the gardens at the back of the house. As Roper stood, a few paces inside the doorway, the bed was between himself and the main bay window. The dressing-table was opposite him and slightly to his right, more or less in line with the foot of the bed. The bed was made up, and neat. So, since Mrs Pumfrey had been naked under her dressing-robe, perhaps she had just been going to have a bath—or had just come from it. Green velvet

drapes, fringed and slightly theatrical, would have closed
off the bays at night and made the room cosy.

It was plainly a woman's room, perhaps even a sanc-
tuary, for there were two chintzy armchairs either side of
a gas fire in the hearth, a small coffee table, a bookcase
and a portable television set. The rest of the house had a
fusty, Edwardian ambience. This was fresh and white and
bright. The glass top of the dressing-table was littered
with bric-à-brac: hairbrushes, a comb wedged in the bris-
tles of one of them, several bottles of perfume, none of
them cheap, what looked like an updated version of an
artist's water-colour box and which probably contained
make-up materials, two nineteenth-century cylindrical
vases of soapstone porcelain, probably Worcester, but
both too frail to be used as bludgeons; and anyway, their
shape wasn't right. An ashtray with half a dozen hairpins
in it—but that was of cut lead crystal and shaped like a
boat with two blunt ends.

There came a grunt from the SOCO.

'Found something?' asked Roper.

The SOCO was kneeling upright and shining his handlamp over whatever lay on the floor ahead of him in front
of the dressing-table. 'Now there's a thing,' he said. He
lifted his reading glasses up into his hair. 'There's a rug
here that looks a dead ringer for the one downstairs in
that bag… Watch where you tread.'

Roper moved up to the foot of the bed and looked over
the SOCO's shoulder.

It was, indeed, a dead ringer: colour for colour and pile
for pile. Whether it was also size for size and shape for
shape and therefore identical was as yet impossible to say,
since the one in the bag downstairs would stay wrapped
up until the boffins across at the forensic laboratory had
had a good look at it. And perhaps this rug too, because

suddenly a possible scenario had sprung into Roper's
mind and once lodged there wouldn't go away again.

'Mills,' he called loudly.

Mills' footfalls thudded around the gallery. He came at
the run and stopped short at the doorway with both hands
gripping the frame.

'Sir?'

'Get Mrs González up here, son. And try not to frighten
her.'

'Right.' Mills' trainers sounded as if they were bound-
ing down the stairs three or four at a time. There came
another resounding thud as he landed in the hall, then a
squeak of rubber on parquet as he turned for the kitchen.
He was too fast in every way was DC Mills, Roper decided. If he'd spent a few more minutes last night in quiet
contemplation and observation of the scene downstairs,
and perhaps even looked around up here, he might not
have allowed Dr Cresswell to coerce him into that precipitate conclusion.

Mills and Mrs González came back together. Mrs González was clearly built for perpetuity rather than swift action. She was breathing heavily after her climb up the
stairs.

'It's all right, Mills,' said Roper. 'You can go back to
Inspector Price…and Mills…'

'Sir?'

'Walk, son. You'll think better.'

Mills' young and unused face flushed darkly again.
'Yes, sir,' he said, waited a moment then turned and went
back to join Price on the other side of the gallery.

Roper waited for Mrs González to get her breath back.
'I need your help, Mrs González,' he said.

'*Sí?*'

'There's a rug here, Mrs González.' Roper beckoned

her to the foot of the bed. She came anxiously, almost as if she expected to see another body lying on it.

Roper pointed down at the rug between the end of the bed and the dressing-table. 'That one.'

She nodded. *'Sí.'*

'Is it like the one in the bag downstairs, Mrs González?'

'Sí,' she said, nodding again. 'Is same.'

'Same? How…same?'

Her forehead corrugated as she hunted for the right words among her sparse vocabulary.

'Is same,' she said. 'Mrs Pumfrey buy two…two same.' She held up two fingers. 'Two same, like this one.'

'One for upstairs and one for downstairs?'

She shook her head. 'For here,' she said. 'Two for here. For bedroom. One here.' She pointed to the one at Roper's feet. 'And one for bed.' She turned slightly and pointed to a spot on the carpet on the door side of the bed where the SOCO had already been.

'But that one is gone,' said Roper. 'The one beside the bed. Yes?'

'Sí,' she agreed, nodding. 'Gone. Is downstairs. Mrs Pumfrey say to Carlos to take it down when she catch shoe. So Carlos take it down and put on carpet to cover holes.'

'Did they ever get changed over?' Roper held out his hands, crossed them at the wrists, then uncrossed them and crossed them the other way again to show her what he meant. 'This one go downstairs and the one downstairs come up?'

She shook her head. 'One downstairs have marks… coffee.'

'Coffee stains?'

She nodded eagerly. She always seemed to become irrationally pleased whenever she and Roper got on the same wavelength. 'Mrs Pumfrey drop coffee. Carlos try to take out mark…with bleach.' She shrugged at the domestic inadequacy of the human male. 'Make worse.'

Then the SOCO said casually, 'There's a stain on this one too, Super,' and switched on his handlamp and aimed its bright white beam at the edge of the rug nearest the bed.

There was a greyish-brown stain, about the diameter of a teacup, and several smaller stains dotted around it. The large stain had a pale halo around it which might have been caused by a bleaching agent.

'*No.*' Mrs González was shaking her head insistently. 'No. This not from up here.' She pointed down at the rug. 'This from *downstairs*.'

'You're sure about that, Mrs González?'

'*Sí,*' she said, nodding furiously now. 'I sure. This one from *downstairs*. The one up here…no coffee…no mark. Is clean.'

And that was the moment when Roper became even surer that Mrs Pumfrey had been killed *upstairs* after all. And if she had been, then she could have been rolled up in the rug and either carried or slid down to the bottom of the stairs with the two Spaniards, high up in the fastness of the roof gables, not hearing a thing except their television. The two green rugs then changed over. It would not have been difficult. It was certainly imaginative, but not difficult. It also meant that whoever had killed Mrs Pumfrey must have known the layout of the house uncommonly well to have been aware of the similarity between the two rugs. And perhaps even to have known that there was little likelihood of their being disturbed on a Friday night.

Mrs González was adamant. Her English might have tended towards the pidgin but she was certain about the

two green rugs. She knew every carpet and rug in the
house as well as she knew her own children. She, or her
husband, vacuum-cleaned each of them twice a week,
three times some of them, and the carpet and rug in Mrs
Pumfrey's bedroom every day, except at weekends. The
stained green rug had been demoted to the foot of the
stairs after Mrs Pumfrey had caught her heel in the crimson carpet a month or so ago. The unstained one had
stayed up here. In front of the dressing-table where the
stained one now was.

'You say that Mrs Pumfrey kept her contact lenses in
the dressing-table, Mrs González?'

'*Sí,*' she said, pointing to the top left-hand drawer.
'*Ahí.*'

Roper snapped on a pair of latex gloves and drew the
drawer open a few inches. Close to the front, and prominent, were two identical contact lens cases in white plastic. They had been crudely numbered 1 and 2 in red nail
varnish on their lids, as if she perhaps wore them on alternate days and needed to differentiate between the in-
dividual pairs. One contained a pair of lenses; the other
was empty. Both sets of recesses were engraved L and R.

According to Mrs González, Mrs Pumfrey was practically blind without her contact lenses. And contact lenses
weren't exactly cheap. Assuming that one had dropped
out on to the carpet, would not Mrs Pumfrey have popped
the matching lens from the other box into her eye to look
for the lost one before she trod on it, or perhaps even
replaced both lenses with the pair from the second box,
since the dropped lens would have to be cleaned before
it ever went back in her eye and she wouldn't have wanted
to mix up the pairs?

And that question begged another.

Would Mrs Pumfrey, visually incapacitated by at least

fifty per cent, have gone down a half-dark staircase wearing only one contact lens, when a replacement was so close at hand?

Well, yes, she might have done. Even in the dark, the stairs would have been familiar. Someone might have rung the doorbell, someone she might have been expecting. She had had, according to the pathologist, the equivalent of two single Scotches in the immediate hours prior to her death. They might have made her a little careless.

Roper made a note of the optician's name and address, stuck on the little gold labels inside the lids of both cases. It might be useful to know exactly how inadequate Mrs Pumfrey's eyesight had been.

He put the two plastic boxes back in the drawer.

'I'd like you to do something for me, Mrs González,' he said.

'Sí?' She seemed more than glad to help out now that she had got to know him, and perhaps because she had genuinely liked Mrs Pumfrey and saw in Roper someone who looked as if he were determined to get to the bottom of things.

'You know this room well, Mrs González?'

'Sí.' She nodded. 'Everything in here, I know; I clean.'

'Good,' said Roper. 'Now I want you to stand just where you are, and have a good look around. Take your time. I want to know if anything has gone from here. You understand?'

'Sí,' she said. 'I understand.' She solemnly closed her eyes for a few moments, presumably to compose herself, then opened them again as she turned to face the doorway. She slowly revolved then in a series of little shuffling movements, plainly taking to heart that Roper had told her to stay exactly where she was.

She had turned through a semi-circle and was facing

the window to the left of the dressing-table when she suddenly flung up an arm with a pointing finger at the end of it and cried triumphantly, '*Ahí!*... There!' And before Roper could stop her she had stepped over the boundary of white tape and into the bay recess and was stabbing excitedly at the window-sill. 'Here,' she said. 'Was here. Is gone...ashtray. On window. You understand...?'

There was a circular cork coaster where she was pointing to on the window-ledge; clearly it had been put there for something to stand on.

'You haven't taken it downstairs...or your husband?'

She shook her head to both. It was not an ashtray easily hidden or overlooked. If the square she drew in the air with both hands was anything near the right size it was a monument of an ashtray, a foot or so square; and even then, when Roper managed to dampen her enthusiasm, she refused to hold her hands nearer than eight inches from each other. She was very sure. And thick it was so: the tips of her thumb and forefinger demonstrated a depth of some two inches.

'So it was heavy?'

'*Sí.* Ver' heavy.' She mimed lifting it to show how weighty it had been.

Roper drew her back over the tape and sat her on the edge of the bed and gave her his pocket-book and ball-point.

'You draw it for me, Mrs González? Make a picture?'

'Not good.'

'Try,' he said.

She drew a shaky square, with a circle in the middle of it, and a pair of lines going from each outer corner to the circle to represent the depressions where a cigarette would be laid. Persuading her to draw a side elevation was a little more difficult. Roper drew a rectangle. She

shook her head and took back the ballpoint and turned
the uprights of the rectangle into chamfered slopes. It was
so. Smaller at the bottom than it was at the top. And it
wasn't *cut* glass like the one on the dressing-table. It was
uniforme—smooth. Mrs Pumfrey read in bed at night—
Mrs González mimed an open book with the palms of her
hands—and smoked cigarettes. Last thing, before she
turned out the lights, the ashtray was taken to the window-
ledge and put behind the closed curtains whence Mrs
González took it in the mornings to empty it. And now
that ashtray was not here, but only the cork coaster upon
which it stood until Mrs Pumfrey put it on her bedside
cabinet each night. Nor was it on the cabinet now, or
anywhere else in the room by the looks of it.

Which made Roper more certain than ever that Mrs
Pumfrey had been killed up here in her bedroom. The rug
that was now downstairs had been taken from up here.
One of Mrs Pumfrey's contact lenses had been found under the dressing-table. And the ashtray, a particularly
heavy ashtray, any corner of which would have been not
only sharp but triangularly prismoidal, could have caused
the kind of indented fracture of the skull that had killed
Mrs Pumfrey. And, empty on the dressing-table, had been
a jeweller's box that had once contained a pair of valuable
earrings.

'Do you know where the safe is, Mrs González?'

'*Sí*...is there.'

And that, too, was only a couple of paces away, built
into the floor under the window and scarcely hidden under
a flap of carpet, and a rectangle of plywood to stop the
carpet collapsing into the recess of the combination dial.
The door showed no signs of having been forced. As safes
went, it wasn't much of one. A good thief with his wits
about him could have levered the little contraption from

out between the joists with only a case opener and a little determination, and carried it away without a great deal of trouble. If the job had been done properly, it might be several days before someone noticed the safe missing, let alone the jewellery in it.

ROPER WAS BACK in the kitchen. Beside him was a cup of tea that Mrs González had pressed on him, in his hands was the cigarette lighter that had been found last night on the rug beside Mrs Pumfrey at the foot of the stairs. It was a Colibri, made in Italy, gold-plated, a man's lighter rather than a woman's. Engraved into an embossed rectangle on one side was a heart struck through with a Cupid's arrow and the letters S and B intertwined with the ends of the arrow either side of the heart.

It didn't feel right. It didn't fit in with the smart clothes that Mrs González had shown him upstairs in Mrs Pumfrey's wardrobe. It was a good lighter, but not an expensive one, and Mrs Pumfrey's tastes had clearly been expensive if her clothes were anything to go by. And the Cupid's dart and the initials, they were just a mite too chichi. Assuming that William Pumfrey was Bill, and Mrs Pumfrey Stella, and that they were giver and recipient, or vice versa, of the lighter, was logical enough on the face of things. Except that, from what Roper had so far gleaned about the pair of them, theirs was not the kind of marriage which was likely to revolve around romantic gestures. Pumfrey would never have bought this lighter and had it so engraved. And if he had been the recipient he would probably have discarded it at the first opportunity.

Roper took a token sip of the tea.

'Had you seen this lighter before last night, Mr González?'

González shook his head. So did his wife. Not that that

meant the lighter wasn't Mrs Pumfrey's. It might have been given to her by someone else and kept out of sight in her handbag where her husband was unlikely to find it. A woman who was unlikely to succumb to a romantic gesture from her husband was highly likely to succumb to another from elsewhere, or make one of her own, again elsewhere. Or perhaps it wasn't Mrs Pumfrey's at all. Perhaps somewhere else there was another S and another B and one or other of them had visited the house and left it behind and Mrs Pumfrey had only used it because it was the nearest one to hand.

'You gave it to Mr Pumfrey last night?'

'Yes, sair,' said González. 'He say it no his. He look and give it back and say t'row it away with the rug.'

Roper dropped it into an evidence bag to take away with him. With evidence so thin on the ground he could afford to disregard nothing, even a lighter with probably a dozen sets of fingerprints on it, none of which might be even remotely significant.

Then he recalled the earlier conversation he had had in the kitchen, and only now realised that something had not been quite right about it.

'Mrs Pumfrey has a sister, yes?' he asked.

Mrs González nodded. 'She live across street.'

'When we talked about Mrs Pumfrey's visitors…' He paused to let Mrs González catch up with him. '…you did not mention her…you did not say her name. Why was that?'

She lifted her broad shoulders and let them fall again. 'She is doctor's wife… But she *never* come here.'

'Never?'

'Not since we are here, sair,' said González. 'We have seen her only in the street. She never speak, never smile.

Nothing.' He, too, shrugged at the strangeness of Mrs Cresswell.

Price came down the single step from the hall.

'Anything?' asked Roper.

'Not a thing,' said Price. 'And this place is about as impregnable as a paper bag with the alarms switched off.' The door and window locks downstairs were all new but all of the upstairs windows could be opened with nothing more sophisticated than a table-knife. And there were at least three rooms upstairs where a breaker could have gained entry without even a ladder.

'But they didn't?'

'I don't think so,' said Price. There was no disturbed dust on any of the window-sills and no muddy marks on the carpets beneath them. And few housebreakers were given to clearing up after themselves. And it had rained so heavily last evening that the surrounding grounds were a morass.

'So what do we do now?' said Price.

'Mills can stay here with the Scene of Crime man,' said Roper. 'We'll drive over and see Dr Cresswell.'

Who, if nothing else, was probably guilty of making a gross professional misjudgement last night. And whose wife had not crossed the lane in the last three months to visit her late sister. There had to be something odd about that.

FIVE

PRICE LOCKED THE CAR and joined Roper on the grass
verge outside Dr Cresswell's thatched, ivy-clad and white-
stuccoed cottage. The wind had strengthened with the
dark. It blustered along the lane and made it feel like
winter all over again. There was rain in the air too.

Roper pushed open the front gate and started up the
path. On the left, in front of a closed garage, stood a red
Toyota with a DOCTOR sticker plastered at the top of
the windscreen. Under the porch, a coach lamp lit a
wooden plate labelled SURGERY and Cresswell's brass
professional plate a few inches below it. The three steps
down from the porch were fitted with a galvanised tubular
handrail, presumably for the benefit of Cresswell's older
patients. Over on the right was a brand-new brick exten-
sion that was probably a surgery.

Price bowed a thumb against the bellpush. The bark of
a distant fox was carried on the wind, and another, closer
to hand, replied to it.

The door was opened just far enough for the bedrag-
gled-haired woman who had answered Price's summons
to peer around the edge of it. 'I'm sorry,' she said curtly.
'The surgery is shut.'

The door would also have been if Price hadn't pressed
the flat of his hand against it.

'Detective Superintendent Roper, madam. County
CID.' Roper held out his warrant card. 'I rang Dr Cresswell earlier. And this is Inspector Price.'

She scarcely looked at the card. 'You'd better come in

then, hadn't you,' she said, and grudgingly opened the door wider.

She watched them wipe their shoes on the doormat. She was somewhere in her middle thirties, drab and slovenly. Roper presumed that she was someone Cresswell had in to clean the surgery after hours. He would certainly never have employed her as a receptionist.

'He's along there,' she said, with a jerk of her head towards the end of the passage.

'Thank you,' said Roper. His encouraging smile met no response. 'Mrs Cresswell about too, is she?'

'I am Mrs Cresswell,' she said dully, to his mild surprise. She certainly didn't look the part, even given that it was a weekend and a woman was entitled to slop about in old clothes in her own house if the fancy took her. But then shock took different people different ways, so perhaps that was it, and accounted for the vague, listless expression she wore and the shabby clothes that looked as if she had bought them second-hand at a church bazaar. He had hoped to talk to her as well as her husband this evening, but had the distinct feeling that he might as well talk to a dummy in a shop window. Perhaps tomorrow. Another twenty-four hours might see her over the worst of it.

She lifted curiously bright, glittering eyes. 'They're saying she might have been murdered,' she said. 'Stella.'

'Yes, it looks likely, Mrs Cresswell,' said Roper sympathetically. 'I'm deeply sorry.'

She shrugged, a gesture of the kind that says: Oh, well, it can't be helped, can it? and shuffled off back along the hall in her carpet slippers. Roper thought that she was leading the way to wherever Cresswell was, but she turned into a room on the left and more or less closed the door of it in his face.

Price hoisted a surprised eyebrow.

Roper turned. The door behind him was marked WAIT-ING ROOM. 'Try in there.'

Price led the way in. The room was newly decorated, a dozen steel-framed chairs ranged around the walls and a battered cherrywood dining-table in the middle of it stacked with magazines and children's books.

The door facing them, glass-panelled and with light showing through the slats of a venetian blind behind it, looked likely. Roper tapped on it.

'Come in,' a male voice called from the other side.

Cresswell was at his drug cupboard and topping up his visiting box. He glanced at his watch like a man rushing for his train. 'Great God,' he said. 'I'm sorry… I don't know where the time goes. Superintendent Roper, is it?'

'Yes, sir.' Roper showed his card again. 'And this is Inspector Price.'

Cresswell gave the card a passing glance and handed it back again. He was in his shirt sleeves, the jacket of his working suit hung over the back of the executive swivel chair behind his desk. Slim, grave and fortyish, he more than made up for his wife's lack of style.

Briskly he arranged a chair at the front of his desk and drew another away from beneath the window for Price.

'Please,' he said, with a businesslike flap of his hands towards the two chairs as he dropped into his own.

He steepled his fingers under his chin as Roper and Price settled themselves and unbuttoned their raincoats. As Price took out his pocket-book, Cresswell said, 'You just beat the County Coroner by a short head, Superinten-dent.'

'How's that, sir?'

'Five minutes after you rang, he did… Apparently he'd been trying to get hold of me all day. I felt the winds of his displeasure. Which is, I presume, the reason why you gentlemen are here?'

'Yes, sir, regrettably,' said Roper. 'The post-mortem on Mrs Pumfrey threw up a few anomalies. We've been asked to make a few more enquiries. And there's to be another post-mortem. A Home Office man. Tomorrow.'

It seemed to take a while for Cresswell to come to terms with that. 'I see,' he said, solemnly, momentarily dropping his hands to draw his blotting-paper closer to him, then lifting them again. 'It all seemed very cut and dried to me. Stella had fallen down the stairs and fractured her skull on the newel post at the bottom. There was blood on the post and one of her slippers hooked on the carpet on the upstairs landing. All the signs were right.' His hands briefly parted company to show how final and straightforward had been his diagnosis at the time. 'I saw no point in seeing the accident any other way.'

'No, sir,' agreed Roper. 'You wouldn't have.' But you should have, he thought. Like DC Mills, Dr Cresswell had been a touch too quick off the mark last night. 'You took a good look at the injury to Mrs Pumfrey's head, did you, Doctor?'

'Yes, I did,' said Cresswell. 'I saw a depressed fracture.'

'The shape didn't strike you as perhaps not quite right? And it was a very deep wound, sir.'

Cresswell seemed to lose a little of his assuredness. 'No. To be honest, it didn't. But then I wasn't looking for what you people call a suspicious circumstance.'

'Whatever caused Mrs Pumfrey's injury had a sharp corner, sir. Like the top of a pyramid…with three sides. Probably heavy. There was no projection like that on either of the two downstairs newel posts, you see, sir, so we're considering a weapon of some kind. Something makeshift. An ashtray. Something of that sort.'

'My God,' said Cresswell, now plainly distressed. His hands had fallen to his lap. 'How bloody—bloody awful.'

'We haven't come across anything conclusive as yet,' said Roper. 'But Inspector Price here found one of Mrs Pumfrey's contact lenses under the dressing-table in her bedroom. And the rug that she was lying on when you saw her wasn't the one that was usually downstairs. They'd been changed over. Some time after Friday lunch-time. The body might have been moved before you saw it.' He paused to let Cresswell work out the further implications for himself. 'Just a theory, sir.'

Cresswell had slumped back in his chair. 'I should have noticed,' he said. 'That's to say I did notice, but it didn't strike me as unusual at the time…she wasn't wearing her lenses… It should have occurred to me… I looked into her eyes, too…'

'So she wasn't wearing either lens?'

Cresswell shook his head. 'No,' he said. 'I'm certain.'

'And there's a glass ashtray missing from Mrs Pumfrey's bedroom,' said Roper. He held the palms of his hands some eight inches apart as Mrs González had done. 'Pretty hefty. So big.'

Cresswell shuddered. 'Please,' he said. 'I'd rather not know how. Who the hell would want to do that to Stella?'

Roper doubted that anyone had *wanted* to. It had simply happened; in the heat of the moment, as the cliché had it.

'When you examined her last night, Doctor, any idea how long she might have been dead?'

'Difficult to say,' said Cresswell, frowning. 'That wasn't my most immediate concern. The body was certainly cool, but then it's always a cold house over there.

I'm only guessing, of course, but I'd hazard only an hour or so.'

Which was probably as good a guess as any.

'You knew Mrs Pumfrey well, sir?' asked Roper.

'Naturally,' said Cresswell. 'She was a patient…and my wife's sister. I could hardly not know her well.'

'As a patient, were you treating her for anything?'

'Not since Christmas,' said Cresswell. 'She was very hale.'

And that wasn't true. According to Mr and Mrs González, it had been around Christmas time that Mrs Pumfrey had taken to the bottle. It would have been almost impossible for Cresswell, not only Mrs Pumfrey's doctor but a relative, not to have noticed some kind of change in her mental and physical condition. When people suddenly took to drink, it showed.

'I'm surprised you should say that, Dr Cresswell,' said Roper. 'That she was hale. I gathered that she'd become depressed…since Christmas.'

'Then if she had, she concealed the symptoms uncommonly well,' said Cresswell. 'I never noticed, and she certainly never consulted me about it.'

Roper wasn't sure whether to believe him or not. Families often closed in at times like this to protect the dear departed; for the time being, he gave Cresswell the benefit of the doubt.

'When did you last see your sister-in-law alive, sir?'

'Thursday,' said Cresswell. 'Up at Crow Hill. I was just going into the bank as she was coming out.'

'And what about your wife? Would you know when she last saw Mrs Pumfrey?'

For a moment, Roper had the distinct impression of looking at Cresswell through the flap of a letter-box that was suddenly snapped shut.

'Not for some weeks,' said Cresswell. And it was as if the letter-box had snapped open again, or had never closed but Roper had only imagined it had. And since he knew that he hadn't imagined it he was forced to the conclusion that Cresswell, for perhaps the second time in less than a minute, was being deliberately evasive. And it wasn't as if the questions of Mrs Pumfrey's health and when Mrs Cresswell had last seen her were particularly relevant to the manner of her death. They had been merely routine questions routinely asked. Cresswell need only have said yes, I know she was depressed or whatever, and yes, my wife saw her on Friday afternoon, or whenever, and Roper would have been satisfied. But Cresswell had denied the first suggestion and been too vague in his answer to the second. Roper was no more psychic than the next man, but thirty-odd years of coppering had given him a finely honed instinct to recognise when he was being side stepped.

'Some weeks, sir?' said Price, who was equally adept at reading signs, glancing up from his note-taking.

'Is it important?' asked Cresswell.

Yes, he *was* being evasive, Roper decided.

'Only as background information, sir,' said Price.

'It must have been several months,' said Cresswell. Then he finally decided to come clean and said, reluctantly, 'They quarrelled, you see. My wife and Stella. Ridiculous, really. Sarah…my wife, tried to patch it up. But Stella wouldn't have it.'

'Fair enough, sir,' said Roper, and wondered why Cresswell had wanted to keep it such a secret. 'Getting back to Mrs Pumfrey's contact lenses: just how bad was her eyesight?'

'Very poor,' said Cresswell. 'Without them, she couldn't read a book at six inches in bright sunlight.

That's why she had two pairs. She was terrified of losing one.'

Which made it even more unlikely that Mrs Pumfrey would have come downstairs into a darkened hall with one lens missing. She would have been, even clinically speaking, nearly half blind.

From the tail of his eye Roper took in the smart new surgery, the professional credentials framed on the wall, the glittering hi-tech equipment and several boxes of what looked like electronic gadgetry. It all seemed very slick and expensive. From the outside it had looked only a modest country practice. It was clearly a profitable undertaking.

'She drank, sir,' said Roper. 'But I expect you knew that…as her doctor.'

'Only lately,' said Cresswell, cautiously. 'I smelled whisky on her last night…that's why I thought… well…you know.'

'But you just told me that she was hale,' said Roper.

'She was a little depressed,' said Cresswell. 'But not clinically so. And I know for a fact that she wasn't drinking so much as she was a few weeks ago. She certainly wasn't an alcoholic.'

'So you *did* know something was wrong?'

Cresswell shifted uncomfortably in his chair. 'Yes,' he admitted grudgingly and at some length. 'It might have been a man. But I'm only guessing, so that's not for the record.'

'A lover you mean, sir? Not Mr Pumfrey?'

'God, no,' exclaimed Cresswell, with a sudden and unexpected vehemence. 'All that man ever wanted off Stella was her money. He'd have bled her white if she'd let him.'

And thereby, thought Roper, probably hung another tale.

'So she had a man-friend, did she, Dr Cresswell?'

'Yes, we think she did,' said Cresswell. 'Discreetly.'

'Did anyone ever mention a name?'

'Not that I know of,' said Cresswell. 'As I said, she was very discreet. I don't think even Bill knew...my brother-in-law.'

'But you did know, sir,' said Roper.

'No, not exactly... My wife told me. She could have been mistaken, of course. She saw Stella a couple of times with a man. And put two and two together.'

In Roper's opinion, when many people put two and two together their wishful thinking was a sight less accurate than a spot of honest-to-goodness arithmetic. From what little he had seen of Mrs Cresswell so far he wouldn't have set great store on her reliability.

'Would she have mentioned any of these affairs to your wife?'

'I doubt it,' said Cresswell. 'As sisters go, my wife and Stella weren't close. Not the way sisters usually are. And certainly not lately.'

For a man of science, Cresswell was remarkably liberal with his generalisations. Roper had twice in his time charged a sister with the murder of her female sibling; on one occasion the weapon had been an axe. And that wasn't the way sisters usually were, either.

'Was your wife Mrs Pumfrey's only sister?'

'Yes.'

'No brothers?'

'None.'

'You mentioned that Mr and Mrs Pumfrey didn't get on, Dr Cresswell,' hazarded Roper. 'You prepared to expand on that?'

'There's nothing to expand. Bill was broke when he married Stella. She set him up in two businesses. He lost both of them. End of story. Except, I suppose, that he inherits her half of the estate.'

Or not, thought Roper, as the case might very well be.

'And the other half, sir?'

'My wife,' said Cresswell. 'At least, I presume so.'

'Have you any idea of what the estate might amount to?' asked Roper. 'Out of interest, sir?'

'A hell of a lot,' said Cresswell. 'You know the price of property these days.' Into his voice had crept a barely disguised rancour. It was almost as if he didn't expect very much of his sister-in-law's estate to come to his wife. And yet if Stella Pumfrey had seen her husband lose her money on his businesses, and if their relationship had been as sour as everyone, including Pumfrey, said it was, then sheer vindictiveness might have led her to make a will solely in favour of Mrs Cresswell despite that quarrel they had had; blood being thicker than water, as the old saw had it.

Cresswell glanced again at his watch.

'You in a hurry, sir?' asked Roper.

'No, not exactly,' said Cresswell. 'I've got an elderly couple to see, and a young woman in the next village has just gone into labour. A bit like your job, I should think. All quiet one five minutes and an emergency the next.'

'Understood, sir,' said Roper. The few minutes with Cresswell hadn't been entirely wasted, and neither he nor his wife were likely to go far. There were still a lot of questions floating about, mostly the frank, brutal ones which couldn't be asked yet because this still wasn't officially a murder inquiry. 'We'll call back tomorrow. And perhaps we can have a word with your wife then, too.'

'Yes, indeed,' said Cresswell. 'She's taken it rather badly, of course…my wife.' He had risen; so had Roper.

'We'll make it tomorrow evening, sir,' said Roper, buttoning his raincoat.

'Fine,' said Cresswell.

'And there's one last question, sir,' said Roper, as Cresswell opened the door to show them back to the waiting-room. 'Would you know if Mrs Pumfrey had any enemies?'

'Enemies? Enemy enough to want to kill her you mean?' said Cresswell. He shook his head. 'Good God, no.'

MRS GONZÁLEZ LET THEM IN. The hall was ablaze with light.

'Mr Pumfrey still about, is he?' asked Roper.

'Sí.' She pointed across to the sitting-room.

Roper and Price started towards it, but then a voice called, 'Super', from the gallery.

It was the Scene of Crime Officer, leaning over the gallery balustrade. 'Have you got a minute?' he said.

Roper and Price struck off towards the stairs, reached the gallery and followed the SOCO into Mrs Pumfrey's bedroom. The SOCO closed the door behind them.

'What have you found?' asked Roper, for the SOCO had clearly found something.

Four identical cork-tipped and filtered cigarette ends. The SOCO had found two under the foot end of the bed and the other two behind the left-hand back leg of the dressing-table. There had also been signs of cigarette ash trodden into the carpet between the dressing-table and the bay window to the left of it. These, however, were the least of his finds.

'And someone's done a tidying-up job, sir. On the dressing-table.'

He had meticulously cleared the glass top of its clutter. He picked up his handlamp from the bed and shone it obliquely along the empty expanse of glass. The lamp showed up several circular, white chalky smears. When the lamp was briefly switched off the smears disappeared. Illuminated again, they reappeared.

'It's ben washed over, sir,' said the SOCO. 'And I've asked Mr and Mrs González; he gave it a polish over with a proprietary window cleaner on Friday. He says he left it shining—like the mirrors.' He moved to the window-ledge where the ashtray had been, and where he had laid out all the odds and ends that had been on the dressing-table. In his latex-gloved hand, between a finger and thumb, he picked up by the neck a bottle of perfume. He shone his lamp obliquely across it. It, too, was faintly smeared with the same chalky whiteness.

'And there's this, sir.' He put down the phial and picked up a flask of skin lotion. The flask was made of opalescent pink glass, squat and bulbous with a pattern of sunrays moulded outwards from the manufacturer's circular black and white label. 'See it?'

A tiny, rust-coloured bead, half the size of a pinhead, adhered to one of the recessed sunrays. The SOCO flashed his lamp. The flask was smeared, like the perfume bottle and the glass top of the dressing-table.

'And here,' said the SOCO, dropping to a crouch beside the front, left-hand leg of the dressing-table and shining his lamp on a white porcelain castor. 'This one's a dilly.'

Roper got down on his hands and knees. On the lower circumference of the castor wheel was a pink stain with dark edges, like a tear, as if a runnel of blood had been overtaken and diluted by a rolling drip of water. As its base, where the castor was impressed into the carpet, the stain suddenly broadened where the carpet had acted like a piece of blotting-paper.

'Any blood on the leg of the dressing-table?' asked Roper.

'Might have been,' said the SOCO. 'But that's been wiped over, too.' He shone his handlamp over the cylindrically tapered leg above the castor. The polish showed whitish vertical smears. And at the top was a tiny scrap of orange rag… 'It looks more like paper,' said the SOCO. He reached into his box for a pair of tweezers and a glass. It wasn't rag. It was too haphazardly fibrous. 'Definitely paper.'

'Try the lavatory, Dave,' Roper said to Price. 'Find out what colour bog paper they use in this place.'

Price was gone for only a minute. He came back into the bedroom with a rectangle of toilet paper.

It was orange. It seemed that whoever had killed Mrs Pumfrey had known the layout of the house as well as their own.

SIX

WITH THE AID of several Polaroid photographs he had taken, the SOCO carefully reconstructed the arrangement on top of the dressing-table. The fragment of toilet paper, the perfume bottle, the flask of skin lotion, the castor—and the washed leg of the dressing table, all were, and had been, on the left-hand side of it. Like the cigarette ends and the ash on the carpet.

Roper stood by the foot of the bed and contemplated what was obviously, now, the scene of the crime. There couldn't have been much blood. There was none on the nearby wall or curtains, nor on the carpet round about. Contrary to popular mythology, blood did not fly everywhere of its own volition. Travelled blood, in most cases, tends to have been flung from the weapon. A maniacal multiple stabbing could fling blood over floors, ceilings, walls, doors and make the average domestic kitchen look like an abattoir after a hectic day's business. That hadn't happened here. The mirrors of the dressing-table showed no smears. So it was probable that only one blow had been struck, and the ashtray, if the weapon had been that ashtray, had not been waved about afterwards, in the manner of what the tabloids called a frenzied attack. So one blow then. And Mrs Pumfrey had collapsed, probably already dead, on to the green rug that was now on its way in a van to the forensic laboratory. And the ashtray, or whatever—Roper still had to take account of that whatever—still in the killer's hand, had been raised only once, perhaps to strike again, perhaps in horror at the terrible

consequences of that first blow, just high enough—to hip
level?—to spatter some blood on the glass top of the
dressing-table and a few of the pots on it, and splash a
few drops down the front left-hand corner of the woodwork and on to the white china castor.

The shock of it, unless the villain was a psychopath,
must surely have followed in the instant. Even Roper, who
had been looking at mutilated bodies for thirty years, still
felt his stomach shrink when he had to crouch down and
touch one. That kind of horror swiftly turns to panic. Murder's been done, a life taken. The dead body wasn't a
vicarious image on the television that you could switch
off and it would go away. It was here on the floor, it had
weight and substance and its life's blood was seeping out
of it and it wasn't tomato sauce, and if it wasn't already
dead it very soon would be. The choices were few. Two.
Run like hell and pray to God that nobody saw you arrive
here. Or try to cover up the worst thing you've ever done
in your life and try to make it look like something else.
Like an accident.

You still the panic. There's a mess. It's got to be
cleared up. A few handfuls of toilet paper from the lavatory, quickly dampened under the tap in the handbasin
of the bathroom next door to it—you knew where it was
because you'd been here before. Back to the bedroom.
Wipe everything with blood on it, and a few other things
just to be sure, but missing a few spots because you are
out of breath and not thinking right because your brain's
slipped temporarily out of gear. You don't notice you've
missed a little bead of red in the moulded pattern of a
bottle of lotion, nor that you've let water dribble down
and around a white china castor because you were in too
much of a hurry to get down on your hands and knees
and look underneath it.

Then, thinking you'd cleared up everything, not noticing the smears you'd left behind, and the fragment of toilet paper caught up in the woodwork, you folded the rug around the body, perhaps lashing it with something, and towed it, bump, bump, bump, down the stairs. Changed the rug over and Bob's your uncle.

But it wasn't going to work. It rarely did. Murder was like a bad marriage. You did it in haste and sweated over it at leisure; and remembered the old adage of being sure your sins would find you out. Eventually. Somebody somewhere was sweating.

'How about dabs?' asked Roper.

'All over the bloody place,' said the SOCO. Except the odds and ends with the smears on them. The SOCO had lifted several dozen prints on to sticky acetate tape. Perhaps the fingerprint analysis could identify a few for certain when he had taken samples from Pumfrey and Mr and Mrs González.

'So he was wearing gloves,' said Price; since whoever had done the cleaning up would have had to hold the items in question while he—or she—did so.

'Likely,' said the SOCO. 'Could have been a professional breaker. Perhaps she went for him.'

'Those smears look powdery,' said Roper.

'I'll take a few scrapings. See what the lab says.'

'Good,' said Roper. 'Burn some midnight oil if you have to. I'll sign your overtime chitty.'

'Right,' said the SOCO; he twitched his spectacles back to the bridge of his nose and got back to work again.

BE IT A WOMAN, a second-hand car punter, or a bit of valuable lead on a church roof, it was Brian Seymour's pride that he could recognise an easy lay when he saw one. This one was still wet behind the ears. Under the

street-lamp in Cawnpore Terrace, Seymour watched him
wistfully circle the Escort and trail a caressing hand over
the bodywork, much filled with resin and glass fibre, the
result of a brush with a lamppost, although he wouldn't
find that out for a thousand miles or so, until it started to
fall out, by which time Seymour would be long gone from
here. An exit which was rapidly becoming a matter of
urgency.

'You had it long?' asked Carter, a.k.a. PC Carter of
Crow Hill police station, but presently in mufti in jeans,
roll-necked pullover and nylon anorak.

'Couple of weeks,' said Seymour, padding around behind him. 'Me auntie left it to me in her will. The old girl
was a schoolteacher. Retired. Nice old lady she was too.'

Carter could almost hear the slow swell of violins. 'A
runner, is it?'

'Sweet as a bell,' said Seymour. Under the lamplight
he leaned in through the driver's window and released the
bonnet catch.

Carter lifted the lid the rest of the way. 'Battery looks
a bit naff,' he observed.

'So you fork out another twenty quid,' said Seymour.
'Or a mate of mine can do you a good second-hand one
for another five. Three months' guarantee.' A crescent of
naked white swag belly hung out between the bottom of
his white T-shirt and his black trouser belt. The crescent
seemed to swing about quite independently of any movement Seymour made.

'You couldn't chuck it in?' asked Carter hopefully.
'The other battery from your mate?'

'I'm a bit like yourself, squire,' said Seymour.
'Strapped for cash. If I was in the business of selling
motors, I'd have probably put a new one in. But I'm not,
see?'

Cater stepped back on to the pavement. 'Yeah, sure,' he said. 'Only I've just started this new job. And the pay's not all that much. It's a lot to fork out. It's got to be cash, has it?'

Seymour shrugged sympathetically. 'Got to be cash, squire. Sorry.'

Carter stood back a little further, and sighed in the manner of a man watching the deal of a lifetime slip through his fingers. 'Sorry, Mr. Seymour. I'm wasting your time.'

Seymour, likewise, saw Carter slipping through his fingers. And that was something he couldn't afford. Besides the Escort he still had two other motors to offload before he could make himself scarce.

'Look,' said Seymour chummily, 'I'll do you a favour. I'll knock off fifty quid... I still want cash, though. How about I get the keys and you give it a turn round the block. Can't say fairer than that, can I?'

Carter smiled his most boyish smile. 'Sounds very fair to me, that does, Mr Seymour. Very fair indeed.'

THE LIGHTS BURNED LATE in Chief Inspector Lambert's office overlooking Crow Hill High Street. From downstairs came a hubbub of conversation and the clatter of locker doors as the middle watch went off duty and the night shift took over.

Lambert handed back the photograph of Mrs Pumfrey's gold and garnet earrings to Roper.

'What are they worth?' he asked, around the unlit pipe he was champing at.

'Pumfrey reckons a couple of thousand,' said Roper. 'I reckon nearer four. At auction, they might fetch five if somebody wanted 'em badly enough.' Antique furniture was more his line, but he knew quality when he saw it. Each earring was a triangular pendant with a delicate gold trellis infill. At each corner of the triangle, with a larger one at the apex, was a rose-cut garnet. At each intersection of the trellis was another, but more diminutive stone, equally finely cut. They were probably hand crafted, probably unique.

'So why didn't Jack the lad take the box?' asked Lambert.

'Probably forgot it in his panic,' said Price. 'He had a hell of a lot to do in the few minutes after he'd killed Mrs Pumfrey.'

'If he did take them,' said Roper, always cautious, 'he's going to have a hell of a job getting rid of 'em. Unless he knows a bent collector of nineteenth-century French jewellery... I'm more interested in this.' He slid the lighter across Lambert's desk.

Lambert picked it up, stretched the plastic of the evidence bag tighter over its front face and held it under his desk lamp. 'The initials fit,' he said.

'Her husband's never seen it before,' said Roper. 'Nor have the servants. According to Pumfrey, she used a Ronson. The SOCO found it in her handbag, with a new flint and topped up with gas.'

'But it was beside her when they found her,' said Lambert.

'It still wasn't hers,' said Roper.

'Perhaps a boyfriend gave it to her and she kept it under wraps.'

Roper had earlier considered that himself; it was still a possibility, but his doubts about it were growing. Mrs González had too free an access to Mrs Pumfrey's bedroom, was often sent upstairs to fetch down a handbag that Mrs Pumfrey had forgotten to bring down with her. The handbags were frequently open when Mrs González collected them. And since the Pumfreys, apart from shar-

ing the same roof, lived quite separately, would she have
bothered, or needed to have bothered, to keep the lighter
out of sight of her husband for fear of raising his suspicions? Would she, indeed, have been concerned about any
such suspicions? Such was the state of their marriage that
Roper doubted it. She probably wouldn't have cared a
damn.

'What I reckon,' said Roper, 'is that someone left it in
the house, that Jack the lad saw it on her dressing-table,
thought it was hers and used it to tart up the scene at the
bottom of the stairs. With the cigarette. Incidentally, if the
SOCO's right, there are only four or five sets of dabs on
that lighter. And one of those is mine. By rights, it should
have been plastered with 'em.'

'Wiped beforehand then,' said Lambert.

'Very likely,' said Roper. The snag with trying to make
a murder look like something else was invariably the
temptation to overdo the evidence. There were very few
well-used cigarette lighters with only a couple of fingerprints on them. The Ronson in Mrs Pumfrey's handbag
had been smothered with them. It would have been clev-
erer to have left that one beside the body.

'So it's a full-blown murder inquiry,' said Lambert.

'Definitely,' said Roper. A half-hour ago, on the telephone, the Assistant Chief Constable (Crime) had agreed
with him. Mrs Pumfrey had been murdered. Tomorrow's
second autopsy on her was only going to establish how,
and even that, so far as Roper was concerned, was more
or less a foregone conclusion. Mrs González and her husband, and the SOCO, had all but ransacked every room
in the house during the course of the evening. The dust-
bins too had been turned over and emptied. Wherever that
glass ashtray was, it wasn't in the house; it might, of
course, have been buried in the garden, in which case it

might never come to light again. If the murderer had taken it with him—or her—then it was probably miles away by now, smashed to fragments and scattered. After its last use, it was hardly likely to be sitting about somewhere as an ornament, least of all in the murderer's own house.

'Will you want any personnel?' asked Lambert.

'I'll use my own people,' said Roper. Price was already on hand. DS Makins and DS Rodgers would be reporting in the morning, and also WDS Hackett who was new to the county but had come from the Devon and Cornwall Force with excellent provenance. Sexual equality was all very well, but nobody could size up a woman like another woman, and Roper wanted Hackett with him when he interviewed Mrs Cresswell tomorrow and, later on, Mrs Pumfrey's little coterie of women-friends.

'How about DC Mills?' said Lambert.

It was on the tip of Roper's tongue to say not on your life, but strictly speaking Mills was Lambert's business.

'Later,' said Roger. 'If I need a local leg-man.'

At eleven o'clock, as voices and slamming car doors down in the street proclaimed that the pubs were turning out, Roper and Price were settling themselves in a spare office a few doors along the passage from Lambert's. Graced with a fresh coat of paint, a desk, two chairs and a coatrack, it was a cut above the usual kind of office, frequently the station file-tip, that was made over to them on their occasional wanderings around the county. Lambert was going to have another desk and a couple more chairs brought in tomorrow.

They compared notes and thoughts over another cup of coffee, and toyed with a few 'what ifs..?' Like Roper, Price had a hunch that the cigarette lighter wasn't Mrs Pumfrey's. It would be interesting to find out if that crumpled cigarette, dropped into the kitchen pedal-bin last night by Mr González and rescued from it this evening by the SOCO, had ever been near Mrs Pumfrey's mouth, or, like the lighter, had been planted with little regard to its antecedence.

'Whoever it was knew the layout of the house,' said Price. 'Or they came in through the downstairs and were pretty quick off the mark to spot the similarities between the two green rugs.'

'Aye,' said Roper, around a cheroot he was lighting. 'I reckon you're right the first time. It was someone who knew the place.'

'And took the earrings—and left the box behind,' said Price, over his coffee cup. 'Doesn't ring right, that.'

'Perhaps she was wearing them at the time,' said Roper. 'And forgot to take them off.'

Price's thick institutional cup, descending towards its saucer, froze a couple of inches below his chin. 'A woman?'

'Why not?' said Roper. 'She knew plenty. And one in the most particular.'

Price's cup completed its descent to its saucer. 'Mrs Cresswell?'

'Why not?' said Roper again, sipping and speculating. 'We've missed something, haven't we? According to Mrs González, before the house was Mrs Pumfrey's it belonged to her mother. So Mrs Cresswell would have known it inside out, wouldn't she? She and Mrs Pumfrey would have been brought up there as kids, wouldn't they?'

'I hadn't thought of that,' said Price.

'Don't worry about it,' said Roper. 'I've only just thought of it myself. Let's say on Friday night she goes across to see her sister. Let's say she has another go at patching up that quarrel, and let's say they do patch it up. And she says—or Mrs P says: how about a bit of a drool

over Mummy's jewellery? Mrs C tries on Mummy's rose-
cut garnet whatnots in front of the mirror, decides her
need's greater than Mrs P's. And pow!... The ashtray's
handy. Mrs P's back's turned...'

'And the dirty deed done she has to go like the bloody
wind,' said Price.

'Right,' said Roper.

But Price was already shaking his head. 'No,' he said.
'That's not like you, Super. Never proceed beyond the
evidence at hand... I quote.'

Roper lifted his shoulders. 'It's only a thought,' he said.

At midnight he was alone and looking down from the
window at the empty rainswept High Street, and the so-
dium lamps patchily gilding the wet pavements, his last
cheroot of the day in one hand and another cup of too
sweet coffee in the other. From downstairs came an occasional rumble of voices and the clack of a typewriter.
This was his winding-down time. Except that it was difficult to wind down with a murder in the wings. It had
been a hasty murder, too; and not premeditated, the signs
were all wrong for that. And the questions that could not
have been asked today—now yesterday according to the
clock over the jeweller's shop across the street—because
at the time they would have been too rashly precipitate,
as Mrs Pumfrey's murder had been, would certainly be
asked later on today. Had Pumfrey been where he said
he'd been last night? And could he prove it? If anybody
had a motive, then perhaps Pumfrey had. Or Mrs Cresswell, the sister. A down-at-heel sister living beside an
obviously wealthy one. A grudge or two in that direction
wasn't unlikely. Murder wasn't a woman's crime, but
there were exceptions that broke the rule. So why not Mrs
Cresswell? Roper had only seen her briefly but he recalled, with hindsight, a woman old and shabby before

her time and perhaps with deliberation rather than a trick of genes. There had been something about her...more than just shock? The way she had shrugged off—literally shrugged off—the bloody murder of her only sister. The strange bright glitter in her eyes, in an otherwise deadpan, vacant face...

And her husband. Vague and evasive. No much, but enough for both Roper and Price to pick it up. Was he protecting his wife? Did he know something, or had he guessed something...?

Roper pulled himself together. It was late, he was getting old, his mind was wandering. Price was right. It was never wise to indulge in the luxury of stepping over the barrier between the physical and ascertainable facts and the jungle of the imagination. But still, Mrs Cresswell *had* seemed a strange sort of woman—

It took him a moment to find the ringing telephone...behind the metal wastepaper-tub in the corner a few feet from the window, its spiral of flex glued to the new white paint of the skirting board...nobody seemed to do a proper job any more.

'Roper,' he said. There was paint on the mouthpiece too. Paint all over the bloody thing.

'You sound a touch tart, Superintendent. Am I interrupting something?' The bland voice was Craig's, from the Forensic laboratory.

'You know what happens when you put paint on plastic, Mr Craig?'

'It takes a bloody long time to dry?' suggested Craig.

'Bloody right,' said Roper, breaking off briefly to wrap a handkerchief around the barrel of the handset. 'What can you do for me?'

'A fair bit,' said Craig. 'The messy green rug you sent us. The blood on it's group AB; as was Mrs Pumfrey's, according to the post-mortem report. And as were the samples the Scene of Crime Officer scraped from the lady's dressing-table castor. Can't be certain, of course, that it was from Mrs Pumfrey, but give us a couple of days to do some more definitive tests and we can tell you precisely.'

'What's the frequency of group AB?' asked Roper.

'In the UK,' said Craig, 'about two or three per cent. So if it's a question of betting your hard-earned pension, I'd say you were on to a fairly safe gamble.'

'And the rugs match?'

'Fibre for fibre,' said Craig. 'So says our spectrophotometer.'

'Bully,' said Roper. 'Don't suppose you came across a contact lens too, did you?'

'We did indeed,' said Craig, causing Roper yet more satisfaction because the question had only been a chance shaft. 'Or rather the remains of one. The gel type. We didn't immediately recognise it for what it was. It had been trodden into the rug.'

'And how about dabs on the stuff that was on the dressing-table?'

'The SOCO was right,' said Craig. 'There aren't any on the things that were washed. And those white smears on the glass top, they seem to be some kind of mild abrasive. Like scouring powder. Not a great deal, though. I've got a couple of technicians coming in tomorrow. I'll get them to work on it and hopefully be able to tell you exactly what it is.'

'And how about that cigarette they found beside her?'

'It was messy.'

'It would be,' said Roper. The gooey residues of several meals had been tipped into the kitchen waste-bin after the cigarette. 'Any traces of saliva or lipstick on it?'

'Absolutely none,' said Craig. 'But we did find traces of the same white powder on it.'

And that was all.

Apart from the scouring powder, Craig had told him little that Roper hadn't already guessed; although final confirmation that Mrs Pumfrey had been struck down in front of her dressing-table had to be the finding of that other contact lens. One lens might just have dropped out. The chances of the other dropping out simultaneously were surely remote.

'WHERE THE HELL have you been?' raged Bernard Cresswell. 'Do you know what the bloody time is?' He had arrived home to an empty house at half past eleven. There had been a used cereal dish in the hearth by the dead fire and an opened romantic novel straddling the arm of the chair where she usually sat; it was now a quarter past midnight. She looked as if she'd been swimming in her clothes.

'Out,' she said. 'I felt like a walk.'

'In the rain?'

'It wasn't raining when I went.' Her grey skirt was saturated, her bare ankles splashed with mud, her short red jacket black and glistening at the shoulders. Her hair hung like wet strings. 'I could ask where you've been come to that.'

'You know where I've been,' he said. 'You always know where I am.'

'No, I don't,' she said defiantly. 'Not always.' Her hands, stuffed into the pockets of the red jacket, dragged it down from her shoulders and made her look pregnant. Like a child, she took one hand out and wiped the back of it across her wet mouth.

'You're walking mud into the bloody carpet,' he said.

'So what? You don't have to clean it, do you?' She turned away and went over to the sideboard.

He watched her pour a brandy. It looked a large one. 'You're getting like Stella,' he said.

'Oh, but I am,' she said, turning and lifting her tumbler. 'Cheers. I'm just like Stella.' She sipped. 'That's why you married me, wasn't it? A surrogate Stella.'

'I didn't know Stella when I married you.'

'No,' she retorted, 'but you bloody got to know her in the end, didn't you?'

'Believe that,' he said tiredly, 'and you'll believe anything.'

'Oh, but I do believe it,' she said. 'It's bloody true.'

'I keep telling you—'

'And I don't believe you.' She shrugged her wet shoulders. 'So there's no point in arguing about it, is there?'

He went across and unbuttoned the red jacket. She put up no resistance. When he moved behind her to take it off she merely shrugged one arm out then transferred the tumbler to the other hand for the second sleeve. Apart from the shift of the tumbler, she might have been a dummy being undressed in a shop window.

'Skirt too,' he said.

'Why?' she said. 'Am I going to get lucky?'

'Come on,' he said irritably. 'For Christ's sake.'

She unbuttoned and unzipped the skirt, pushed it down around her feet, then kicked it aside on the carpet.

He moved away and stooped to pick it up. Then clicked his fingers.

'Now your shoes,' he said.

'You used to like me keeping them on,' she said, with a hideous attempt to be arch. 'You see, I still remember little things like that.'

'I'll hang these up in the kitchen,' he said. 'And get you a towel.'

'Yes,' she said, flourishing a hand airily. 'Good idea.'

But he didn't move, except to arrange the sodden jacket and skirt more neatly as they hung from his fingers. Then he said, 'The police are coming again tomorrow, Sarah.'

'I know,' she said blithely. 'You told me.'

'Last night; they'll probably ask you where you were.'

'They'll probably ask where you were, too,' she said. 'They aren't stupid.'

'I can't prove where I was,' he said. 'Can you?'

She lifted her glass again. 'Cheers,' she said.

'*Can* you?' he said.

'I was here,' she said. 'I was here—on my own—like I always am.'

'The fire was out,' he reminded her. 'You never let the fire go out.'

She shrugged. 'I told you,' she said. 'It got too hot in here.'

He started towards the door to the passage, stopped at the opening, then turned back to face her again. Her wax-white ears protruded through her wet black hair. They looked as if they had been stuck on with adhesive, like an afterthought.

'Did you kill Stella, Sarah?' he said, willing her to look at him. 'I have to know before the police come again. I have to know what I ought to tell them.'

She swirled the remains of her brandy in the tumbler, and watched it settle. Then she lifted her face and smiled at him with bright mischievous eyes.

'Now, there's a funny thing,' she said. 'Do you know... I was going to ask you that very same question... How about playing truth or dare?' She stalked towards him in her mud-stained black stilettos, stopped a foot away and lifted a hand to grip his chin and rock it viciously from side to side with her eyes narrowed. 'Truth or dare, Bernard. How about it?'

He took hold of her wrist and forced her hand away. 'Why do you do these things to me, Sarah,' he said between gritted teeth. 'Why? Why do you pretend?'

She smiled sweetly.

'Because I loathe you, Bernard,' she said. 'Isn't that reason enough?'

SEVEN

AND THEN IT WAS Easter Sunday morning and the sharp end of a new day. A watery yellow sun glittered on the wet pavements and was fighting a losing battle to dry them; according to the weather forecast it would be raining again by lunchtime. On the desk in front of Roper was a photocopy of the sketch plan of Mrs Pumfrey's bedroom that Price had made yesterday.

'And that's about it,' said Roper, to the recently arrived Makins, Rodgers and WDS Hackett, all three of whom were crowded together on the other side of the desk. Behind Roper, Price was perched on the radiator under the window. 'The lady was murdered. Her husband didn't get on with her, she'd had a row with her sister a few months back and there's an expensive item of jewellery missing. And Dave and I reckon that whoever did it knew the house like the back of their hand. So it has to be somebody fairly close to Mrs Pumfrey—or somebody who'd once worked there.'

'How about the two Spaniards?' asked Makins.

'They don't fit the bill,' said Roper. And perhaps that was another precipitate conclusion, but somehow he didn't think so. 'I think they're both on the up and up. And both of them genuinely liked Mrs Pumfrey.'

'Does Pumfrey stand to inherit?' asked Rodgers. 'That's as good a motive as any.'

'Or the sister?' asked DS Makins.

'Or it's simpler than that,' said Roper. 'We could just be looking for a knowledgeable housebreaker who got caught, panicked, and perhaps put up a fight that went the wrong way.'

'And the husband's got an alibi,' added Price. 'So he's probably out of it.'

WDS Hackett, dark-haired, and wearing regulation spectacles and a smart black suit, had the Colibri lighter in its plastic envelope and was turning it over speculatively. 'Could whoever planted this have known that it wasn't Mrs Pumfrey's, sir?'

'I'm not with you, Sergeant.'

'Well…could he have left it behind knowing who it *did* belong to? A frame job.'

'Could be,' agreed Roper. It was a line of thought that had not so far occurred to him. So much else had been designed to deceive, so why not the lighter?

Mills' photographs, already passed from Rodgers to Makins, were passed now to Hackett. She turned the photograph of Mrs Pumfrey lying on the rug so that the face was the right way up.

'This lover she was supposed to have,' she said. 'Could he have done it? Perhaps he'd cooled off and Mrs Pumfrey was threatening to tell his wife.'

And that was a thought, too. Emotional blackmail was not the least of motives.

He stretched an arm across the desk as the phone rang, carefully arranging his fingers to miss the still-sticky patches of white paint. The caller was Mr González. He was speaking from a box in the village, and from the way he was puffing and blowing it sounded as if Mrs González had made him run all the way to it.

'It is my wife, sair. She make me telephone you. I say it is only a little thing. She say important. She say to me you tell her to tell you if anything missing from house.'

'I did indeed, Mr González,' said Roper. 'She's noticed something else, has she?'

'*Sí*, yes, sair. I tell her it not important, that you are busy man, but the gloves have gone from the bathroom—of rubber, sair. For cleaning the bath. She use them on Friday—in the morning—and she say for sure she put them back in cupboard. You understand, sair?'

'Yes, I understand, Mr González.' So that's how the killer had come by his gloves, and why he hadn't left his prints on the stuff he had cleaned on the dressing-table. And perhaps those white smears that Forensic had thought were scouring powder in fact were exactly that, perhaps residues of the stuff left on the gloves after their last use in the bathroom by Mrs González. 'That's very important, Mr González. Does your wife know the make of these gloves? And where they were bought?'

González sighed. 'She will know, sair. But I did not think to ask her. I did not think it was important.'

'Don't worry about it, Mr González. I'll be talking to your wife again fairly soon.'

He put the phone back on its rest with a feeling that another little piece of the jigsaw had been slotted into place.

'There's a pair of rubber gloves missing,' he said. 'They were the ones Mrs González used to scour the bath. And if she's right, the villain took 'em away with him.'

'Pity,' said Price; because the outside of the wrist of at least one of the gloves would probably bear an excellent set of the villain's dabs, since he must have been bare-handed when he'd hauled the first one on, or he wouldn't have needed to wear them in the first place.

And it was very likely that he had known where the gloves were stored. Which made it even more certain that he had known the layout of the house. Or she, of course.

And again Mrs Cresswell wandered into Roper's mind; there had definitely been something adrift about Mrs Cresswell...

'Right,' he said. 'We'd better get started.' He took out his wallet and from it the business card that Foyle, the solicitor, had given him yesterday evening. He passed it back over his shoulder to Price. 'Fix yourself an appointment with Mr Foyle, Dave. I've got a feeling he's a family friend as well as the solicitor. Find out what he knew about Mrs Pumfrey's private life, and who she's left all her assets to. Make sure you tell him we're on a murder inquiry, and if he won't talk without a warrant tell him we'll get one. And you, Peter,' this to Rodgers, 'sort out a telephone directory and find a Mrs Hubert. She lives down in Little Crow. According to González, she was a close friend of Mrs Pumfrey's. Fix up an appointment with her and find out what she knew about Mrs P, and generally chat her up. And you'd better let her know that I might have to come along and see her later. Take Sergeant Hackett with you.'

'Will do,' said Rodgers.

'How about me?' said Makins.

'With me, George,' said Roper. 'We're going down to see Mr Wainer.' Who had given William Pumfrey a lift home from the Country Club on the night in question.

LIME COTTAGE was a few hundred yards beyond Chalk House. It was white and thatched and sprawling, as if it had been added to over the years, but sympathetically, as an estate agent would say, so that none of the additions looked out of place. Several leaded windows stood open to catch the fresh morning air. Makins hauled on the handbrake.

Roper stepped out on to the grass verge. Despite the

sun the ground underfoot was still soggy after the last two days of torrential rain. He held the front gate open for Makins.

'Bet this place is worth more than a few shillings,' muttered Makins as they started together up the crazy-paved front path.

'Aye,' said Roper. The cast-iron door-knocker was in the shape of a horse's head. He rapped it down twice. The instant response was a barking dog that raced up the hall and hurled itself against the door, followed by a woman's voice shouting, 'Shut up, Baskerville, for Christ's sake. Sit! Sit!' But when the door was opened, the dog, an overweight, drooling boxer, still wasn't sitting, but rearing up eagerly on its hind legs and dribbling spittle, while the woman strained to haul it back by its studded collar and looked in imminent danger of losing the struggle.

'It's all right,' she said, still straining. 'He doesn't bite. You're the police, are you?'

'Yes, madam. Superintendent Roper, County CID, and this is Sergeant Makins.' Roper showed his warrant card.

'You'd better come in,' she said breathlessly, still wrestling with the splay-legged boxer, finally twisting it off balance so that it flopped to its side behind her on to the carpet. Before it could scrabble to its feet again she had quickly closed the door behind Roper and Makins. 'Now sit!'

The boxer sat, with its ears pricked and its wagging stump of tail a blur. It regarded Makins amorously.

'I'm sorry about that,' the woman said. 'I'm Mrs Wainer.' She was lean, attractive and fortyish, and wore her grey slacks and loose black pullover with that careless elegance that betokens moderate wealth. 'My husband's de-sludging the fish-pond. Will you go through, or shall I call him in?'

'We'll go out, Mrs Wainer,' said Roper. 'I fancy a bit of fresh air myself.'

She led them along the passage, the panting boxer bringing up the rear, and into a sitting-room, then out of a pair of open French doors on to a paved patio. She pointed towards a fringed yellow sunshade that was just visible above a hump of lawn in the middle distance.

'He's there,' she said. 'By the umbrella... Would you like a cup of tea?'

'No, thank you, Mrs Wainer.'

'I'll leave you to find your way, then.'

'Yes,' he said. 'Thank you.'

He and Makins took the three stone steps down to the path along the lawn. Over on his left was a new clay tennis court in a cage of wire netting. There was clearly a lot of money to be made in the antiques business around here.

As they topped the rise, their first sight of Wainer was a kneeling figure in an old army pullover with leather shoulder patches, jeans and a pair of green wellington boots. With his right sleeve rolled up, he was grubbing about in the bottom of a pond and bringing up handfuls of black slime that he was tossing into a yellow plastic bucket on the flagstones beside him. The haft of the yellow sunshade was spiked through a white-painted wrought-iron table with four matching garden chairs ranged about it. On the table, a few plants in pots were laid out on an old newspaper.

Roper cleared his throat as he and Makins started down the short flight of stone steps to the sunken garden. Wainer glanced along his shoulder, then rose with a final flick of another handful of slime into the yellow bucket.

'Superintendent Roper, is it?' he said, moving a pace

to one of the chairs, over the back of which hung a thread-bare red towel. 'I'm Lance Wainer.'

'How do you do, sir,' said Roper. He introduced Makins while Wainer dried his right hand and forearm on the towel. He was a tall, narrow, brisk-looking man, forty or thereabouts.

'Do sit down, won't you.' With the hand that held the red towel he gestured towards the wrought-iron chairs around the table. 'Dreadful business. I take it that's what you're here about? The Mrs Pumfrey thing?'

'Yes, sir,' said Roper. He and Makins ducked under the fringe of the yellow sunshade. Wainer draped the towel over the chair-back again and sat down opposite them. He reached among the plant pots and brought out a packet of cigarettes and a lighter. Both Roper and Makins declined the proffered packet. Roper measured Wainer while he lit his cigarette, his hand cupped around the lighter flame against a momentary breeze that came across the garden. A face that was lean like the rest of him, sharp bright eyes and a thin mouth; he had that kind of jerky élan that is often the hallmark of the ex-military.

With a flourish, Wainer let his lighter snap shut and exhaled smoke up into the bright sunshine.

'Nice place, sir,' observed Roper, by way of a gambit.

The thin mouth smiled. 'It suits,' said Wainer. 'We like it. It's very quiet.'

A soft padding footfall at the top of the steps heralded the reappearance of the drooling boxer. Wainer clicked his fingers at it and it came down all the way. It snuffled fondly around Makins' shoes, trailed a friendly festoon of spittle across his left trouser leg then lurched around to deposit the rest on Wainer's knees as it gazed soulfully up at him and had its ears scratched.

'So how can I help you, gentlemen?'

Roper went immediately to the nub of things. 'You drove Mr Pumfrey home early on Saturday morning, so he tells us, Mr Wainer. That's right, is it, sir?'

'It is indeed,' said Wainer. 'Just after one o'clock. The ambulance was already there for poor Stella. I offered to go into the house with Bill, but he declined the offer. He told me he could manage. I watched him go up the front steps. Then I drove back across here. I rang him a few minutes afterwards. I was concerned, you see, about that ambulance. Carlos, that's Stella's Spaniard, answered the phone and put me on to Dr Cresswell. He told me that Stella had fallen down the stairs and was dead. I couldn't believe it.' He shuddered distastefully. 'Ghastly business. Still haven't got over it.'

His concern looked genuine enough. The boxer, bored with having its ears scratched, mooned away and flopped down by the pool where it continued to dribble somnolently over the flagstones. Wainer leaned forward and dropped his lighter on to the newspaper. From behind Roper came a distant burst of girls' laughter and the thunk of tennis-balls against rackets.

'Warming up for the season,' said Wainer proudly, jerking his head towards the top of the steps. 'Tennis crazy, the pair of them. The elder one's rather good.'

Roper presumed that the girls were Wainer's daughters.

'You know Mr Pumfrey well, do you, Mr Wainer?'

'We were in the army together,' said Wainer. 'Bill was my commanding officer. We did two tours in West Germany together. He resigned his commission when he married Stella. Nice chap.'

'So you go back a long time together.'

'Twenty years,' said Wainer. 'I suppose that is a long time.' He reached between the plant pots again, and this time produced an old glass ashtray. 'Man and boy, you

might say.' He rolled his cigarette on the rim of the ashtray.

'And how about Mrs Pumfrey? Knew her fairly well,
too, did you, sir?'

'Yes, indeed,' said Wainer. 'In fact I knew her before
Bill did. I introduced them to each other.'

'How about Friday night, sir?' asked Roper. 'With Mr
Pumfrey all evening, were you?'

'No,' said Wainer to Roper's surprise, because certainly
Pumfrey had led him to believe that he had. 'No. Not *all*
evening. He came into the club bar at about eleven fifteen.
He joined our little school—'

'This club, sir…?'

'The Country Club,' explained Wainer. 'Actually, it's
the Old Mill Country Club. About ten miles down the hill
from here. Near Sturminster Newton. On the B3092.'

While Makins wrote that down, Roper mulled over that
questionable time of eleven fifteen, when Pumfrey, according to Wainer, had arrived at the club. The pathologist's estimated time of death for Mrs Pumfrey could easily be adrift a couple of hours either way, apart from the
fact that Mr and Mrs González had noticed the effect of
the electric carving knife on their TV at ten and González
had found Mrs Pumfrey's body at twenty minutes past
midnight. She could have been killed at any time during
those two hours and twenty minutes. Besides which, according to Pumfrey, he had met up with Wainer that evening at *eight* o'clock. Roper opened his mouth to frame
the obvious question, but Wainer was marginally quicker.

'Well, to be honest,' he said, glancing surreptitiously
up the steps and hunching forward over the table, 'I *had*
seen Bill before. Earlier that evening. About eight o'clock.
At the club.' But then he broke off and drew back again
into his chair. 'Look, I'm sorry,' he said, with an apolo-

getic wave of his cigarette. 'I'm talking out of turn. Forget I spoke.'

He glanced across at Makins, who was sitting with his ballpoint poised over his pocket-book waiting for Wainer to continue. 'This can't be off the record, can it, Sergeant?' he said. When Makins didn't reply, Wainer's hopeful gaze repeated the question to Roper.

'It depends, sir,' said Roper. 'Have you spoken to Mr Pumfrey since Mrs Pumfrey's death?'

'Yes,' said Wainer. 'Yesterday morning. He'd just come back from the mortuary.'

'Not since?'

'No,' said Wainer. 'Not since. I got the impression he preferred his own company for a few days. Can't blame him, in the circumstances.'

'No, sir, quite,' agreed Roper, although from what he had found out so far it seemed to him that Pumfrey was not in need of a great deal of consolation to help him through his mourning. 'So you don't know that Mrs Pumfrey's death was the result of foul play?'

The skin tightened abruptly on Wainer's face. 'Christ, no,' he said. 'I didn't.' And if he did, he was a better actor than most. A hand, not so steady now, extinguished his cigarette in the ashtray. 'Are you sure?... Yes, I suppose you must be, otherwise you wouldn't be here, would you? Stupid question, really.'

'No, sir, not necessarily. And we aren't absolutely certain ourselves yet. We think someone gained entry to Mr Pumfrey's house late on Friday night, and perhaps Mrs Pumfrey caught him at it.'

'I see,' said Wainer; to be fair to the man, he certainly looked aghast. 'Christ, that's terrible. We had no idea it was anything like that. When I phoned Bill, he thought Stella had simply taken a nasty tumble down the stairs.'

'That could still be the way it happened, sir,' said Roper, not quite truthfully. 'But if it wasn't, of course, the first person we have to clear is Mr Pumfrey himself. Just a question of routine elimination.'

'Well, I can do that gladly,' said Wainer. 'I know where he was for most of the evening.'

'Good, sir,' said Roper. 'We'd be obliged.'

Wainer pushed the ashtray away again. He seemed to do everything with a quick showy flourish, as if he were about to perform a conjuring trick.

'Eight o'clock,' he began, after considering for a moment or two. 'I'm sorry, I can't be nearer than that. That's about the time I first saw Bill. He was talking to Jackson…he's the club steward. They were in the dining-room. I hadn't seen Bill come in through the bar so I presumed he'd used the back door. That's on the car park side of the club. Bill disappeared then for a few minutes; the next time I saw him he was in the gents'. I suppose it would have been about a quarter past eight. He was a bit embarrassed. I hadn't seen him, he said. If Stella asked, I hadn't seen him. I said, fine, okay. I suspected he was engaged in a little extramural activity, if you know what I mean. Anyway, I didn't press. He went back to the dining-room and I went back to the bevvy I'd left in the bar.'

'You said that was about the time you *first* saw Mr Pumfrey, Mr Wainer. I take it you saw him later?'

'Not saw, exactly,' said Wainer. 'I didn't see him again until ten thirty, or thereabouts, but I knew he was still here. It was the Scotches and the pony chasers. Ever half hour or so, the waiter came to the bar for a pair of those. And a Martini. I presumed the Martinis were for Bill's companion. And then, at half past ten, I happened to

glance out of the window of the billiard-room and saw
Bill in the car park seeing a woman into his car.'

'Happen to know the lady, did you, sir?'

'No,' said Wainer. 'I only saw her silhouette. But I
think she was wearing a fur coat.'

'Could she have been a member of the club?'

'Hardly,' said Wainer. 'Given the circumstances.'

'But her name would be in the club guest book, would
it, sir?'

'No,' said Wainer. 'He would only have to have signed
a guest in if he'd brought her into the bar.'

'So presumably, when you saw them in the car park,
Mr Pumfrey was taking this lady home?'

'I got that impression,' said Wainer.

'And then he came back,' said Roper.

'Yes,' said Wainer. 'About eleven fifteen, it was. Perhaps a little beforehand.'

Which was more or less a blueprint for a flawless alibi.
Sturminster Newton was about ten miles south-west of
Little Crow. Given the appalling weather conditions of
Friday night, and the dangerous wet state of the winding
country roads between here and there, Pumfrey, if he was
sensible, wouldn't have done the journey in much less
than twenty minutes each way. He had left the Country
Club at ten thirty and reappeared again at eleven fifteen,
which only left him five minutes in which to return home
and kill his wife. And whoever had tidied up that bedroom
had needed a lot longer than five minutes.

'And you drove Mr Pumfrey home, sir.'

'I did,' said Wainer. 'I insisted. He got on to doubles
when he came back. I told him to leave his car in the club
car park and I'd drive him down to pick it up whenever
he felt like it.'

'Which you haven't done yet?'

Wainer shook his head. 'No,' he said. 'Not yet.'

Roper pressed him a little further for a better description of Pumfrey's Friday night companion, but Wainer could only recall that she wore a chunky fur coat, and was on the tall side for a woman. Not that the vague description mattered. The lady was certainly known to Pumfrey, and in the circumstances he was hardly likely to be reticent about her name if it came to the point.

EIGHT

ROPER POKED HIS HEAD around CI Lambert's office door. 'You got a minute, Laurie?'

'Be my guest.' Lambert was in civilian clothes, and rooting through one of the drawers of his filing cabinet. 'Take a pew.'

'It's only a quickie,' said Roper. 'I won't keep you.' He waited while Lambert sorted out the file he was looking for and slammed the drawer shut.

Like Roper's office, Lambert's, too, reeked of new white paint. He went over to his desk and dropped the file into a wire tray. 'Right,' he said. 'Ask on.'

'Pumfrey,' said Roper. 'I was driving home last night and running through things; and I remembered something you said yesterday, about not liking the man.'

'Bloody right,' said Lambert with some feeling. 'I've had a lot of aggravation from William Pumfrey.'

'Like what?'

Lambert gestured to his visitor's chair, and sat down himself. 'We've had several epidemics of break-ins,' he said. 'Started last summer. Down in Little Crow mostly.' He pushed an ashtray across the desk as Roper brought out his packet of cheroots. 'Three or four of the smarter houses got done, then the Pumfreys' place. Then in October it happened again. That time it started with the Pumfreys' house. Then the Pumfreys were done again on Christmas Eve. And we never did find the culprits.'

'So Pumfrey isn't exactly enamoured of coppers,' said Roper, over his lighter flame.

'You can say that again,' said Lambert. Pumfrey's wrath had extended to the writing of at least four angry letters to the Chief Constable, two of which had rebounded in the general direction of Lambert.

'They've got a burglar alarm down there,' said Roper. 'Didn't it work?'

'They didn't have one the first time,' said Lambert. 'It was the insurance company that told Pumfrey to get one fitted.'

'What about the second time?'

'It worked,' said Lambert. 'Only there was no one in the house to hear it.'

'And the Christmas job?'

'Pumfrey and his missus both told my DI that they'd switched the alarms on before they went out. Only according to my DI, they hadn't. They're still swearing they did, or rather they were until poor Mrs Pumfrey copped it. I don't doubt Pumfrey will carry on doing battle.'

On the first two occasions, the Pumfreys' insurance company had made a settlement. The third occasion was still the subject of a lot of correspondence.

'And the last time was at Christmas,' said Roper. 'Nothing like it since?'

Lambert shook his head.

'So perhaps it started again last Friday night,' said Roper. 'And it all went wrong.'

'Possible,' agreed Lambert. The first illicit entry to the Pumfreys' house had been through a forced downstairs window. The second entry had been made through the jemmied back door of the kitchen; the door and its locks had been replaced. But that had proved no deterrent, since the entry on Christmas Eve had been affected by the same route and the Pumfreys had arrived home to find it minus one gilt-framed nineteenth-century water-colour and what

Lambert referred to as 'some kind of Chinese pot'. The
total haul from the Pumfreys' house alone stood at twenty
thousand pounds, and from all the burglaries in the same
series some twenty-seven thousand. So Pumfrey and his
wife had been by far the most severely hit, and it was
little wonder that he was writing strong letters to the CC
in order to get some action.

At eleven o'clock Makins drove him back to Little
Crow, DC Mills in the back seat with Lambert's burglary
file on his knees. The more Roper had thought about them
the more significant those break-ins had become. There
had been three series of them so far; so why not a fourth,
beginning last Friday night, the victims again the Pumfreys.

ROPER STOOD OUTSIDE the kitchen door, new and bright
yellow now, brown and rotting according to DC Mills'
photographs, at the time of the second burglary last October. It had been Mills and his DI who had come to
investigate it. Behind Roper, a small army of boiler-suited
cadets, working under two sergeants, were searching the
rear gardens for the ashtray, although it was Roper's
hunch that they weren't going to find it. It was long gone,
that ashtray.

The unofficial camera that Mills carried about with him
in furtherance of his hobby was inclined to make Roper
warm a little towards him. The original door had clearly
left much to be desired. Its lower quarters showed the
splits, shivers and peeling paint that were the visible
symptoms of wet-rot. The mortice lock had been badly
fitted and was almost an antique, and the only door-bolt,
fitted near the bottom of the door, had homed into a sheet
metal stirrup which in its turn had been screwed to the
door frame that had also rotted near the bottom.

'Didn't need much jemmying, did it?' said Roper.

'No, sir,' said Mills.

In fact Mills' photographs showed only a few dents in the woodwork around the area of the mortice lock, and they weren't deep; and it looked as if the door and the jamb had simply been sprung apart the quarter inch or so needed to release the mortice bar from its plate in the door frame. A knowledgeable child could have done it without too much trouble, and made hardly a sound. And the newly fitted burglar alarm had been triggered, and no one had heard it.

The window where the first entry had been effected last summer was again at the downstairs back of the house, the left-hand window of the dining-room. There was no photograph because Mills had still been in uniform then, pounding the pavements down in Weymouth, but he had mugged up on the incident in the light of the second burglary.

'Any glass broken?' asked Roper.

'No, sir,' said Mills. 'They used a knife or something to ease off the sash catch and climbed in over the window-sill.'

'And the insurance company paid up?' said Roper, eyebrows lifted.

'Yes, sir,' said Mills. 'Apparently.'

'Remind me to ask Pumfrey who he insures with,' said Roper. 'I could use a soft touch like that myself.'

The downstairs windows, however, had been immediately made secure, or as secure as sashed windows could ever be, and the alarm system had been fitted since.

At Christmas, the third break-in at the Pumfreys' had again been via the door to the kitchen, only on that occasion it hadn't been forced. Mrs Pumfrey had sworn that she had locked it, and both she and her husband agreed

with each other that the burglar alarm had been switched
on before they had gone out. She had stood by the stairs,
where the control box was secreted, and seen the green
neon light come on as her husband had clicked the switch.

'Did they go out together?'

'Yes, sir,' said Mills.

'And stay together—and come back together?'

'Yes, sir,' said Mills. 'I heard 'em both tell DI Spenlow.
It was some sort of business lunch. I suppose they had to
put up a public front.'

That sounded likely. From what Roper had gleaned, the
Pumfreys would not have gone out in each other's company unless they'd had to.

And on that third occasion, what had been stolen was
the object referred to by Chief Inspector Lambert as 'some
kind of Chinese pot'. It had been, in fact, a nineteenth-
century *famille rose,* Cantonese vase valued, according to
the insurance inventory in Lambert's file, at five and a
half thousand pounds. The French water-colour, stolen at
the same time, had been worth another four thousand
pounds. Neither the vase, some four feet tall, nor the water-colour, eighteen inches by thirteen over its gilt frame,
had been exactly pocketable, and the vase would not have
been exactly portable either, so that that burglary at least
must have been carried out by a villain with transport, or
more likely two villains, and one of those had to have
been an expert. An untutored eye glimpsing an old *famille
rose* vase would probably have dismissed it as a piece of
colourful old junk. Whoever had knocked off the Pumfreys' house, on that occasion at least, had certainly
known his business.

And last Friday night might have been a repeat of the
Christmas episode; there had been no signs of a forced
entry. The only difference had been that the house had

not been empty and the burglar alarm had certainly *not* been switched on. There had been not a mark on any of the window-sills, nor any signs on the woodwork around the windows and doors that showed they might have been tampered with. It sounded almost like an inside job. And that Mrs Pumfrey had interrupted it, to her bloody-ended detriment.

Pumfrey was his same abrasive self. 'I thought you were supposed to be investigating the murder of my wife, Superintendent.'

'I am, sir,' said Roper.

'About time you and your people came up with something, isn't it?'

'Time will tell, sir,' said Roper blandly, refusing to be ruffled. 'Time will tell.'

And hopefully it would. It usually did.

ROPER SAT AT ONE SIDE of the old whitewood table in the kitchen and Mrs González at the other. His arms encircled a mug of tea she had brewed for him, despite his protestations.

'How did Mrs Pumfrey spend her evenings, as a rule, Mrs González? Was there any kind of pattern… routine…something she did regularly?'

'She read, she smoke, she watch television, she bath, then she go to bed.'

'Did she go out some evenings?'

Mrs González shook her head. 'Two…three times, since we have been here. No more. She very quiet lady. Not much for going out. People come to see her, but she don't go out.'

'She took her bath at a regular time, did she? The same time every night?'

'No. Not at exact same time. But always before she just

go to bed. And sometimes in morning. Mrs Pumfrey very clean lady.'

Roper forebore to smile in the face of Mrs González' earnestness. 'How about Friday night?' he hazarded. When Mrs Pumfrey had been found she had been totally naked under her dressing-robe. Ergo: she might either have been on her way to the bath or have just come from it.

Mrs González suddenly grimaced, and slapped her forehead. 'Ah, *sí;* I forget! We hear water…water box in roof very noisy. Very noisy and very slow. It fill water box in airing cupboard.'

'This water,' said Roper. 'Was it running for very long on Friday night?'

'*Sí,*' she replied. 'Long time.'

'Long enough to fill a bath?'

She nodded more vigorously. '*Sí.* Ten minutes. More. Long time. Carlos say pipes are…' The word failed her; she made a circle with her hands, then closed them together, looked desperate.

'Clogged? Corroded?… Never mind.' Roper hurried on. 'I do understand.' Then he asked the crunch question: because if Mrs Pumfrey had drawn that bath *after* she had made her chicken sandwich he could put the time of death closer still. 'When, Mrs González? What time was it? Roughly?'

She could not remember. Few witnesses ever could; but Mrs González took her failure to heart.

'Was the football still on the television?'

Yes, it had been, she remembered that much.

'The first or second half? Do you remember?'

She shrugged. She had no interest in football, even when Real Madrid were playing. She would fetch Carlos. Carlos would know.

But Carlos did not, at least not exactly. Except that the game was into its second half. The programme had started at nine thirty, so that the first half would have been over by ten fifteen. Adding ten minutes to that for the interval would have made it ten twenty-five. It wasn't much, but at least it got Roper a half-hour nearer.

'How far into the second half, Mr González? Roughly?'

González thought about ten minutes, but admitted that he was only guessing and did not really want to commit himself. He agreed with his wife that all the hot water taps in the house ran with much slowness, and that to run enough hot water for a bath took the best part of ten minutes. Which would have made the time that Mrs Pumfrey had stepped into it some time around ten forty-five. But neither González nor his wife had heard the water draining away, so it was impossible to say how long she had been in the bath.

Then Mrs González took Roper upstairs to show him the bathroom. It was huge and luxurious, like an advertisement in the Sunday supplements, with bath, separate shower cubicle, handbasin and bidet, and lushly carpeted. But for all the elegant showiness, when Roper turned on the hot water taps, the result was a mere trickle. The flow of cold water was only marginally faster.

The cleaning materials were stored in a low cupboard that extended from the head end of the bath. It was in this cupboard that the rubber gloves were usually kept. They had been in there on Friday morning because Mrs González had worn them to clean the bath. She also remembered putting them back in the cupboard afterwards. And now they were gone, like the glass ashtray.

IT WAS MIDDAY, and despite the forecasters the weather had held. Rodgers and Hackett were back after their in-

terview with Mrs Hubert. The sun was turning the office
into a greenhouse and making the smell of new paint po-
tent again. On Tuesday, after the Easter holiday, the con-
tractor's workmen were coming back to replace the venetian blinds which they had taken down for their painting
operation. In the meantime, Roper assumed, it was his lot
to be either roasted alive or sit in a constant draught from
the open window behind him. For the time being he had
settled for something in between.

'She'd known Mrs Pumfrey for about ten years,' said
Hackett, her open pocket-book on her lap. 'Ever since the
Huberts moved down here after Mr Hubert's father died
and left him the family business. She last saw Mrs Pumfrey on Friday evening at about half past seven.'

'Alive, presumably?'

If Hackett noticed the acerbic quality of the question
she showed no sign of it. 'Yes, sir,' she said.

'I like to know these things, Sergeant. They're important.'

'Yes, sir,' said Hackett. 'I'm sorry. According to Mrs
Hubert, Mrs Pumfrey was in her underclothes and dressing-robe. She was going to have a whole evening of just
flopping about; that's what she told Mrs Hubert. Mr Pumfrey was out; probably with a woman, so Mrs Pumfrey
said. She was quite used to his affairs, apparently.'

'How about *Mrs* Pumfrey's affairs?'

'Mrs Hubert did point a cautious finger, sir,' said Hackett. 'She said she saw Mrs Pumfrey up here in the town
a couple of times with Dr Cresswell.'

'And she would have, wouldn't she?' said Roper.
'Cresswell was her brother-in-law.'

'She did say the doctor and Mrs Pumfrey looked a bit
close on both occasions, sir,' broke in Rodgers. 'But when

I pressed her, she said it was only an impression she'd got. Said she wasn't into scandal-mongering.'

Roper made a note on his jotter. Whether Mrs Hubert was scandal-mongering or not, it was something he would have to sort out with Cresswell himself. An ex-man-friend, even if he was a brother-in-law, might easily have an axe to grind.

'Did she have anything to say about Pumfrey?'

'Not a great deal,' said Hackett. 'But when she did, she kept referring to him as "poor old Bill". I got the idea they rubbed along pretty well together. And it was her opinion that the Pumfreys' marital problems were mostly the fault of Mrs Pumfrey.'

Mrs Hubert had suspected that Mrs Pumfrey was drinking a little more than usual, but she was never quite certain. She had first noticed this last Christmas. She and her husband had gone to the Pumfreys' for Christmas lunch and a general get-together—the Cresswells had been there, too, and Mr and Mrs Wainer. Pumfrey, already deeply into his cups by the time the guests arrived, became practically comatose by four o'clock and disappeared upstairs. His absence made everyone edgy, and it had not been the most pleasant gathering that Mrs Hubert remembered. At some time during the evening Mrs Pumfrey had found occasion to go to the kitchen. Mrs Cresswell had followed her shortly afterwards, and all the guests had heard their raised voices slanging each other like a couple of fishwives from across the hall. Cresswell went out of the room, presumably to calm things down in the kitchen. Only Mrs Pumfrey returned, naturally flustered, and told everyone that the Cresswells had gone home because Sarah Cresswell hadn't been feeling well. The two sisters quarrelled a lot, or so had stated Mrs Hubert. They didn't seem to get on at all, although Mrs Hubert suspected that the cause of the rift was Mrs Cresswell rather than Mrs Pumfrey. Although Roper recalled, according to Cresswell, that it had been *his* wife who had tried to patch up the quarrel...

'...definitely a strange woman.'

'She said that, did she?'

'Quote,' said Rodgers. 'Our Sarah is a very strange lady.'

'She takes rambles on her own at night, apparently,' said Hackett. 'In tatty old clothes. And doesn't talk to anybody unless she really has to. Mrs Hubert thinks Dr Cresswell's taken her up to London a couple of times to see a friend of his who's a psychiatrist. On the quiet, of course.'

'I take walks at night,' said Roper. 'Clears my mind.'

'*She* does it whatever the weather,' said Hackett. 'When Mrs Hubert saw her out wandering last night, it was raining stair-rods, she was covered in mud and she wasn't even wearing a raincoat. Mrs Hubert stopped and asked her if she wanted a lift, but Mrs Cresswell shook her head and carried on walking. Didn't say a word.'

'Perhaps she doesn't like Mrs Hubert,' said Roper. Although Mrs Hubert was probably right. 'How about that lighter?'

'We showed her the Polaroid,' said Rodgers. 'She thought the lighter was Mrs Pumfrey's. But when we pointed out the engraving on it, she changed her mind.'

'Pointed out?' said Roper. 'It's twice life-size, that picture.'

'I think she needs glasses,' said Hackett. 'Only they'll spoil her image.'

'She did make a suggestion, though,' said Rodgers. 'The initials fit the Cresswells. Bernard and Sarah. Mrs Cresswell packed up smoking six months ago.'

Roper made a note of that.

'Mrs Hubert seem reliable, did she?'

'She was a bit uptight when we arrived,' said Hackett. 'Nervous…you know?'

Roper set little store by that. Most folk were when the law came calling.

'And her husband turned up while we were there,' said Hackett. 'Wanted to know what the hell we were doing about his burglary.'

Roper made a note of that, too. It was still possible, and becoming likelier, that the Little Crow housebreaker and Mrs Pumfrey's killer were one and the same.

ROPER PUSHED THROUGH the swing-doors of the mortuary and smelt the familiar cocktail of antiseptic and formalin and hospital floor polish float up to meet him. From a room on the left came the clatter of a metal bucket on tiles, the flopping of a wet mop and a cheerful, if out of tune, male voice declaiming that the sun had got his hat on.

Roper rapped on the open door. He had to do it twice, the second time louder, before the singing stopped and the mop ceased swinging, and the spry, wizened little figure in a green boiler suit and wellingtons caught sight of him in the doorway. He held up an admonitory finger before reaching inside his boiler suit to switch on what was obviously a hearing aid in his shirt pocket. Then he wriggled the earpiece more firmly into his ear and gave an experimental tap on the microphone under his boiler suit. That the device was still working seemed to surprise him. 'Yes, guv'nor?' he enquired cheerily, his head tilted to one side like a querulous little bird. 'Which one are you for?'

'Police,' said Roper, holding out his ID. Still clutching

his mop handle, the cleaner trailed it behind him as he sloshed across the wet tiles to take the card.

'Thought you were a bit flash for an undertaker,' he said, beaming around a set of overly large false teeth as he handed the card back again. 'Looking for a client in partic'lar, are you, guv'nor?'

'Examination theatre,' said Roper, tucking his card away. 'Someone's doing a second post-mortem on a Mrs Pumfrey. Can you point the way?'

'Theatre two, guv'nor. Second door on your right. Come to watch, have you?'

'Hopefully not, old lad,' said Roper. 'Thanks.'

The sun already had its hat on again as he skirted a stainless steel body-trolley then a standing yellow notice bearing a warning about floor polishing in progress.

When he poked his head around the swing-door of the theatre, Wilson was alone, sitting on a high stool beside a workbench and bent intently over what appeared to be an array of small white stones laid out on a piece of black paper. Wilson was delicately poking them together, like pieces of a jigsaw puzzle, with the ends of a pair of tweezers. There was no sign of Mrs Pumfrey's corpse, to Roper's relief. Mortuaries made him all too aware of his own frail mortality.

'Got yourself a new toy, I see,' he said, from the doorway.

'A nice little puzzle,' said Wilson, still intent on pushing the fragments of bone together. 'Do come in, Mr Roper. Long time no see.'

'Not half long enough,' said Roper. 'How goes it?'

'Oh, the poor lady was clobbered all right,' said Wilson. He sat upright, hitched his horn-rimmed spectacles from his hair and down on to the bridge of his nose, then stretched an arm for a covered Petrie dish standing beside an autoclave at the back of the bench. He held it out on the palm of one hand and lifted the lid with the other. '*Et voilà,*' he said.

Roper joined him at the bench and took the dish. He held it under the bright light of the illuminated stand magnifier that Wilson had been using to help him assemble his jigsaw. He saw three minute splinters of glass, one with what appeared to be a fragment of pinkish-grey meat adhering to it.

'Find another piece of glass with an identical refractive index,' said Wilson, 'and you've got your weapon.'

'It was an ashtray,' said Roper, passing back the dish.

Wilson lofted his eyebrows approvingly. 'You've found it then?' He capped the dish and put it back beside the autoclave.

'No such luck,' said Roper. 'It's still only a guess. But there's a bloody great ashtray missing from Mrs Pumfrey's bedroom. It was there last Friday lunchtime, and gone by Saturday afternoon.' He sketched its size between his hands. 'So big,' he said.

'Looks about right,' said Wilson. 'It had to be something heavy to cause the amount of penetration that it did, and perhaps with an edge or a sharp corner. I'll show you the X-rays.'

He stepped down from the high stool and led the way to an illuminated X-ray viewer further along the bench. A large yellow Kodak envelope lay beside it. One X-ray negative was already on the screen and leapt to brightness as Wilson switched on the illumination. It showed in black and grey, in profile, the most intimate secrets of Mrs Pumfrey's skull, several gold crowns on her lower back jaw, a steel pin retaining another nearer the front, and, more trenchantly, the hole at the top of her skull and the mangled mash of her brain in the area beneath it.

'Struck from the back, do you think?' asked Roper.

'I thought so at first,' said Wilson. 'But the initial penetration was here.' A latex sheathed little finger rose and indicated the lighter grey area of the wound near the back of the skull. 'Then it sliced forward towards the forehead. Death was probably instantaneous.'

'Hopefully,' said Roper.

'Indeed,' agreed Wilson, with a sympathetic twitch to the corner of his mouth. Wilson, in Roper's opinion, was a good 'un. He knew his gruesome business backwards, forwards and sideways, and he never fluffed his lines in court. If he had a fault it was caution; but then Roper had that too.

'And these are from the ultrasonic scan,' said Wilson. For the X-ray negative were substituted two from the Kodak envelope. To Roper, they were even less intelligible than the X-ray. 'She had an extraordinarily thin skull,' said Wilson. 'This one,' he pointed to the left-hand negative on the viewer, 'is looking down at it. Three radiating cracks; didn't show on the profile X-ray, of course. That's where the wound originated—this is the general site, by the way.' The latex-clad finger traced the boundary of the fracture. It was approximately an isosceles triangle, with the major apex of the triangle nearer the back of the skull and the jagged base of it more or less parallel with Mrs Pumfrey's forehead. Three fine, white radiating lines showed the probable point of impact at the apex. 'And these are those shards of glass,' said Wilson. 'Here, here, and here.' The fingertip indicated three white dots where the ultrasonic echo had been reflected back more strongly than they would have been from the far softer and more acoustically absorbent tissue of the brain. All three were close to the point of impact. 'It was a forward-moving,

slashing blow,' said Wilson. 'Forward-moving in relation
to the poor lady, of course.'

'Somebody fairly tall then,' proposed Roper.

'Or poor Mrs Pumfrey was stooping…or kneeling
down, perhaps. I'd say that was likelier. But whichever,
it was a hefty chop on someone's part. And there might
have been two blows,' said Wilson. 'She might have
warded the first one off.' He put up another X-ray, this
one taken at the initial post-mortem examination. It
showed the chip of bone displaced from the ulna of her
right forearm. 'Perhaps she saw the blow coming and
lifted her arm…so.' Wilson dropped almost to one knee
and raised his right forearm to protect his head as Mrs
Pumfrey might have done. The thumb of his left hand
demonstrated the downward sweep of the glass ashtray.
'She would have bled profusely.'

'I know,' said Roper. 'We've got a rug. The pile was
all glued together with the stuff.'

Wilson returned to his stool at the other end of the
bench and showed Roper the four or five fragments of
Mrs Pumfrey's skull that he had so far reassembled. The
point of impact was quite apparent, at the tip of one of
the fragments, as an indentation, with tiny flakes of loose
bone at its edges.

'Why didn't the other pathologist find all this out?'
asked Roper.

'Simple,' said Wilson. 'He wasn't looking for anything
untoward, not initially. According to Mrs Pumfrey's doctor, she had fallen down the stairs. And since he was Mrs
Pumfrey's regular GP, my predecessor saw no reason—
at first—to question the diagnosis. But when he saw the
depth of the penetration, he showed uncommonly good
sense and advised the County Coroner. Thank your lucky
stars he did.'

'I could have done without the work,' said Roper.

'So could I,' agreed Wilson. 'I can think of better things to do on a sunny Easter Sunday…ah, George.' Wilson had turned as the cleaner's cheerful face appeared around the edge of the door.

'Black and very sweet like last time. And a few biscuits. How about you, Mr Roper? He makes a very virile cup of coffee, does our George. Don't you George?'

'Do an' all,' said George.

'Not for me, thanks,' said Roper, to George's evident disappointment.

George's face disappeared again.

'How about you?' asked Wilson. 'Any of your chaps come up with anything?'

'Not yet,' said Roper. 'Except I think the husband's already counting his chickens, Mrs Pumfrey's sister's seen a psychiatrist a couple of times, and the doctor who signed the body away on Friday night was Mrs Pumfrey's brother-in-law.'

'Oh, that's naughty, that last one,' said Wilson. 'It would have been wiser in the circumstances to have called in a second opinion. Perhaps he acted in all innocence, though.'

'Maybe,' said Roper.

'And if he didn't?'

'Who knows, Mr Wilson,' said Roper. 'If we could read minds we wouldn't be stooging around here, would we?'

NINE

THERE WAS A SCREECH of brakes, a squeal of tyres, the horrendous thud of metal crumpling against metal, and shattering glass. A woman screamed. The time was exactly one fourteen on Easter Sunday afternoon, there was no doubt about that. Traffic accidents involving police vehicles are rare, but when they occur they are more precisely documented than most.

Roper had returned to Crow Hill police station at ten past one. There were two more desks in the office and three more chairs. Makins was pinning up the photographs that Mills and the SOCO had taken at Chalk House and Hackett was typing a transcription of her own and Rodgers' notes of their interview with Mrs Hubert. Like the eye of a cyclone, there came a lull in every murder inquiry, the dead time, when there was nothing much to be done and nowhere to go and nobody was quite sure what questions to ask next.

He hung up his raincoat on the coatrack.

'Dave Price not back yet?' he asked, as he wedged himself into what little space there was now between his desk and the window.

'He phoned about an hour ago,' said Hackett. 'He was stopping off in Dorchester for a bite to eat. He said Foyle turned out to be a dead end. He didn't mind telling Dave about Mrs Pumfrey's will, but he wouldn't discuss the Pumfreys' private life. He pleaded ethics.'

'And Dr Cresswell phoned,' said Rodgers. 'He'd like to call in and see you—before you go along and see him tonight, that is. He said it was very private and confidential. I said you'd be free at four o'clock.'

Roper glanced at his watch. It was eleven minutes past one. 'Did he say why?'

'It sounded a bit urgent,' said Rodgers. 'He said it wouldn't take more than ten minutes. I told him if you couldn't make it, I'd ring him back.'

'I'll see him,' said Roper. It would be interesting to know what Cresswell had to say that could not wait until six o'clock, when Roper had an appointment with him at his cottage.

'Nothing at the mortuary then?' asked Makins.

'Not a lot,' said Roper. Afterwards, Wilson had taken him along to see the body. Mrs Pumfrey had been a good-looking and well-set-up woman in the prime of life. Statistically, at least, she had had thirty years more of it left to her. Instead, she had been transmuted into a refrigerated cadaver in a drawer of the public mortuary, which was no kind of justice at all in Roper's reckoning.

Nor was it any kind of justice that his own thoughts kept returning to Mrs Cresswell, and those gold and garnet earrings, and a mental picture of Mrs Cresswell trying them on in front of Mrs Pumfrey's dressing mirror, with Mrs Pumfrey standing beside her. It wasn't fair on Mrs Cresswell, and perhaps as ideas went it would never get off the ground; the earrings and Mrs Pumfrey's murder might be entirely unconnected. Pumfrey had said that the earrings were probably about the house somewhere, which was a remarkably cavalier approach for someone whose house had been burgled three times in a few months, but it was Roper's guess that the earrings had left the house last Friday night, and with Mrs Pumfrey's killer. And if they had not been stolen, but given, their most likely recipient was, again, Mrs Cresswell, perhaps as a peace of-

fering after the quarrel the two of them had had in the
kitchen at Christmas. Roper had learned at his first inspector's knee, many years ago now, that the motives for
murder were as many as all the days that were numbered
in Paradise. But, in the end, the genealogy of all of them
could be traced back to but four antecedents: panic, pas-
sion, prejudice and greed.

'Whose turn to get the coffees in?' said Makins.

'I'll go,' said Rodgers. 'How about you, Super?'

'Leave me out,' said Roper. 'I think I'll knock off for
some lunch.'

But it was one fourteen now and Rodgers didn't even
get as far as the door with the tray in his hand. Like
everyone else in the room he froze as the screech came
up from the High Street, then the high-pitched squeal, and
then, with awful inevitability, the slam of metal into metal
and the sound of glass tinkling to fragments. The woman's
scream came somewhere towards the end of the sequence.

Roper scrambled to his feet. Makins was first to the
other window. For a few moments more, Crow Hill
dropped back into the somnolent quiet of a Sunday afternoon.

To the left of the station was a pedestrian crossing. An
open-mouthed woman, mercifully still on her feet, was
standing paralysed a few feet in front of a grey Ford Escort—Dave Price's Escort—that looked as if it had been
shunted a couple of yards across the zebra stripes by a
rust-infested white van with a collapsed front end and
steam gouting from its smashed radiator. The back of the
grey Ford was hull down on its springs under the weight
of the front of the van which had climbed partly up the
Escort's back end under the momentum of the impact.

By the time Roper reached the street a WPC was already steering the shaken woman into the station, and

white-faced Price had kicked his door open and was advancing grimly towards the driving cab of the white van.

He beckoned with a crooked finger. 'You,' he shouted angrily. 'Out!'

The other driver, unable to open his own jammed door, had to climb down on the near side. Short-armed, short-legged, and with a head that was mostly overgrown greasy black hair and beard, his gross body looked as if it was straining his clothes dangerously close to bursting point.

'You hurt?' asked Price.

'No, I'm all right. Look I'm—'

'Good,' said Price, one hand already diving into his jacket for his pocket-book. 'What's your name?'

'Seymour,' said the other. He looked alarmedly around at the sea of navy-blue uniforms that had erupted about him. 'Look, I'm sober,' he protested. 'It was an accident. I just wasn't thinking for a couple of seconds. I was just driving the van over to a bloke who's going to buy it. It was an honest-to-goodness bloody accident.'

'You all right, Dave?' asked Roper, breaking in at Price's shoulder.

'Fine,' said Price, although he didn't look it. 'Do you mind stepping into the station, Mr Seymour?'

Only then did it dawn on Seymour that Price, too, was a police officer, and it looked for a second as if he was going to make a run for it. But then his shoulders slumped, and he made his way between the arcade of blue uniforms that opened up before him as he crossed the pavement and mounted the steps to the station.

It took an hour. Seymour, it transpired, had been stone-cold sober, and an examination of his van showed that his brakes had been sound and the treads of his tyres just within the legal limit. It seemed that Price had stopped at the pedestrian crossing to let the woman across the High

Street, and Seymour had simply braked too late and
ploughed into Price's back. The charge was merely one
of driving without due care and attention, a modest
enough beginning for the event that was to provide the
first substantial lead towards finding the murderer of Stella
Pumfrey.

AT HALF PAST TWO Price was restored to his former calm
self and relating the gist of his interview with Jack Foyle,
down at Portesham earlier in the day.

Mrs Pumfrey's will, according to Foyle, was a veritable
hornet's nest of impracticalities, due mainly to the fact
that it had to hinge about the will of Mrs Pumfrey's late
mother.

Chalk House, it turned out now, was not the property
solely of the late Mrs Pumfrey. Her position there was
one only of trusteeship. Under the terms of the mother's
will, the house and its contents were to be shared equally
between Stella Pumfrey and her sister, Sarah Cresswell.
The house could not be sold without both sisters agreeing
to it, and if there was a sale then the proceeds were to be
equally divided. The contents of the house were the subject of similar conditions.

The jewellery, however, had been disposed of more
quaintly. Again, Mrs Pumfrey had been its trustee. And
the collection was not to be broken up until Mrs Cresswell, the younger sister, reached her forty-second birthday, after which the items were to be shared equally between any children that she and Mrs Pumfrey might have
had between them—or between Mrs Pumfrey and Mrs
Cresswell equally should that progeny not have been
forthcoming. Which it had not, in either case.

'So now who gets what, exactly?' asked Roper.

'Half the house to William Pumfrey,' said Price. 'And

the other half and all the contents and jewellery to Mrs Cresswell—who also has the right to sell off the place once the will's been probated. Pumfrey won't have a say in the matter.'

'But he will get a pretty hefty cut,' said Roper. 'Or will he?'

'Hefty's right,' said Price. 'About half a million, even after inheritance tax.'

Mrs Cresswell's share would be even more, nearer three-quarters of a million; and Roper could not immediately think of two people with a better motive for murder than that.

ON THE DOT of four o'clock, Dr Cresswell was shown up by a WPC, and made manifest the lack of room in the temporary office.

'It *is* rather private, Superintendent,' he said, glancing pointedly around at Hackett and Makins and Rodgers. 'I'd hoped to see you alone.'

'It's all right, George,' Roper said to Makins, as Makins rose to lead the others out. 'We'll use Chief Inspector Lambert's office. This way, Dr Cresswell.'

Like everywhere else that afternoon the passage was quiet; and Lambert had taken the afternoon off, so that it was only from habit that Roper rapped on the office door and bent his ear to the panel before stepping in. He heard a quick rustle of papers from inside and a couple of swift, carpeted footsteps; and opened the door just in time to see the door closing softly on the adjacent CID room.

'Take a chair, Doctor,' he said, catching a whiff of skulduggery. 'I'll be right with you.'

He opened the door to the CID room. The only person in there was DC Mills, just about to drop his behind on his chair.

'Nothing to do, Mills?' asked Roper.

Mills' dark face flushed as he looked up. 'No, sir,' he said. 'Not a lot. Just paperwork. I'm on stand-by.'

'Yours or Mr Lambert's paperwork?'

The flush deepened. 'I only went in to drop a report in Mr Lambert's filing tray, sir.'

'A report about what?'

'On street car-dealing and clocking,' said Mills. 'A bloke called Seymour down in Little Crow.'

'You'd better have a word with Inspector Price, then,' said Roper. 'He's just had a brush with a bloke called Seymour. Could be one and the same.' And so saying, he reached behind him for the door lever and stepped back into Lambert's office while the flush was still on Mills' face.

'Sorry about that,' he said as he sat down on the opposite side of the desk from Cresswell.

Cresswell smiled thinly back. He was in an anorak over an old tweed sports jacket and looked as if he had aged ten years since Roper had last seen him. He was clearly a worried man.

When Roper offered him a cup of tea he shook his head abstractedly and mumbled vaguely, 'No. No... But thank you all the same... I know how busy you must be.'

Roper lit a cheroot and crabbed his hand across the desk for Lambert's glass ashtray. A long uneasy silence ensued.

'It's about Mrs Pumfrey, is it, Dr Cresswell?' he prompted, when Cresswell seemed to have forgotten what he had come for; or was even perhaps wishing that he had not come at all because it was certainly looking that way.

'Yes,' said Cresswell, at last, looking up miserably. 'Well, no...not exactly.'

Roper waited. Outside in the street, what sounded like

an articulated lorry growled by and made the building
shake.

'To come to the point, Superintendent,' Cresswell began again, visibly wracked as he cast about for the right
words as the lorry went from hearing. 'I've come about
my wife.'

THERE ARE MANY FOLK who prefer to make their confes-
sions to a back. It avoids eye contact and implies an im-
personality on the part of the hearer, much as the fretted
screen serves a similar purpose in a church confessional.

Apart from a couple of teenagers, locked in a secret
embrace in the shadowy doorway of the jeweller's shop
opposite, the High Street was deserted again.

'You think your wife went out on Friday night, Doctor,'
said Roper. 'But you can't be sure?'

'She goes out often at night,' said Cresswell, to Roper's
back. 'And I am *sure* she went out on Friday night. Her
hair was wet... I'm certain about that. And the curtains
weren't drawn. And she'd let the fire go out, too.'

'Perhaps she simply went for a walk,' said Roper.

'I think she went over to see Stella,' said Cresswell.

'And supposing she did?' asked Roper. 'Why should
that worry you, Dr Cresswell?'

Silence. Time was suspended. Nothing stirred anywhere.

'Well, sir?' asked Roper, when the silence had dragged
on until it was like the shriek of chalk on a blackboard.

'My wife...' Again there was an agonised pause. 'My
wife pretends to be ill, Superintendent,' said Cresswell.

'Pretends, sir?' Roper turned slowly and perched his
behind on the window-ledge. 'Why should she pretend?'

'She hates me,' said Cresswell.

'A strong word, sir,' said Roper. 'Hate.'

'Oh, she hates me all right,' said Cresswell. 'She wouldn't be doing it otherwise, would she?'

'Doing what, sir?' asked Roper patiently.

Cresswell looked up and at last met Roper's gaze, and made some attempt to pull himself together. 'She's feigning some unidentifiable mental illness, Superintendent. She pretends to forget things.'

'We all forget something at some time, sir,' said Roper.

Cresswell twitched one corner of his mouth peevishly. 'This is cold-blooded cussedness, Superintendent. I know. I *do* know. She does it to discredit me. She has perfectly good clothes. She won't wear them; she prefers to wander about looking like a bloody tramp. When I've patients in the waiting-room, she sometimes goes in there and starts dusting—in a bloody apron; I've a cleaning woman who comes in each morning and does an excellent job. And sometimes, if she knows I'm going out to see a woman patient, she'll ring the woman up to see if I've arrived; and half an hour later ring up again to see if I'm still there.' For a moment, Cresswell ran out of wind. 'She thinks I'm knocking them all off—to put it bluntly.

'And sometimes,' he continued, after something else came to mind, 'she gets to the checkout in the supermarket and tells them she's got no cash…and I have to drop everything and drive up there and bail her out. And each time, I've checked her handbag. She *always* has the money—or a credit card.'

Roper still waited patiently for Cresswell to get to the point, because he still had not.

'And what you're telling me has a bearing on the death of Mrs Pumfrey, does it, sir?'

'Yes,' said Cresswell absently. 'I'm not certain, of course. She won't tell me, you see.'

'You still haven't answered that question I asked you

earlier, sir,' said Roper. 'Perhaps we should start with that and work on from there.'

'What?' said Cresswell, frowning as he tried to remember what that question was. 'I'm sorry. What question?'

'You told me you thought your wife might have gone across to see Mrs Pumfrey on Friday evening. I asked why that worried you.'

With his head down, Cresswell considered that at some length. Then he looked up wretchedly and said, 'I didn't tell you the exact truth yesterday, Superintendent... I'm sorry.'

Roper waited again in silence, careful not to prompt, and wondered if Cresswell knew the possible extent of his wife's inheritance.

'I told you that my wife hadn't spoken to Stella for several weeks. It was several months. Christmas Day. Last Christmas afternoon, to be exact. That's when the row was between Sarah and Stella. And it wasn't Stella who kept the feud going, it was my wife. Stella tried to patch up the silly business several times, but Sarah wouldn't have it.'

'What was this quarrel about, sir?'

'Me,' said Cresswell. 'It was about me. She's very jealous...my wife is. Stella had lent me some money; a few thousand. It was for the new surgery; the old one simply wasn't big enough. I already had an overdraft from the bank. Halfway through the building I decided I wanted some changes, and it was easier to borrow the extra cash from Stella—and cheaper. Stella offered, I hasten to add. I didn't ask her.'

'And this loan from her sister upset your wife, I take it?'

'God, yes,' said Cresswell vehemently. 'She accused Stella and me of having an affair.'

'And had you?' asked Roper.

Cresswell sighed. 'No, of course we hadn't,' he said. 'But there were circumstances that made my wife think we had.'

'And when was this, sir?' asked Roper.

'Last December,' said Cresswell. He had been attending a three-day medical conference in London. Unknown to him, or Mrs Pumfrey, the two of them had spent two nights sleeping in the same hotel. They had met, quite by chance, in the foyer of the hotel, on the third evening.

Mrs Pumfrey had been on her way out, Cresswell had suspected, from the way she had been dressed, to meet a man-friend. Their conversation had only been brief. Mrs Pumfrey had then gone out and Cresswell, after a couple of drinks in the bar, had retired to his room for an early night. It had occurred to neither of them that each had left the hotel telephone number with Sarah Cresswell in the event of an emergency.

'...she rang me,' said Cresswell. 'At three o'clock in the morning. What I didn't know was that she'd rung Stella's room only a couple of minutes before...and of course she didn't get an answer. She said to me: I'd like to speak to Mrs Pumfrey, please. I was half asleep and didn't recognise her voice; at least, not at once, and that made it worse. She called me a lying bastard, she knew Stella was there, she said. Then she slammed the telephone down. When we got back here, Sarah taxed us both... Stella told her, yes, she had been out of her room that night, and with a man, a man she'd gone to London to meet, a long-standing affair. I denied it, too; but Sarah didn't believe either of us. She's given me hell ever since.'

It was thin evidence. If Cresswell and Mrs Pumfrey had been conducting an affair they would hardly each have given Mrs Cresswell their hotel telephone number. But there was more to it; there often was.

On two previous occasions, Mrs Cresswell had seen, admittedly at some distance, the figure of her sister stepping into Cresswell's car up here in Crow Hill High Street. On the first occasion, Mrs Cresswell had mentioned this sighting only casually. Cresswell told her she must have been mistaken; he had been out on his rounds, and nowhere near Crow Hill High Street. A few weeks later Mrs Cresswell made a similar sighting, and mentioned it less casually. And, again, Cresswell told her she must be mistaken; at the particular lunchtime he had been at the infirmary again, nowhere near Crow Hill High Street.

And then, a week or so afterwards, had come the episode of the mutual hotel booking.

But nor was it as simple even as that. This was Mrs Cresswell's second marriage. Ten years ago, having shared with her sister their mother's not inconsiderable liquid assets, she had woken one morning to find herself a widow, and broke. Her husband, so the police later stated at the inquest, had aimed himself and his Mercedes, at some one hundred and ten miles an hour, off the road and straight into the wall of a derelict roadside café as a way of ending it all. Not only had that gentleman gone through all her money at more or less a stroke but had also made over the marital home as surety for other debts besides without her knowledge. This, and the fact that another lady surfaced at the inquest and proclaimed herself to be the late husband's 'fiancée', had been sufficient to put Sarah Cresswell, as she was now, into a nursing home that specialised in mental disorders. In the event, Stella Pumfrey had paid the bills for the nursing home, and Dr Cresswell had moonlighted there as its physician between his spells as a house doctor at a nearby hospital. Romance blossomed and the marriage took place. As marriages went, this one had gone well, but Mrs Cresswell's first experience had left her with a strong feeling of insecurity.

'But despite your wife's suspicion, sir, you and Mrs Cresswell went across to Christmas lunch at your sister-in-law's house.'

'We always went over there at Christmas. A sort of standing invitation. A few days before Stella rang up and asked us to go across again. I didn't want to go the way things were. But to my surprise, Sarah did. I thought she wanted to make her peace with Stella. But she only went over there to have a blazing row with her, more or less in public. Several of our friends were there, you see. Since then, it's only gone from bad to worse.'

Cresswell scratched intently at something on the back of his right hand. 'And that's why I had to see you privately, Superintendent,' he said. 'D'you see?'

Still wary of prompting the man, or, worse, putting words into his mouth, all Roper dared to venture was, 'No, I'm sorry, Dr Cresswell, you still haven't made yourself clear.'

Cresswell looked up miserably. 'It's possible,' he said, 'just possible, that my wife might have killed Stella... *That's* what I've been trying to tell you. Do you understand now?'

TEN

WHEN ROPER CAME BACK Cresswell was still hunched forward in Lambert's visitor's chair and looking like death. Between his hands was a crumpled linen handkerchief, and when he glanced up Roper saw that his eyes were tired and blood-shot, and the man himself was almost at the end of his tether; so that Roper, still not a totally conditioned cynic, even after thirty years of plying his trade, felt a genuine upsurge of sympathy. There could not be many men, this Easter Sunday afternoon, wedged in the kind of cleft stick in which Dr Cresswell found himself.

'Try and get this down you.'

Some of the tea slopped over into the saucer as Cresswell reached up for it. 'Thank you,' he said. 'I'm sorry about all this.'

Roper moved around the desk to sit in Lambert's chair, and watched Cresswell sip gratefully at the hot sweet cup of tea. Finally, Cresswell had had all he wanted of it, half turned to put the cup and saucer on the desk and dabbed at his mouth with the crumpled handkerchief.

'You were out yourself on Friday night?' asked Roper.

'Yes,' said Cresswell. 'It was a hectic evening. I was called out soon after seven on a maternity case; then I went on to a patient with terminal cancer. The old lady had refused to go into hospital. She died while I was with her.'

'So you finally got home when?'

'About quarter past midnight.'

'And your wife's hair was wet. Perhaps she'd washed it.'

'Her shoes and skirt were wet, too,' said Cresswell. 'It wasn't just her hair… And the fire was out.'

'Was it raining when you got back indoors?'

'I don't think so,' said Cresswell. 'To the best of my memory, the rain stopped around here just before midnight… She was drenched.'

'Did you ask her where she'd been?'

Cresswell nodded.

'And what did she say?'

Cresswell shrugged defeatedly. 'Nothing,' he said. 'She won't tell me anything. It's almost as if she wants me to believe she did kill Stella.'

'And you think that's possible, do you, sir?'

Cresswell rocked his head from side to side. 'God knows,' he said. 'What I do know for certain is that she detested Stella absolutely. Perhaps even more than she hates me.'

'Is she violent…your wife?'

'Only verbally,' said Cresswell. 'She didn't used to be…but just lately, she's absolute hell to live with.'

'If your wife did kill Mrs Pumfrey, Dr Cresswell…and I stress that *if*…she would have had to get into the house. Do you think Mrs Pumfrey would have let her in? After this row you said they'd had?'

'Oh, yes,' said Cresswell, reaching again for his teacup. 'Whatever anybody tells you about Stella, she was a good sort. Help anybody. She was soft… And, anyway, Sarah's got a door key. I told her she ought to give it back…in the circumstances. But she never did.'

Roper's eyebrows had gone up. Another key to the Pumfreys' home might be just the evidence he was looking for.

'You're saying Mrs Cresswell had a key to Chalk House?'

'Keys,' said Cresswell, stressing the plural. 'A Yale and a Chubb. She was always in and out of there. It was her house, too, you see. Well…half of it was. Stella…well, lived there with Bill…and she was brought up there… Stella…and Sarah of course.'

'So your wife was free to walk in and out, more or less as the fancy took her.'

'Yes,' agreed Cresswell. 'But of course she didn't, not unless Stella knew she was coming… And to keep an eye on the place when neither Bill nor Stella was there.'

'Until last Christmas,' said Roper.

'Yes,' said Cresswell. 'It all stopped then.'

'What happened when Mr Pumfrey had the door locks changed?'

'Stella sent a new set of keys through the post.'

'I see,' said Roper, as a whole new can of worms to open was set before him. 'Which means your wife could have let herself in to Chalk House on Friday night; and no one in there need have been any the wiser.'

'Yes,' said Cresswell. 'That's it exactly.'

And if anyone had known of Mrs Pumfrey's routine, who more knowledgeably than her sister? Mrs Cresswell would have known that the servants had Friday evenings off, that Mrs Pumfrey took a bath at roughly the same time each night. And known that house as well as her own. And, for her own part, spent Friday evening between seven o'clock and midnight ostensibly on her own and unobserved.

'You didn't go home between calls on Friday night?' asked Roper. 'Or phone?'

'Why do you ask that?'

'I only wondered if you might have seen or spoken to

your wife some time during the evening,' said Roper. 'It would help us to fix a time.'

'No,' said Cresswell. 'I didn't. I was with Mrs Sefton—that was the delivery—until nine o'clock. Then I went along to old Mrs Bentley; she died at a quarter to eleven. The nurse laid her out, then I told her she could go home. I stayed behind until the Coroner's Officer and the undertakers came.'

'Which was when?'

If Cresswell realised that his own movements on Friday night were being questioned he showed no sign of it.

'The Coroner's Officer…about ten to midnight, and the undertakers a few minutes afterwards,' he said.

'This Mrs Bentley; I take it she had a husband?'

'No,' said Cresswell. 'She'd been a widow for the best part of twenty years.'

'Was there some other relative in the house?'

'No,' said Cresswell. 'She lived completely alone. There's a nephew up in Suffolk…it was the nephew who was paying for the private nurses…the old lady refused to go into hospital…she thought that if she left her cottage she'd get squatters in. They get these funny ideas, old folk.'

So Cresswell had been alone with the mutest kind of witness, a corpse, for the best part of an hour last Friday night. And, more relevantly, during the hour that straddled the probable time of death of his sister-in-law. Even assuming that the nurse had taken half an hour to wash and lay out the body, then Cresswell had still had more than thirty minutes to play with. And that had been time enough and plenty.

'Where did this Mrs Bentley live exactly, Dr Cresswell?'

'In Little Crow,' said Cresswell. 'About two minutes' drive from the surgery.'

And still Cresswell seemed unaware that he was scuttling himself deeper into the mire of suspicion with every word he uttered.

Then, sitting at the desk, and now with a notepad in front of him, Roper took Cresswell again through the events of Friday evening and night and carefully jotted down the times as Cresswell repeated them, and from time to time chipped in with a question or two. The answer to one in particular astonished him.

'You're saying, Dr Cresswell, that when you told your wife that her sister was probably dead, she replied *"good"*?'

'Yes,' said Cresswell, nodding. 'And then she smiled.'

'You're sure about that?'

'Absolutely certain,' said Cresswell. 'She actually smiled.'

'And how has your wife been since?'

'Blank,' said Cresswell. 'Exactly the way she was before.'

But still he denied strenuously that his wife was the victim of any identifiable disorder. It was her way of breaking him, her way of paying him back for his alleged affair with her sister.

'Have you ever had your wife examined professionally?'

Yes, he had. Twice. And she had gone willingly. And succeeded in making him look a fool on both occasions. Both psychiatrists had drawn him aside afterwards and asked him why he was treating his wife like a backward child; because she wasn't.

'And last night, she suggested you might have killed

her sister. What do you think caused her to draw that conclusion, Dr Cresswell?'

'She phoned Mrs Bentley's house, so she says, and didn't get a reply, so she presumed I wasn't there. She thinks I was across at Stella's—'

Roper looked up sharply at that.

'I keep telling her, she must have dialled the wrong number.'

Yes, she might have done; on the other hand she might have dialled the right one.

'When?' asked Roper. 'Did she mention the time?'

'Yes,' said Cresswell. 'Half past eleven—at least, that's what she tells me.'

'And where did she ring from? Have you asked her that?'

Cresswell had not thought to do that; but Roper would, when he saw the good lady at six o'clock. On a previous occasion, or so alleged Cresswell, his wife had drawn the wrong conclusion from a telephone call. Had she, on this occasion, drawn a correct one?

ROPER WATCHED Cresswell's despondent back descending the stairs to the duty desk and the street. After thirty-odd years in the Force, this was the first time a man had come to him with the suggestion that his wife was a murder suspect. He might, of course, be right. He might equally be wrong. It could even be possible that Cresswell himself had killed Mrs Pumfrey, and was trying to hive off the blame on to his wife. He wouldn't be the first doctor to have murdered a patient, and certainly wouldn't be the last.

When Roper returned to his office he found Mills in there closeted with Dave Price.

'And you think he's a bigger villain than that?' Price was saying.

'Yes, sir,' said Mills. 'I'm bloody certain he is. Only I need a warrant and an expert witness.'

'If you need an expert witness then you can't be certain,' said Price.

But Mills was certain enough. The subject of the conversation was Mr Seymour whose white van was presently in the station yard waiting to be towed away for repairs; if it didn't fall apart from rust in the meantime. Last night, one of Lambert's uniformed officers—out of uniform—had called at Seymour's house on the pretext of buying a car, of which Seymour had three for sale despite the fact that he had denied being a dealer. The supposedly intending purchaser, one PC Carter, had been allowed to test-drive all three vehicles. Once out of Seymour's sight, PC Carter, suspicious of the mileage displayed on the odometers, had observed that the numerals on these instruments were all out of alignment within the rectangular aperture of the speedometer in which they appeared. It was also PC Carter's opinion that two of the roadworthiness certificates that Seymour had shown him last night had been tampered with. It also became evident to PC Carter that Seymour was in a hurry to move on and that he was worried about something, although the latter was only a hunch on Carter's part.

DC Mills had paid a similar visit to Seymour's house before he had come on duty this morning. On the pretext of being a potential buyer, he had sat in the same three vehicles that Carter had tried out last night. Mills, too, thought that the odometers had been tampered with—and that Seymour seemed in an unwarrantable hurry to sell.

'Anything known about him?' asked Roper.

'Not on our sheets here,' said Mills.

'Tried Records?'

'No, sir.'

'Give 'em a go,' said Roper. 'You might get lucky.' Then to Price, 'I'm off down to see Mrs Cresswell, Dave. With Hackett.'

'Right,' said Price, as Roper reached for his raincoat, the mundane subject of Mr Seymour already forgotten.

WITH HALF AN HOUR to spare before he interviewed Mrs Cresswell, Roper had dropped in on William Pumfrey, referring to the visit, somewhat euphemistically, as a 'courtesy call'.

It might only have been surprise that fleeted across Pumfrey's face when he answered the doorbell, but whatever it was it took him a moment to recover from it.

'I was just going out,' he complained. 'What do you want exactly?'

'It won't take long, sir. A few minutes.'

Grudgingly, he let them in, but only as far as the dimly lit hall.

'Going to collect your car, sir?' Roper asked amiably.

'Yes, I am, in fact,' said Pumfrey. 'Wainer's on his way over shortly to drive me down there. So what *do* you want?'

'I've been thinking about your wife's earrings, sir,' said Roper. They had started to niggle at him, those earrings, not so much the articles themselves as Pumfrey's curious disregard of their loss. An odd reaction in a man who was presently pursuing a sharp correspondence with the Chief Constable about a similar matter. 'Come to light, have they, sir?'

'No,' said Pumfrey. 'Perhaps a word with González might frighten them back. Or his wife, of course. Before they go.'

'Go, sir?' asked Roper. A lifetime student of human nature, he doubted that the species came more honest than Mr and Mrs González.

'I've put them under notice,' said Pumfrey.

'I see, sir,' said Roper. He had guessed that might happen. It had only been a question of when. He was, however, surprised at Pumfrey's alacrity. He waited for Pumfrey to ask him about the results of the second post-mortem examination on his wife; but Pumfrey was plainly in too much of a hurry for that, or perhaps he had forgotten it had even happened.

'And that's all you've come to say, is it?' asked Pumfrey curtly.

'No, sir, not quite,' said Roper, to Pumfrey's increased irritation. 'We spoke yesterday.'

Pumfrey lifted a querulous eyebrow. 'I'm not suffering from loss of memory, Superintendent.'

Roper declined to bridle. He had little doubt that William Pumfrey would be objectionable even on his deathbed.

He smiled winsomely. 'Perhaps just a temporary loss, eh, sir? Only when we talked yesterday, you told us you'd met Mr Wainer at the Country Club at eight o'clock on Friday night.'

'I did,' agreed Pumfrey.

'That's what I meant about your memory, sir,' said Roper.

Pumfrey's eyes narrowed, and he pinned Roper with the kind of chill stare with which he might, years ago, have transfixed one of his army subalterns. 'Are you calling me a liar, Superintendent?'

'According to Mr Wainer, sir, you and he met in the gents' toilet of the Country Club at eight fifteen on Friday night. And again in the bar at eleven fifteen.'

'You'd call me a liar for a quarter of an hour?' retorted Pumfrey.

'No, sir,' Roper replied. 'But as I remember, you implied when we spoke yesterday that you and Mr Wainer were together all evening. And you weren't, were you, sir?'

'I was under the same roof,' said Pumfrey testily. 'And I certainly never said that I spent the *evening* with him. He knew I was in the club. From your point of view I'd say that was sufficient.'

'No, sir,' said Roper. 'The point is, Mr Wainer only saw you briefly on two occasions during the course of the evening.'

'I was with him when Stella died,' retorted Pumfrey. 'That's really all that matters, isn't it? Or isn't it…?'

'That's the trouble, Mr Pumfrey,' said Roper. 'We aren't quite sure yet when Mrs Pumfrey *did* die. Ascertaining the time of death isn't an exact science, you see, sir. And you were seen in the club car park at half past ten. Apparently in company.'

Pumfrey was momentarily deflated. 'I see,' he said. 'You've obviously been checking up on me. My God…'

'Perhaps we could all sit down and go over a few points again, sir.'

Pumfrey hooked aside the cuff of his black pullover and regarded his wristwatch. 'Yes,' he mumbled irritably. 'Very well. If we have to.'

He led the way into the huge sitting-room. There was no fire in the grate and the room looked even drearier without it. Roper and Hackett made themselves comfortable on the leather settee. Hackett brought out her pocketbook.

'All right,' snapped Pumfrey, standing with his back to the empty fireplace. 'Let's get on with it, shall we?'

'Do you mind telling us who the lady was, sir? And at what time you left her?'

'I did not kill my wife, Superintendent.'

'That isn't what I asked you, sir,' said Roper patiently. 'For your sake, as much as ours, we have to know exactly where you were between ten thirty and eleven fifteen when you met up again with Mr Wainer.'

'The lady has a husband, Superintendent.'

Roper had already guessed that for himself. 'We're very discreet, sir. If the lady vouches for your whereabouts at the relevant time on Friday night, then she ceases to be of interest to us.'

'Otherwise you'll suspect me of murdering my wife, is that it?'

'You're missing the point, Mr Pumfrey,' said Roper, stifling his own impatience now with difficulty. 'All the time we're wasting at the moment is giving your wife's murderer a better chance of slipping further away. And we're not magicians, sir.'

'All right, all right,' snapped Pumfrey. 'But I insist on an undertaking from you that you approach the lady with the utmost discretion.'

'Fair enough, sir,' said Roper. It had occurred to him that Pumfrey both looked and sounded an unlikely lover, but he had long since given up the study of the human race's choice of bedfellows. If a woman somewhere loved the unpleasant William Pumfrey she probably deserved him.

'Her name is Hubert,' said Pumfrey, grudgingly, and addressing himself particularly to DS Hackett. 'She lives in Priory Lane.'

'And her telephone number, sir?' asked Hackett, her ballpoint not even stuttering momentarily over the pocket-book, whereas Roper's nose had lifted like a scenting fox.

'Crow Hill 3972,' said Pumfrey.

Roper's nose had stayed up. For someone who lived in the same lane, he was surprised that Wainer hadn't recognised Mrs Hubert standing in the car park on Friday night. He might, of course, have merely been being circumspect. Alternatively, he was a liar. It also seemed to Roper that it had been careless of Pumfrey, to say the least, to be conducting an affair with a neighbour's wife in a place so public as the Country Club where any of his friends—or hers—were likely to see them.

'Where did you go, sir?' he asked. 'When you left the club at ten thirty?'

'I drove Mrs Hubert back to her car,' replied Pumfrey.

'Which was where, sir?'

'Up at Crow Hill,' said Pumfrey. 'In the public car park behind the library.'

'Where you arrived when, sir?' asked Roper. It all sounded messy and complicated and hole in the corner; but then illicit affairs usually were untidy things…

'I can't be certain,' said Pumfrey. 'But I suppose around ten to eleven.'

It sounded about right, even given an error of five minutes either side.

'And you and Mrs Hubert parted company when?'

'It was eleven o'clock,' said Pumfrey. 'I heard the town hall clock strike just as Mrs Hubert got out of the car.'

Which, if it was true, finally provided Pumfrey with a gilt-edged alibi. He would have had his work cut out to drive back to the Country Club by eleven fifteen, let alone stop off to kill his wife and clear up the mess in the meantime.

SHARON MOFFAT raised her sharp little face tartly as the shadow fell over her table by the window of the Wimpy bar. It was Macho Man again. They never gave up, some of them.

'Mind if I sit down?' he said.

She looked pointedly around at the dozen or so empty tables between the window and the counter. 'Only if you have to,' she said. 'I'm waiting for somebody.'

'That's all right,' he said. 'I'll help you wait.' He wound his bottom half under the table and sat down opposite her. He fished a packet of cigarettes from the breast pocket of his expensive leather bomber jacket and offered her one. She shook her head. 'Didn't see you in the paper shop this morning,' he said.

'No,' she said. 'You wouldn't have.' He had real bedroom eyes. Quick and dark and knowing. He had managed to find excuses to come into the newsagent's three or four times a day to chat her up. It had been going on for the best part of a fortnight. She had never seen him before that. She didn't tell him that she'd phoned old Johnson this morning and told him she'd quit. The dark eyes fixed her again through a veil of cigarette smoke. She looked away and glanced out of the window. From here in the Wimpy she had a clear view of the entrance to the public car park. Her plan had been to watch him turn in there and keep him waiting a few minutes; instead, it was she doing the waiting. He had promised to be in the car park at a quarter to six. It was already five to. Nobody had ever stood her up before, and she didn't like it. It boded ill for their future relationship.

'You're Sharon Moffat,' said the voice across the table. 'Right?'

She only smiled. She didn't reply. She would have liked to know how he had found out her name, but she certainly wasn't going to ask.

'I'm a copper,' he said. 'We've got ways of finding out things like that.'

'Oh, yes?' she said, lifting one eyebrow. 'I thought it was something you'd brought in on your shoes.'

The dark eyes smiled across the table at her, but to little effect. Sharon Moffat had been fending off unwelcome attentions since she was thirteen and considered herself something of an expert. She lowered her empty cup, and tilted her wrist to look at her new Easter present. It was a minute to six.

He clicked his fingers for service, and ordered a filtered coffee.

'How about you?' he said.

'The same,' she said. Damn it, if she was going to be kept waiting she might as well do it in comfort. And it might not do him any harm should he happen to glance this way and see her with someone else. Serve him right.

The waiter shuffled off.

'You've got great hair,' he said. 'Great everything.'

She smiled. The older man was all very well, but Sharon Moffat had always preferred to keep her options open. And he was good-looking in a way. Sort of intense. And he obviously fancied her like hell, or he'd have sloped off by now with his tail between his legs.

Their coffees came.

'I will have a cigarette after all,' she said.

He opened the packet. She plucked one out with a show of polished crimson talons. He struck his lighter and she contrived a brush of fingers. She drew smoke into her mouth and let it seep seductively out. 'Thanks,' she said.

He put his cigarettes away again, folded his arms and leaned forward and fixed her with those hot dark eyes.

'You off duty?' she said.

'Meal break,' he said. 'I'm waiting for information. From Hendon.'

'Hendon?'

'The central computer,' he said importantly. 'It's where we keep records.'

'Oh,' she said, tilting her head and sending him her most mysterious smile. 'That sounds interesting.'

'I CAN'T FIND a bloody clean shirt,' snapped Clive Hubert.

'Try the bloody wardrobe,' retorted Mrs Hubert.

'I'm looking for a blue one. It isn't bloody there.'

'Hard luck,' she said. 'You'll have to wear a different bloody suit then, won't you?'

'I'm bloody late already, for Christ's sake!'

'Then you'll have to be later, won't you? Who is she, by the way? Anybody we know?'

He raised a rigid finger in contempt.

'Yes,' she sneered. 'And up yours too, lover.'

ELEVEN

ROPER AND HACKETT wiped their shoes on Cresswell's doormat. A premature dusk had brought the rain that the forecasters had promised, a cold, depressing drizzle which, according to the experts, would see out the rest of the Easter holiday all over southern England.

Cresswell himself closed the door behind them and took their wet raincoats. The sound of a knife scraping a plate, then the flap of a waste-bin lid came from the kitchen.

'I haven't mentioned this afternoon,' Cresswell muttered under his breath. 'And I'd prefer to be with her, if that's all right.'

'We'd prefer it too, sir,' said Roper, standing aside in the narrow passage, then ushering Hackett ahead of him as Cresswell led the way towards the back room into which Mrs Cresswell had retreated yesterday. It was a sitting-room, a fire blazing in the grate and folk-weave curtains drawn over the doors to the garden.

'My wife decided we'd eat before you came,' explained Cresswell, still under his breath. 'Bad timing, I'm afraid. Please sit down. My wife usually sits in that chair.' He nodded towards a grey armchair on the side of the fireplace nearest the curtains. Roper motioned Hackett to the one opposite, and for himself picked the end of the settee closest to her.

Cresswell took the other end of the settee after giving the fire a rake with a poker.

'We enjoy a coal fire,' he said, inconsequentially, as he lowered himself.

'I like them myself, sir,' said Roper, to fill the uncomfortable silence.

Cresswell fidgeted impatiently with his wristwatch. 'I'd better go and remind her you're here.'

'No rush, sir,' said Roper, and Cresswell, who had started to rise, sat down again.

Cutlery clattered in the kitchen. A drawer out there was slammed shut. The sounds served to heighten the tension.

'You will be...?' Cresswell began to ask, but changed his mind; but then changed it back again. 'Well...you know?'

'I'm never in a hurry, sir,' said Roper. 'It doesn't pay.'

'No,' said Cresswell. 'I suppose it doesn't.'

Hackett took her pocket-book out of her briefcase, then stood the briefcase back on the floor beside her chair. The small room was cosily furnished, if a little untidy. A stack of library books on the floor beside Mrs Cresswell's chair hinted that she was either a prodigious reader or a literary grasshopper. Two soapstone vases on the shelf above the fireplace were identical to the ones Roper had seen in Mrs Pumfrey's bedroom. Family heirlooms perhaps, and Mrs Pumfrey and Mrs Cresswell had been left two each.

Cresswell stiffened as a door shut in the passage.

Roper rose. Belatedly, so did Cresswell. Roper could almost feel the air twanging.

Her slippered footfall stopped in the doorway. She was a little smarter today in a white pullover and black slacks, although she wore no make-up and her dark hair had been carelessly dragged back and clubbed untidily at the nape of her neck. She smiled brightly at Roper as if she were pleased to see him.

'Superintendent Roper, Mrs Cresswell,' he said. 'I called to see your husband yesterday.'

'Yes,' she said. 'Yes, I remember you. Good evening.'

'And this is Sergeant Hackett.'

The bright smile was switched to Hackett. 'Hello.'

They all sat down, Cresswell still looking anxious and his wife clearly enjoying being the centre of attraction.

'We've come about your sister, Mrs Cresswell,' said Roper.

'Yes,' she said. 'I know.'

Roper lifted his face and regarded her. She sat on the edge of her armchair with her hands pressed together between her knees. In the flicker of the firelight, her eyes had that same unnatural glitter that he had first noticed yesterday.

'Do you mind telling us something about her?'

'There's nothing much to say, is there?' she said, as if her sister's death was of no consequence to her. 'She's dead, isn't she? She was murdered, wasn't she?'

'Sarah, for God's sake,' railed Cresswell.

'Well, it's true,' she retorted.

Roper waited patiently. Cresswell had not been far wrong this afternoon when he had talked of his wife's hatred of him. It was an emotion she seemed to possess in some quantity.

'Did your sister have any enemies, Mrs Cresswell?'

'Yes,' she said.

'Who?'

'Me,' she said.

'And why was that?' asked Roper.

She made a sideways flick of her head towards her husband. 'She was screwing Bernard here. And I didn't like that. Sort of incestuous, don't you think?'

There was a long and uncomfortable silence. Roper waited for Cresswell to make some kind of protest, but sensibly he did not.

Roper started again. 'When did you last see your sister, Mrs Cresswell?'

'Friday,' she said. 'Friday night.'

Roper felt his skin prickle. 'What time on Friday night?'

'Eleven,' she said. 'About.'

From the tail of his eye, Roper saw Cresswell's clasped hands tighten as his worst suspicions were confirmed.

'About?'

'It might have been earlier. A few minutes.' She spoke with blithe unconcern, as if she were completely unaware of the jeopardy in which she was placing herself.

'She came here, or you went to her?'

'I went over there.'

'And you left her when?'

'I can't quite remember,' she said, regarding him with an almost elvish pleasure. 'About half past eleven, I suppose. I got back here about an hour before Bernard did.'

Which was probably her way of pointing out to Roper that her husband had been out, too, and that he might be worth asking a few pointed questions of. Because all this pantomime was for his benefit, and not for Roper; and it was working, too. Cresswell sat there perfectly immobile, deathly pale, listening and dreading every word.

'And you went inside? In the house, I mean.'

'Oh, yes,' she said. 'I went in. She invited me. But then she couldn't do much else. She had some things that belonged to me. I wanted them.'

'And she gave them to you?' asked Roper.

'Yes,' she said. 'She had to. They were mine.'

Roper measured his words carefully. If she went on like this he was going to have to caution her. 'What…exactly, did she give you, Mrs Cresswell?'

'Mother's earrings,' she said, and from the corner of

his eye Roper distinctly saw Cresswell flinch. Hackett's ballpoint stilled momentarily over her pocket-book, and even Roper could only keep his face expressionless with difficulty.

'Would you mind showing us those earrings, Mrs Cresswell?' he said.

'Now?'

'Please, madam,' said Roper. 'If you wouldn't mind.'

'CHRIST,' said Cresswell miserably, as a drawer was opened upstairs, then slammed shut again. 'I knew. I bloody knew… I *knew* she'd been over there.'

'With respect, Dr Cresswell,' advised Roper, 'it might be better if you said nothing at all until we've all heard what your wife has to say.'

'But she was there! She must have been the last person to see Stella alive!'

'Or the second to last, sir,' said Roper. He put up a warning finger as he heard Mrs Cresswell starting back down the stairs. The time of death recorded by the pathologist was only the best estimate. It could be wrong an hour either way. But it was a dead certainty that not many people had seen Mrs Pumfrey alive after Mrs Cresswell had.

The slippered footfall scuffed up to Roper's end of the settee.

'Here,' she said, and held out a thick wad of folded paper handkerchief, then returned to her armchair.

Roper carefully lifted aside the folds of paper handkerchief.

And eventually revealed the gold and garnet earrings. He heard Cresswell's sharp intake of breath.

Pumfrey's photograph had not done them justice. They would probably tip the scales at an ounce and a half each.

The gold trellises were unscratched, the stones were pristine, and glittered as they caught the light of the fire. They were the kind of earrings designed to hang from gold keepers. Mrs Cresswell was not wearing gold keepers; nor, as far as Roper could see, were her ear lobes pierced.

'And these are yours, are they, Mrs Cresswell?' he said.

'Yes,' she replied.

Roper carefully wrapped them up again. 'But Mrs Pumfrey didn't give you the box they originally came in?'

'No,' she said.

'I'm surprised, Mrs Cresswell,' said Roper. 'Mrs Pumfrey gave them to you just like this, did she?'

She shrugged. 'She said the box was about somewhere. When she found it, she'd give me a ring. Stella was always pretty careless when it came to losing things.'

'So they were wrapped up like this when she gave them to you?'

'Yes.'

'And do you know where she'd got them from on Friday night?'

'Upstairs,' she said. 'The safe in her bedroom.'

'You went up there with her?'

'Yes,' she said.

'I see,' said Roper, straightening his legs and half rising and stretching an arm to hand them back to her. 'Thank you, Mrs Cresswell.' Her story was plausible; just. Pumfrey had commented on his wife's carelessness too. Perhaps Mrs Pumfrey had gone out on some occasion wearing the earrings, slipped the blue Cartier's box in a drawer for the evening, and when she returned home again forgot where she had put the box; and simply put the earrings back in the safe, wrapped in a couple of paper handkerchiefs until the box turned up again. And perhaps, on Friday night, after Mrs Cresswell had gone home, Mrs

Pumfrey had set to to find the box, and tracked it down; and put it on top of her dressing-table to give to Mrs Cresswell on Saturday.

Seated again, Roper said, 'I'm sure you'll understand, Mrs Cresswell, that I have to ask certain questions. What I need to do most is to put together just how your sister spent Friday evening, and especially the last few hours of it. Do you mind telling me what happened from the moment you went for your walk that night? Any little detail you happen to remember. A strange car parked near your sister's house, a face you might not have seen before…anything of that sort.'

'It wasn't raining,' she said. 'Not at first, anyway. I walked up as far as the church, then back again as far as Sam Hubert's house. I had a lot to think about, you see. Stella and I hadn't spoken a word since Christmas. She'd been screwing Bernard here, like I told you, and we had this bust-up, Stell and me…where are you going, Bernard?'

Cresswell had shot to his feet. 'The bloody surgery,' he said. 'You can see this out on your bloody own, Sarah. If you want me, Superintendent, I'll be across the passage.' And with that he stormed across the room and out of the door, and slammed it shut behind him so hard that it sucked a rolling curtain of smoke into the room from the chimney.

'By the time I got to Stella's it was raining again,' continued Mrs Cresswell, as if nothing untoward had occurred. 'And I rang the doorbell. Stella answered the door herself. We stood there looking at each other, and she said: Christ, you'd better come in. You look like a bloody drowned poodle. Talking as if nothing had ever happened, you know? I went in. We could talk in the sitting-room, she said. Her two tame Spaniards were upstairs watching the telly. I said I hadn't come to talk. All I wanted were Grandmother's earrings. I could wait for the rest of my share, but I wanted the earrings now.'

'Your share, Mrs Cresswell?' asked Roper.

'The jewellery was to set up our kids,' she said. 'Stella and mine. But we didn't have any, and it doesn't look likely now, does it? And, if we didn't, then Stella and I divvied out on my forty-second birthday. I suppose the old girl thought I'd be menopausal by then. All I wanted to do was to jump the gun by a few years. I told her I was going to sell them. I needed the money. And when I'd divorced Bernard, she could have him all to herself, and she could send the rest of the jewellery on to me wherever I happened to be.'

'And your sister simply handed them over to you, did she, Mrs Cresswell?'

'No,' she said. 'Not at once. She said it would have to be done through a solicitor—and the insurance company would have to know. I said, right, I'd sign a receipt for them. Absolving her from all responsibility. And I said I'd make out a receipt for her for Grandmother's diamond pendant so I couldn't ever stake a claim to that. She said I was crazy. The pendant was worth twice what the earrings were. What we ought to do, she said, to be fair, was to wait for a few more years, sell the lot, then split the proceeds down the middle.'

'But you didn't want to wait?' said Roper.

'No,' she said. 'Why the hell should I?'

Roper didn't pursue that. He steered her back carefully to Friday night. After the argument about the garnet earrings, Mrs Pumfrey had gone upstairs to fetch them from the safe, and Mrs Cresswell had followed. Yes, she had heard faintly the sound of either a radio or a television set coming from somewhere upstairs; and, no, she had seen neither of the two Spaniards.

'How about lights, Mrs Cresswell?'

'Lights?'

'Electric lights. Was the house more or less in darkness, or what?'

She thought. 'Dark,' she said. 'Except the landing. And the wall-light just inside the front door. My brother-in-law had developed an obsession about the electricity bills; not that he ever had to pay them, of course. Stella did that, too.'

'So your sister let you into the house, you discussed the earrings and then both of you went upstairs to fetch them. How long did that take, d'you think?'

'About ten minutes, I suppose. Then I made her write out a receipt for me to sign.'

'And where did she do that?'

'On the table by the stairs,' she said. 'Where the telephone is.'

'And what did she write it on?'

'A message pad,' she said.

Her answers were quick, and plausible too. There had been a small table lamp beside the telephone in Pumfrey's entrance hall, and a message pad. And with the hall more or less in darkness, and perhaps exhausted by her sister's behaviour and wanting little more than to get her out of the house, Mrs Pumfrey had turned to the paper and pen nearest to hand—and with a light nearby, and scribbled a receipt.

'And you signed this receipt, did you, Mrs Cresswell?' asked Roper.

'Yes,' she said. 'Then Stella signed the one I'd written, and dated it. She said she was going to put it in the safe, in our mother's pearl-box.'

It all sounded so right; and certainly the business of the receipt could be proved—one way or the other. Whether the exchange had been legal or not was none of his business.

'Then you left the house and came back here?'

'Yes,' she said. 'Straight back.'

Roper tried to fault her, taking her back to the beginning, reworking some questions and embroidering a few others, and generally trying to coax her into a corner where she couldn't get out again, but she was either a clever woman or telling the absolute, ungarnished truth. Although Roper had been plying his trade long enough to know that he could ask questions until hell froze up and still not be sure of getting the truth, the whole truth, and nothing but.

He steered her back to the subject of her joint ownership of Chalk House. Did she have a set of keys to it?

'Yes,' she said.

'Have you ever used them?'

'No,' she said. 'Never.'

'Not even before you and your sister quarrelled?'

'No,' she said. 'I didn't even want a set of keys, but Stella insisted.'

'You didn't use them on Friday night?'

'I told you,' she said. 'Stella let me in.'

Roper left a pause.

'Chalk House has been burgled several times over the last few months,' he said. 'I presume you knew about that?'

She nodded. 'Yes,' she said, 'I knew.'

'We think by someone who had keys.'

'Oh, I *see*,' she said, smiling shrewdly. 'No, I didn't do that. I've got theories of my own about that.'

'Like what, Mrs Cresswell?' asked Roper.

'Like Brother Bill,' she said. 'He had keys. And it was always his stuff that went missing, wasn't it?'

'I didn't know that,' said Roper. And nor had Lambert. And nor had anybody, except, probably, the insurance company. 'Are you certain?'

'Dead certain,' she said. 'That's why Stella always handed the compensation money to Bill. Obvious, isn't it?'

'Nothing of Mrs Pumfrey's ever went missing?'

'No,' she said. 'Never. But I'm surprised you didn't know.'

Roper paused again, but this time to draw breath and think. Mrs Cresswell might be telling the truth, or, on the other hand, she just might be setting up a store of trouble for Pumfrey, for whom she clearly had little time. And, if she was telling the truth, then Pumfrey might indeed be engaged in an insurance fraud of some sort, and perhaps that was why he had found it necessary to show so little concern for the missing earrings. Because if he was involved in some kind of fraud operation he would know who the burglar was—and be aware that that same person, or persons, might have killed his wife.

Or, for far more basic motives, Mrs Cresswell might have. She had been at her sister's house on Friday night, and at the right time.

'I noticed some faded patches on your sister's wallpaper when I was over there. Looked like places where she'd hung pictures.'

'They were,' said Mrs Cresswell. 'She had to sell a few.'

'They weren't stolen?'

'No,' she said. 'She sold them. Clive Wainer arranged for them to be auctioned off. Up in London.'

'With your permission, I take it?' Roper asked, recalling what Price had told him about the mother's will and the fact that nothing could be sold off without both sisters agreeing to it.

'Yes,' she said. 'Last year. She got Wainer in to put a value on some and sold the less important ones.'

'She was short of money?'

'No,' she said. 'Not exactly. But she was having to dip into her private cash to keep the house going.'

'And at that time you and your sister were on good terms?'

'Yes,' she said. 'But I didn't know about her and Bernard then, did I?'

Roper veered away from that. Dr Cresswell wasn't out of the frame himself yet. But something he had noticed: for a few moments just now Mrs Cresswell had let her vindictive façade crumble. Now she had repaired it again. The glassy smile had come back, and it was almost as if she was trying to provoke him into asking her outright if she had killed her sister. She was, he decided, a perverse woman; perhaps with justification, or perhaps not.

'Did you have another quarrel with your sister on Friday night, Mrs Cresswell?'

'We had…' She broke off briefly to find the right word '…let's say an exchange of views.'

'About whether you should have the earrings or not? Or something else?'

'Only about the earrings.'

'Not about your husband?'

'God, no,' she said. 'We'd already been through that at Christmas. All I wanted were the earrings.'

'Which she subsequently handed over to you.'

'The receipt's in the safe,' she said. 'Ask Bill. He'll show it to you.' Again, her bright eyes invited him to ask the outright question. She seemed disappointed when he did not.

'She was your sister, Mrs Cresswell. You don't seem very…'

'Upset?' she broke in. 'That's the word you're trying to think of, isn't it? No, I'm not, in fact. I don't feel anything. She's always had everything. That house. Money. And naturally my husband. Why the hell should I be upset?'

'She was murdered, Mrs Cresswell.'

'Yes,' she said. 'I know.'

'Why didn't you come forward before, and tell the police—or your husband, about the earrings?'

'There was no point,' she said. 'I left Stella alive and kicking. I didn't steal them, you know. Whatever happened over there happened after I left.'

'There was an ashtray,' he said. He sketched its size between his hands. 'So big. Probably in the bedroom somewhere.'

'It was on the bed,' she said.

'You saw it? Did you touch it?'

'No,' she said. 'I didn't.'

'Did you, by any chance, contact your husband on Friday evening? At any time?'

'No,' she said. 'I tried to phone him—at where he was supposed to be. But he wasn't there.'

'What time was that, Mrs Cresswell? D'you remember?'

'When I got back from Stella's.'

'Which was when?'

'I told you,' she said. 'About half past eleven.'

Roper tried one last shot.

'Perhaps you'd show Mrs Cresswell that lighter, Sergeant,' he said to Hackett.

Hackett leaned sideways over the arm of her chair and reached into her briefcase. 'This one, Mrs Cresswell,' she said, rising and crossing the hearth rug and letting the plastic evidence bag dangle between her finger and thumb.

Mrs Cresswell reached up for it, took it, looked at it, felt it, then handed it back again.

'Recognise it, Mrs Cresswell?' asked Roper, as Hackett returned to her chair.

'I can't be sure,' she said. 'But it looks like the one Stella had on Friday night.'

'You saw her using it?'

'No,' she said. 'But it looked like the one that was lying on the telephone table when she was writing out that receipt. I could be wrong. When you don't smoke, one lighter looks like all the others, doesn't it? If it wasn't Stella's it was probably Bill's.'

'SHE WAS DYING for you to ask if she'd killed her sister,' said Hackett, as she buckled herself into the driving seat. It was seven o'clock. The evening had grown chillier and it had started to rain again.

'I know,' said Roper. 'I noticed. What did you think of her?'

'I reckon she was acting up,' said Hackett. 'Mind you, if I thought my old man was screwing about with my sister, I think I'd give both of them a very hard time too. Hell hath no fury; it was more than a poetic observation, that.' She switched on the ignition and reached for the handbrake. 'Where now?'

'Pumfrey's place,' said Roper, because, if he had heard right, William Pumfrey was able to open his wife's safe despite the fact that he denied it. And what he *had* heard right was that everything stolen from Chalk House to date had belonged to that same gentleman; which, to say the least, required an explanation or two. 'One way or another, we've got to get that safe opened.'

But, even as he spoke, a pair of headlights flashed in the driving mirror and a white police Metro pulled up beside them. Its driver was DC Mills and in the passenger seat was Spenlow, Mills' DI. Seymour's records had been faxed from Hendon, and Spenlow had rousted out a magistrate. And procured a search warrant for the house in Cawnpore Terrace.

TWELVE

ROPER READ THE FAX in the pale glow of the courtesy light.

Seymour had ten years' worth of form. Breaking and entering domestic premises, Birmingham, 1979: three months suspended sentence. Birmingham again in 1981; on that occasion he had used a home-made set of keys to enter a warehouse: three months plus the previously suspended three months. In Norwich, in 1983, he had been found guilty of being in possession of a motor vehicle knowing it to be stolen: fined five hundred pounds and placed on a year's probation upon a promise of good behaviour. Clearly a travelling man, 1985 found Seymour taking the sun—and various items of value from several domestic premises—in Southend-on-Sea. On two of these occasions he had again used home-made keys. Another three months, that time in an open prison. In Portsmouth, in 1987, Seymour had been spotted in a front garden by the driver of a roving patrol car. Distributed about Seymour's pockets had been a chisel, a screwdriver, a pen torch and a sheet of adhesive plastic film about a foot square, all items difficult to explain satisfactorily at a quarter past two in the morning. Probation again. Nothing known since.

And now Brian Seymour was here in Little Crow, a man who was a known petty villain with a record of attempted and executed burglaries. He wasn't exactly a high-flown villain—he had been collared too often, nor did he have a record of violence, but circumstances changed, people changed, and who knew what Seymour's reaction would have been on Good Friday night had he been in the process of burgling the Pumfreys' and been caught in the act by Mrs Pumfrey. Panic. The work of a moment.

'Thought we ought to show you that before we nicked him,' said DI Spenlow from the back seat.

'Glad you did, old lad,' said Roper, passing the fax back over his shoulder to DC Mills. 'I'd like ten minutes with him m'self first, if that's all right with you. He could be our man too.' And if he was, the investigation, with any luck, might be wrapped up before midnight. 'Lead the way to Cawnpore Terrace, will you, Mills.'

ROPER AND HACKETT stood huddled against the rain outside the narrow, shabby house in Cawnpore Terrace. DI Spenlow and DC Mills were further along the street in their car.

'Yes?' the woman said, holding the door open against a security chain.

'Roper, madam. Police. County CID.' He held his warrant card in the narrow spill of light coming from the hall behind her. 'We'd like a word with Brian Seymour. He does live here, I take it?'

'Yes,' she said suspiciously. 'What do you want him for?'

'Is he in?'

'No,' she said. 'He went out. About ten minutes ago.'

'Mrs Seymour, are you, madam?'

'Not bloody likely,' she said. 'He lives here, that's all.'

When she had first opened the door her cheek had been swollen with a sweet she had been sucking. From behind her came the sound of a television going at full blast, and the sour smell of a house that has its windows opened all too rarely.

'Perhaps we could talk to you then…Miss…?'

'Mrs,' she said. 'I told you; he's only a lodger. My name's Broadbent. In trouble again, is he?'

'If we could come in, Mrs Broadbent. Just for a few minutes.'

'Yeah,' she conceded grudgingly, 'I suppose so.' She closed the door a fraction and unhooked the chain. 'I knew he was in trouble the moment I saw the bugger.'

'Do you know where he might have gone, Mrs Broadbent?' asked Hackett, as she closed the door behind them and the mixture of damp carpets, stale cooking and cheap perfume made a fresh assault on their nostrils.

'The pub, I expect,' she said. 'That's where he usually is. It's about crashing into that police car, is it?'

'No, that's another matter, Mrs Broadbent,' said Roper. 'We're making enquiries into the death of Mrs Stella Pumfrey; we think Mr Seymour might be able to help us.'

She paled. She was wearing a black skirt that was too short and too tight, and a white nylon blouse with a froth of lace down the front. She was, Roper guessed, only a shade on the right side of forty and doing her determined best to stay there. There was a blob of chocolate mixed in with the thickly applied lipstick on her lower lip.

'You'd better come in here.'

In the cramped little sitting-room she turned off the blaring television. 'I'm sorry,' she said. 'You've caught me on the hop. I've never opened the door to a policeman before.'

'It's all right, Mrs Broadbent,' said Roper. 'I don't think this has anything to do with you. It's only Mr Seymour we want to talk to.'

'Well, thank the Lord for that,' she said. A nervous

hand reached up to the shelf above the gas fire for an opened packet of cigarettes. She offered them.

Hackett declined. 'I smoke cheroots, Mrs Broadbent,' said Roper, 'but thanks all the same.' He struck his lighter for her and held it to the wavering tip of her cigarette. An opened chocolate Easter egg sat in the hearth beside the gas fire.

She turned her head to one side and blew smoke. 'Thanks,' she said. She nodded towards a cheap, two-seater red settee. 'You can sit down, if you want to.'

Roper and Hackett sat side by side on it. Mrs Broadbent perched herself on the arm of an armchair, the cigarette in one hand and the other hand extended towards the hissing gas fire.

'They're saying in the village that Mrs Pumfrey was murdered,' she said.

'It does seem likely,' said Roper.

'But *he* wouldn't have done it,' she said, looking honestly puzzled. 'He does his car business, that's all. And a few jobs for people. He wouldn't kill anybody. He's not that sort.'

'I'm not suggesting he did, Mrs Broadbent,' said Roper, unbuttoning his raincoat. He glanced at his wristwatch. 'So Mr Seymour went out at about five past seven.'

'Yes,' she said. 'About. He went in the car. He just, sort of, took off.'

'Took off?'

She shrugged. 'More or less. He had this phone call, and he went.'

'And he didn't say where he was going?'

'No,' she said. 'The phone rang. It was some man. He wanted to speak to Brian—about a car, he said it was. I called Brian down from upstairs, and went back to the kitchen—I was doing a bit of supper. Next thing I heard was the front door slamming. Made me cross, that did, because only ten minutes before he was moaning about being hungry.'

'Do you know much about him, Mrs Broadbent?'

'No,' she said, with a hint of grimness. 'But I'm beginning to find out, aren't I? Twenty years I've lived in this house. Never had the police in. Not ever.'

'Was Mr Seymour out on Friday night, Mrs Broadbent?'

'Yes,' she said. 'He went out about seven.'

'And came back when?'

'About midnight.'

'About, Mrs Broadbent?'

'A bit afterwards, maybe. Five past, ten past. I was in bed.'

'Did he mention where he'd been?' asked Roper.

'On the booze,' she said. 'He likes his pint, does Brian. And he said he'd been for a Chinese, too.'

Something in her voice. 'But you didn't believe him? About the Chinese?'

She shrugged. 'He might have done. I don't know. He's a bit of a liar when it suits him.'

'How long has he lived here, Mrs Broadbent?' asked Hackett.

'A year,' she said. 'After he'd come across from Portsmouth.'

That would have been around last April. The burglaries in Little Crow had started a few months afterwards.

'Out a lot in the evenings, is he?' asked Roper.

Yes, he was. Especially at weekends. Didn't get home till one or two o'clock in the morning sometimes. Said it was business.

'But you didn't think it was?' asked Roper, detecting a

note of rancour in Mrs Broadbent's voice from time to time.

'No,' she said. 'Not lately.' She didn't have anything to go on exactly, but she had a sneaky feeling that Seymour had found himself another woman. She thought, too, that he was about to make tracks. He'd suddenly got very eager to sell up all the motors he'd got outside; and on Saturday morning he'd come back from Crow Hill with a set of new suitcases. There was never smoke without a fire, was there?

'...and good riddance to him.'

Roper showed her the gold-plated Colibri in its plastic envelope.

'It's a lighter,' she said. She took it and looked at it, and turned it over. 'Yes,' she said. 'It's Brian's.'

'You sure?' asked Roper.

'Certain,' she said. 'Some girl gave it to him, so he said. He lost it.'

'Lost it?'

'Friday morning. He asked me for matches. He'd got an empty box. But no matches. I asked him where his lighter was. He said he'd lost it.'

Roper reached out for the lighter. She laid it across his palm.

'He didn't mention where he might have lost it?'

She shook her head.

'He's got a room here, Mrs Broadbent?' asked Hackett.

To Roper's astonishment, she had the grace to blush. 'No,' she said. 'Not exactly. We sort of share. You know? Well, I s'ppose he's got the front bedroom, in a way,' she added. 'At least, that's where he stores his car bits.'

'Perhaps we could look at that,' said Roper.

'Oh, I don't know,' she said, her forehead puckering.

'It's private. Even I don't go in there. I hoovered up a screw once, by mistake…'

'There are two more officers outside with a search warrant, Mrs Broadbent,' said Roper. 'If you'd let us look around Brian's room, perhaps they wouldn't have to serve it. It's a warrant for the entire house, you see.'

'My things too?'

'Yes,' he said. 'I'm afraid so, Mrs Broadbent.'

THE ROOM REEKED of engine oil. Little more than a box-room, its carpet was littered with the components of a stripped-down car engine spread out on old newspapers. From hooks on the wall hung gaskets, spanners, wrenches, and what looked like an old gearbox stood upright on another sheet of newspaper under the window. Of more immediate interest was a tall wooden cupboard, painted in hideous light green, with a cheap padlock, hasp and staple holding its two flimsy plywood doors together. It wouldn't have kept a baby out; and Roper had a suspicion that the only person it was intended to keep out, or from prying too closely, was Mrs Broadbent.

'Do you know what he keeps in there, Mrs Broadbent?'

'Tools, I think,' she said. 'At least that's what he says.'

'Do you know where he might keep a spare key?'

So far as she knew, there wasn't one. And no, she didn't mind if they opened it. They could break it open, if they liked.

Roper brought out his key wallet and flipped it open. His briefcase key looked the most likely. He stepped over the mess of oily parts on the newspaper. It didn't take long. A couple of fiddles of the key in the padlock, a push, a turn, another fiddle. A click.

One glance inside the rickety cupboard was enough. The top shelf was a miniature Aladdin's cave. Four—no, five—snuffboxes, one of them gilt-mounted, the other four silver, one very nice Edwardian silver card-case, a pair of silver Queen Anne dredgers, a George III, or perhaps George IV, gold and enamel scent bottle, some figurines, two Chelsea and one that looked like Royal Doulton...

'YOU NEVER SAW HIM bring any of that stuff into the house?'

Mrs Broadbent was stiff with rage. She had guessed for some time that Seymour wasn't straight, but she had not, for a moment, guessed that he was also a thief, and that he was using her house as a hiding place for his ill-gotten gains. He was *out*. Tomorrow. First thing. Car parts, suitcases and all.

The three of them sat in her cramped little kitchen. She had brewed a pot of tea. Upstairs now were DI Spenlow and DC Mills, making a tally of the goods in the cupboard and ticking them off against their list of stolen property. Upstairs, too, had been equipment for putting vehicle registration plates together, and a set of fine files and a miniature vice, both of the sort that might be used by a professional key cutter. There was no doubt now that Brian Seymour was a case-hardened recidivist, and perhaps worse, because in his spare time he was also the local gardener and among his clients were Mrs Hubert, Mrs Cresswell, Mrs Wainer and the late Mrs Pumfrey, three of whom, at least, were the victims of the burglary epidemics. Only last Thursday, he had worked over at the Pumfreys' place...in the morning that was...told her he was going over there to tidy up the greenhouses...mind you, she hadn't seen him go, because she'd left him in bed...she had a few early morning jobs...cleaning...two estate agents' offices, and Mr Foyle's office which was

over the top of one of them, although she did Mr Foyle's
office of an evening sometimes…it brought in a bit of pin
money…she'd seen Mrs Pumfrey there a couple of times,
too, evenings mostly…she'd wondered for a time if there
hadn't been something going on there between those
two…you know, between Mr Foyle and Mrs Pumfrey…she always turned up after the office was shut…

'Lately, Mrs Broadbent?' asked Roper, over his teacup,
as his interest was quickened amidst Mrs Broadbent's out-
pourings; because if Foyle and Mrs Pumfrey had been
consorting lately it opened up a whole new vista…

'Oh, no,' she said. 'Not lately. Christmas was the last
time.'

'Christmas?'

Yes, it *had* been Christmas. The day before Christmas
Eve. Mr Foyle had brought her—Mrs Broadbent—a great
big box of lovely chocolates. He was a lovely man, Mr
Foyle, a real gentleman. Only that had been the first time
she'd ever seen him cross.

'Cross with you, Mrs Broadbent?'

'No,' she said. 'Her. Mrs Pumfrey. She turned up just
as he was going home. They had a row. I heard it through
the floor.'

'Through the floor?'

'Well, it sounded like a row,' she said. 'They were
shouting. After she'd come in, Mr Foyle came out and
asked me if I wouldn't mind doing the estate agent's
downstairs first. So I was down there.'

'Do you think Mr Foyle wanted you out of the way?'

Well, yes, she had got that impression. Through the
estate agent's window she had seen Mrs Pumfrey storm
out through the snow after only a few minutes which was
unusual. Mind you, she had wondered sometimes if there

wasn't a lot more going on between Mrs Pumfrey and Mr
Foyle than her eyes had actually seen…you know…

Roper didn't press her. He had heard enough, and he
didn't want her talking too much to Foyle before he himself did.

IT WAS NOT the breakthrough Roper had hoped for. Brian
Seymour might be the epicentre of the Little Crow break-
ins. What he was unlikely to be was the murderer of Stella
Pumfrey, or he would never have left that lighter beside
her. According to Mrs Broadbent, Seymour had lost the
lighter before Friday morning. According to Mrs Cresswell, dubious witness though she was, the lighter had
been on the telephone table in the hall when she had left
Mrs Pumfrey, alive, at around eleven thirty on Friday
night. It looked as if Seymour had dropped it or left it
behind when he had been working in the garden at Chalk
House last Thursday. As a clue to Mrs Pumfrey's killer it
had become a strict non-starter.

But Seymour might still be a useful man to talk to.
Down in Little Crow, DI Spenlow and DC Mills were still
waiting for Seymour to come home, when they would
promptly arrest him. The charge of burglary—or receiv-
ing—would be sufficient to hold him for long enough for
Roper to have a lengthy chat with him. According to DC
Mills, the snuffboxes found in Seymour's cupboard had
been stolen from the Huberts, last December. There had
been no sign of anything stolen from the Pumfreys; although, of course, Seymour had had long enough to fence
all that by now.

But—it was a long shot, a probable among a horde of
impossibles—had Seymour known Pumfrey more than he
would have known Pumfrey merely as that gentleman's
jobbing gardener? Pumfrey could not have killed his wife

but Roper still had that nagging feeling that Pumfrey's losses might not have been all they appeared to be. All three burglaries at Chalk House: '…it was all Bill's stuff that was stolen', so had said Mrs Cresswell. How had Seymour known what was 'Bill's stuff'? Five items had been stolen from various rooms in the house. And they had all been 'Bill's stuff', upon which 'Bill' had probably paid the insurance premiums and would stand to draw the compensation. Which smelled to Roper, as it had earlier, like a fraud of some sort. Seymour made keys; Mrs Broadbent had seen him at it a couple of times, up in that little front bedroom. Had he made the keys to Chalk House, where he was probably a frequent visitor? Or had he been given a set? And had someone else used them? That wasn't impossible, either.

Roper had finally called in on Pumfrey at half past eight, but he was out, and had been since soon after Roper had last seen him, just after six o'clock. According to González, he had gone down to the Country Club with Wainer to collect his car from the car park. Roper, however, had gone upstairs and taken the number and manufacturer's name from the cover of Mrs Pumfrey's safe. The manufacturer was based in Bristol and all DS Makins had been able to raise, because of the holiday and the late hour, had been the telephone answering machine; but he had left a message asking for the service of one of their engineers as soon as possible on Tuesday. Because Mrs Cresswell wasn't out of the woods yet, either, and it gave Roper no satisfaction that his little flight of fancy about Mrs Cresswell trying on those earrings had not been far off the mark. She had been across to Chalk House, if she was telling the truth, between eleven and eleven thirty on Good Friday night. She was vague about both times; but even if she was wrong a quarter of an hour either way,

she had to be either the last or second to last person to
see her sister alive.

Pumfrey himself had ceased to be a suspect. Earlier in
the evening, DS Hackett had phoned the Country Club
and spoken to the steward. He had confirmed Wainer's
statement that he had spoken with Pumfrey in the club at
some time around eight o'clock on Friday night, and that
Pumfrey had brought a guest with him, a woman, fairly
tall, red-haired, he thought, and wearing a dark fur coat.
The description, apart from the fur coat, according to both
Hackett and Rodgers, fitted Mrs Hubert. The steward,
Jackson, had not seen Pumfrey leave with his guest, but
he had seen him come back, alone, at some time around
ten or quarter past eleven. He had left, finally, at about a
quarter to one with another member, a Mr Wainer. Few
alibis came more impenetrable than that; given, of course,
that Mrs Cresswell had seen her sister alive when she said
she had.

And now it was eleven thirty on Easter Sunday night.
The pubs were long since shut, and still Brian Seymour
had not returned to the cottage in Cawnpore Terrace.
Hackett, Makins and Rodgers had gone home, and only
Roper and Price were left. It was raining heavily again,
beating against the windows and running down them and
making it feel as if the entire town was submerged under
water and daylight would never come again.

THE RAIN HAD STOPPED at midnight, but the twisting
downhill road was still treacherously wet. Roper would
never have come this way had Price not needed a lift
home after having his car smashed. There were no street-
lights and every few moments what sounded like a buck-
etful of water was flung up into the Sierra's wheel arches.

At ten to midnight, Roper had made his last call down

to the Sergeant in the communications-room. DC Mills
had radioed in a few minutes before. He and DI Spenlow
were still waiting in Cawnpore Terrace. There had been
no sign of Seymour.

'Watch it,' said Price.

'I've seen it,' said Roper, giving a couple of taps on
his footbrake.

'Looks like an accident,' said Price.

The three fleeting images were caught one after the
other in the quicksilver beams of Roper's headlights. A
youth—or it might have been a girl—in a motor-cyclist's
crash-helmet and with a reflective band across the chest
of a waterproof, frantically signalling, the motor-cycle
propped up on its stand and with its hazard lamps winking
a dozen yards beyond her. And the roof of the car that
looked as if it had slewed off the road and ploughed
straight through a clump of bushes and into a tree.

Roper braked and pulled up on to the verge, scrambling
from the car on one side as Price debouched swiftly from
the other.

'You hurt?' asked Price of the girl—for she was a
girl—who had been standing in the road.

'No,' she said. 'It's nothing to do with us. We've only
just arrived. D'you think you could find a phone and ring
for an ambulance? There's a man in that car. I think he's
dead.' She was breathless and shaking, couldn't have been
more than seventeen or eighteen.

'It's all right, Miss,' said Roper. 'We're police officers.
We've got a radio… You'll be warmer in our car.'

He left Price to it and hurried up the slope of the verge.

The shadowy figure of the girl's boyfriend, helmeted
and waterproofed and with a handkerchief pressed over
his nose and mouth, appeared around the back of the car.
All the doors hung open and there was a stink of exhaust

fumes and soot and human vomit that caught at the back of Roper's throat. Like a wet black snake, a length of hosepipe trailed across the grass and terminated at the car's exhaust outlet. It had not been a crash.

'Please don't touch anything, sir,' said the motor-cyclist.

'Police,' said Roper. 'My Inspector's on the radio now for an ambulance. Anybody in there?'

'Yes, sir,' said the motor-cyclist. 'He's stretched out across the back seat.'

'Dead?'

'I can't find a pulse, sir. And he feels a bit cold.'

Roper ducked in over the back seat, and felt about a hairy neck. The lad was right. The flesh was several degrees cooler than it ought to have been, and there was no pulse. There was another smell too…

'You didn't turn the engine off?'

'It was off when I arrived,' said the motor-cyclist.

Price came running with a torch.

'I know him,' said the motor-cyclist.

'So do we,' said Roper. Nothing could be done. He was no medic, but he recognised a cyanosed face when he saw one. 'Get back on the radio, Dave,' he said to Price. 'Message to DI Spenlow. Tell him he can go home. We've found Brian Seymour.'

THIRTEEN

A QUEUE OF VEHICLES stood at the edge of the verge: crash-tender, ambulance, a Traffpol pursuit Rover whose driver had heard Price over the radio, the police doctor's car and the car of the Coroner's Officer too because, to Roper's mind, this was a suspicious death if ever he had seen one. This side of the carriageway had been closed off with cones and winking hazard lights.

The driver of the Traffpol Rover, a dour sergeant of many years' experience, had ascertained that the ignition of the car—a Y-registered Ford Escort—had been switched on and the choke pulled right out to a fast idle. The engine block was still faintly warm; and a couple of knuckle raps on the petrol tank indicated that the engine had stopped, probably a couple of hours ago, simply because it had run out of fuel.

According to PC Carter, the motor-cyclist, he had caught a glimpse of the Escort in his headlight, and had wondered what it was doing parked there at this time of night amongst the trees and shrubbery. It hadn't taken him long to find out: the hosepipe going in through the open window of the rear door, and the soggy wet newspapers plugging up the remaining space between the window and the door frame were evidence enough. He had opened the driver's door first, expecting to find someone huddled over the steering-wheel. All he had seen first was smoke. In the few seconds it took to clear, he realised that the driving seat was empty. It wasn't until he opened one of the back doors that he saw Seymour lying along the back seat.

'Did you smell anything, son?' asked Roper. 'Besides exhaust fumes?'

'No, sir,' said Carter.

But Roper had, he was sure of it, although that particular smell had blown away now.

The two of them stood in the fresher air by the crash-tender. PC Carter had been to a late-night disco with his girlfriend. Like Roper and Price, he had thought the car had missed the curve in the road, climbed the verge and struck the tree, which it had in fact stopped short of by a yard or so. It was PC Carter who had been instrumental in getting DC Mills to pass a second opinion on Seymour's stock of second-hand cars. The Escort, still reeking of exhaust fumes, inside and out, had been one of them.

'Won't be selling any more, will he, poor bugger?'

'No, sir,' said Carter.

For Seymour was thoroughly dead, and probably had been for several hours, so had diagnosed the police doctor, agreeing with Roper that Seymour's cherry-red face, in its frame of beard and hair, was caused by well-advanced cyanosis, sure indication that Seymour had died of asphyxia.

'Better get your girl home, son,' said Roper. 'There's nothing more you can do here. I'd like a copy of your statement, though.'

'Yes, sir,' said Carter. ''Night, sir.'

''Night, son.'

Roper trudged back through the mud to the Escort, where the fire brigade crew had set up a floodlight.

The trees, the shrubbery, even the wet ground, still

reeked of exhaust fumes. The police doctor was putting his instruments away.

'Suicide, definitely,' he said, looking up as Roper joined him.

At nearly one o'clock in the morning, Roper almost rejoined with a terse 'cobblers'. But he didn't. The police doctor was young and callow; like DC Mills. He didn't know the half of it yet.

'Can I take a look at him?'

'Sure.' The doctor shuffled aside. Roper crouched down beside the stretcher.

Seymour, if he had, had not picked the easiest way to top himself. Roper laid the backs of his fingers against the beetrooty red cheek. It was chill. A trail of vomit ran from the left-hand side of the mouth and seeped into the straggle of beard.

'Drunk, was he?'

'Can't say,' said the doctor. 'I've taken some samples. Tomorrow, perhaps.'

Roper thought not. Seymour, or someone, had arranged all this in the most meticulous detail. According to the tyre tracks, the Escort had been driven off the road, in a straight line, and finished up here amongst the trees and bushes disturbing nary a leaf. The lights had then been switched off—the aluminium pipe at the end of a domestic vacuum-cleaner hose then rammed into the exhaust, the other end passed in through the open rear window—and then the rest of the space between the window and the top of the door frame packed solidly with wet newspapers. Whether these operations had been carried out in that order or not was impossible to say, but they had been carried out. And that they had was evidence enough, in Roper's opinion, that they had been carried out by a reasoning man and not somebody who was three parts witless with alcohol.

'Any cans or bottles in the car?'

'No,' said Price.

'Perhaps he threw them out into the bushes,' proposed the doctor, hopefully if naïvely.

Roper could have told him that suicides, in their desperate extreme, were not usually given to a last tidying up before they finally committed themselves. But again he did not.

He stood up and passed back the torch. 'Where's the Coroner's Officer?'

'Here, sir.'

'I want this noted as a suspicious death,' said Roper. 'All right? Full post-mortem with all the trimmings. As soon as the Coroner likes.'

'If you say so.'

'I say so,' said Roper.

IT WAS NINE O'CLOCK. Another new day. And the District Coroner was in spiky form.

'What authority do you have, Superintendent? Exactly?'

'It was advice, sir,' said Roper, not at his best himself at this hour. 'The man had ten years' previous, the officers around here wanted him on suspicion of theft and sundry other charges, and I wanted him for enquiries I'm doing on a murder investigation.'

'Oh,' said the Coroner.

Oh, indeed, thought Roper. 'So his demise was a bit too convenient, wouldn't you say, sir? Given the circumstances.'

'Perhaps he got wind of all this investigation, and decided to end it all. A few stiff whiskies…'

'If he'd had a few whiskies, sir, I doubt he'd have been able to hide his car the way he did. It was all very neat and tidy.'

'So he was sober, and emotionally disturbed?'

'Or somebody helped him, sir. Somebody who *was* sober.'

'Do you have any evidence?'

'No, sir,' said Roper. 'But believe me, I'm working on it.'

ROPER PUT DOWN the telephone, rose and shrugged back into his raincoat. He had finally got home at three o'clock this morning, and felt as if he hadn't been home at all. His first port of call this morning was Mrs Broadbent, after that Mrs Wainer. Mrs Hubert had phoned the desk downstairs at eight o'clock this morning and left a message that she would be free all day should Roper want to talk to her.

'Give her a ring, Liz,' he said to Hackett. 'Tell her we'll be along about eleven o'clock.'

'What do we do?' asked Makins, speaking for himself and Rodgers.

'Ring around all the local boozers,' said Roper. 'I want to know if any of the landlords saw Brian Seymour last night. And one of you'd better contact Cresswell. Find out when he made that trip to London last December.'

'And then phone Foyle?' said Makins. 'And find out if he was up there as well?'

'You've got it,' said Roper.

AT HALF PAST NINE, with WDS Hackett, Roper was again on Mrs Broadbent's front steps. In the cold light of day, the cottage looked even more unprepossessing than it had last night under the street-lamps. The narrow strip of front garden was a junkyard of old exhausts, rusting engine blocks, batteries, worn-out tyres and the rest of the detritus that was concomitant with the used-car trade.

Mrs Broadbent answered the door. She looked as if she hadn't slept, and she probably hadn't.

'God,' she grumbled. 'Not again. I had policemen here at two o'clock this morning.'

'I'm sorry, Mrs Broadbent,' said Roper. 'There are still a few things we've got to clear up.'

She let them in, and again showed them into the little front room.

'I'm sorry,' she said, presumably apologising for her snappiness when she had opened the door to them. 'It's just that everything seems to have gone wrong all at once. I'm still wondering how I'm going to get rid of all the junk he's left behind.' If she had had a moment of grief, it had passed. There would be other Brian Seymours, as there probably always had been. Mrs Broadbent was the resilient sort. 'Would you like a cup of tea?'

'Shall I make it?' asked Hackett.

'Yes, dear, that'd be nice... Milk's in the fridge. Cups are in the cupboard over the sink.'

She sat down in the armchair facing the window. Roper sat in the one opposite. He lit a cigarette.

'Do they know how the accident happened yet?' she said. Plainly, the officers who had called last night had kept to the euphemisms to avoid distressing her.

'No, Mrs Broadbent,' lied Roper. 'Not yet.' Seymour's Escort was on its way to the vehicle testing shed at the Forensic laboratory, together with a partly melted vacuum-cleaner hose and a half-dozen wet newspapers.

'Nobody else was hurt, were they?'

'No,' said Roper.

'That's good,' she said. A clinking of crockery came from the kitchen.

'You told us, last night, Mrs Broadbent, that Brian had had a phone call. Have you any idea who might have been calling?'

'No,' she said. 'But it was a man's voice.'

She had been in the kitchen peeling a few potatoes. Brian had been up in the front bedroom. He had not wanted to answer the phone all day for some reason.

'...the voice was sort of muffled. Like he was phoning from a long way away. "Seymour there?" he said. Not Brian, he called him Seymour. I noticed that. Curt he was. "Yes," I said, "what do you want him for?" "It's about my car," he said. So I called up to Brian. "Who is it?" he said. "I don't know," I said. "But I've told him you're in, so you'd better come and speak to him." And he did.'

'And then he went out, so you said.'

'Straight out,' she said. 'Didn't even change his clothes. Didn't even say goodbye or I won't be long. One second he was on the phone, the next one he was gone.'

'And that was soon after seven o'clock?'

'Yes,' she said.

'And he didn't come back at all? Or give you a ring to say what time he'd be back?'

She shook her head. 'No,' she said. 'That was the last I saw or heard of him.'

It sounded to Roper as if Seymour had left the house so swiftly last night in response to a summons.

'How had he been the last few days, Mrs Broadbent?'

'Sort of edgy,' she said. 'Twitchy. You know. Like he had a lot on his mind. Didn't even go out on Saturday night for a glass of beer.'

Hackett came in with three cups and saucers on a tin tray.

'Thank you, dear,' said Mrs Broadbent.

Roper gave her a few moments to herself while she sipped at her tea.

'He'd lived here for a year, you say.'

'Yes,' she said. 'Near enough.'

'Did he ever talk about what he'd done before?'

'No,' she said. 'Not a lot. He did tell me once he'd done time, but swore he'd gone straight ever since. But he obviously hadn't, had he?' Her mood switched momentarily back to bitterness, but it passed in the instant. 'But he certainly never did me down, I can tell you that. He always paid his share. He did all this.' A twitch of her head indicated the claustrophobic magenta wallpaper and the hastily applied white paint that had been allowed to run into weeps here and there.

'How did you get to know Brian in the first place, Mrs Broadbent?' asked Roper.

'He was just a lodger,' she said. 'At first. For a little while. He had a girl then. A girl from up in the town. Pretty, she was—common, mind. But it didn't last. She chucked him over. After that, we sort of drifted together... Except...just lately...' Her voice tailed away. 'Well...you know...'

'What's happened lately, Mrs Broadbent?'

Mrs Broadbent blinked down at the cup and saucer sitting on her lap. She sniffed. Perhaps she was not so resilient after all. 'He's been different,' she said. 'Started to go out more on his own. Nights, like. You know?'

'Another woman, d'you think?'

She didn't answer at once. She bent forward and stubbed out her cigarette in a glass ashtray lying in the hearth.

'I tried to think it wasn't,' she said. 'But he'd sort of...lost interest, you might say. And got very close. Se-

cret, like. And worried… He didn't use to worry about
anything. And Saturday—like I said—he came home with
that new set of suitcases. I know he was thinking of moving on. I asked him; he said he wasn't. But I'm still not
quite sure. He'd just got sort of, well…different.'

And perhaps Seymour *had* been going to move on. His
record showed him living a few years here, a few years
there. He had never stayed anywhere very long. And perhaps, scattered around the country, there was a trail of
Mrs Broadbents left behind to either weep for him or wish
him good riddance.

And he had changed; very lately, according to Mrs
Broadbent. Morose, secretive, worried. Was that a sign of
a man falling out of love, and trying not to let the woman
know? Somehow, Roper didn't think so. Men like Seymour were not usually gifted with the finer feelings. When
they tired of a woman, they usually packed their tents and
went. It was a rare one who moped about while he worked
out ways to tell her. And on Saturday he had been still
more bothered about something; on Sunday, yesterday,
distracted enough to run his van into the back of Price's
car; and not wanting to answer the telephone. But, finally,
he had answered the telephone; and that might just have
been the death of him.

THE CHATTY and garrulous Mrs Wainer had nothing but
good to say of Stella Pumfrey. At a quarter past ten in
the morning it could easily have been dusk outside, and
from where Roper was sitting he could see the rain bounc-
ing high off the patio like miniature fountains.

But she didn't like Bill Pumfrey. Not that she had said
so in so many words, but her dislike was there all the
same. She and Stella had been school friends.

'…It wasn't a good marriage,' she said. 'And Stella

was on the rebound, which probably made her a bad judge.'

Stella Pumfrey, it appeared, had been engaged to marry, but a few days before the wedding her intended had taken himself off with another woman and dropped from sight. A letter of apology had arrived a month afterwards. From the Cayman Islands, where the erstwhile fiancé was taking a honeymoon with his new bride.

Mrs Wainer, then an army wife—Wainer was serving in West Germany at the time and they were living in married quarters—invited Stella Pumfrey or, rather, Stella Goldring as she had then been, over to Germany for a two-girls-together skiing holiday for a couple of weeks.

Upon their return from the mountains, both Mrs Wainer and Stella Goldring were invited to a ladies' night dinner and dance in the officers' mess. Wainer, a major, had introduced Stella to his colonel, Pumfrey, during the pre-prandial cocktails. A month later, they were married.

'...I think Bill could smell her money. He was a lot older than her, of course, almost fifteen years. It isn't always a good thing, that, is it?'

The Pumfreys had started to go their separate ways some five years ago. Mrs Wainer was not completely certain, but she thought a divorce was in the offing. Sad, really, because Stella was the salt of the earth, help anybody. She had deserved a little more out of life...

And, yes, she did know Brian Seymour—or rather she had. He did a spot of work in the garden for them from time to time. She had heard the news of his accident this morning on the village grapevine.

Trying not to sound as if he were uttering the next question in the same breath, Roper said, 'There have been several outbreaks of burglaries around here, Mrs Wainer. Have you ever lost anything from here?'

'No,' she said. 'Luckily.'

And surprisingly, too, thought Roper. There weren't many antiques on show—perhaps Wainer kept his business and domestic interests apart—but there were a few nice pieces of china lying around, and a bronze and gilt mantel clock, which looked like a Webster, on the shelf above the fireplace. The furniture was smart, and expensive, and there was that new clay tennis-court in the garden, and any intending housebreaker worth his salt could surely have sized the place up from the outside in a couple of minutes and known it was worth his while. It was secluded, too, even from the front, behind its tall hedges that shielded it from the lane.

'Fortunate,' he observed, and wondered just *how* well Wainer had known Brian Seymour.

'Yes,' she said. 'It has been, rather. Every time it's happened, we've been away on holiday and the house has been empty. We've been very lucky.'

I'll say you have, thought Roper grimly.

'Your daughters weren't here, either?' he asked.

'No,' she said. 'They were always away at boarding-school.'

They were going on holiday again; tomorrow, in fact. Just for a week. Morocco. They were taking the girls with them this time. To get some sun. This awful English weather...

'But you weren't on holiday last Christmas, were you, Mrs Wainer?' asked Roper. 'When the last outbreak started? I heard you and your husband had Christmas lunch with the Pumfreys.'

'No,' she replied. 'We'd intended to, but we had to cancel for a few days.' They had eventually got away, to Portugal, two days after Boxing Day, when their daughters' school had finally let the girls out of quarantine; there had been an epidemic of chicken-pox and both had succumbed to it...

And Roper, sitting there nodding and smiling and listening, and generally exuding amicability, began to ponder more deeply a possible relationship between Lance Wainer, antique dealer of some substance, and Brian Seymour, illicit dealer in cars and several times convicted felon, and late of this same parish, who had come to a particularly messy end last night not ten miles from here.

Nothing in Seymour's previous records had indicated that he had specialised in the theft of antiques. His line had appeared to be easily marketable consumer goods, video-recorders, television sets, jewellery. Before arriving in Little Crow, Seymour had operated on a catch-as-catch-can basis. If it was there on show, he nicked it, making his entrances and exits as quickly as possible. But then he had settled in Little Crow. And soon after his arrival, the spates of burglaries had begun, and all that had been stolen, on every occasion, had been antiques. The finding of Mr Hubert's snuff-boxes in Seymour's cupboard was only proof that Semyour was in possession of Hubert's stolen property—at least, in a court of law. And if Seymour had not been the fence—which was unlikely—of those items, then it was reasonable to suppose, given his previous form, that he himself had stolen them and was only biding his time before he offloaded them.

And, given that, it was equally reasonable to suppose that all the other burglaries in Little Crow had been carried out by Seymour.

So, Seymour, amongst his other hobbies, was either an expert on the subject of antiques, or he knew one. And, if he was an expert, he would still have needed someone to fence them for him. And who better than the owner of an antique gallery tucked away in a place like Little Crow?

Like Lance Wainer, who conveniently went to cover whenever his neighbours got themselves burgled. There was a lot of money here, this elegant cottage, that tennis-court, and two-car garage, those expensive holidays three or four times a year. Roper himself intended taking up the antiques business when he retired, but he had no illusions about it. Unless he was lucky most of his living would come from his police pension. Except, of course, Wainer would have a pension, too, from the army, and perhaps he had, on several occasions, made a lucky deal or two. Or, on the other hand, perhaps not...

'Your husband not about this morning, Mrs Wainer?'

'No,' she said. 'He's driven down to the Country Club. He's on the management committee. He went about an hour ago.'

And that, to Roper's mind, might be another example of Wainer making himself conveniently scarce at the opportune moment. He was beginning to have serious doubts about Mr Wainer. He said casually, 'I'd like a few more words with your husband, Mrs Wainer. When would be the best time, do you think?'

'Oh,' she said brightly, 'this evening, I think. Not too late. We shall all be having an early night.'

And, of course, they would be, because tomorrow the four of them were flying south again to catch the sun. Which might be yet another example—in Roper's consideration—of serendipity working overtime again on behalf of Lance Wainer.

'Did you smell anything in there, Liz,' he asked Hackett, as he buckled himself into the seat beside her.

'A rat, maybe?' she said.

'Good,' he said. 'That makes two of us.'

DS MAKINS, connoisseur of womankind in general and self-professed expert on even the innermost arcane workings of the female psyche, would undoubtedly have qualified the tall, flamboyant and heroically bosomed Mrs Hubert as 'seriously tasty', and perhaps even awarded her his ultimate accolade of twenty points for artistic presentation.

Mr Hubert was also in attendance, a man, like both Pumfrey and Lance Wainer, with a touch of the ex-military about him, lean and suave and wearing a meticulously trimmed toothbrush moustache, a smoothie if Roper had ever seen one.

'I thought you were going out,' said Mrs Hubert, with leaden weightiness, as she turned into her lounge with Roper and Hackett behind her.

'I am,' said Hubert, cavalry-twilled, Harris-tweeded and with a trenchcoat over his arm, standing with his back to the fireplace. He otherwise ignored her. 'Superintendent Roper, is it?' he asked, extending a hand. 'My hearty thanks to you, sir. I understand you're the gentleman who found our bits and pieces. Can't say where, I suppose?'

It was a hand, for once, that could not be evaded. It crushed Roper's enthusiastically.

'No, sir,' said Roper, as Hubert continued to pump. 'We're still pursuing our enquiries.'

'Well, wherever you found them, thank you.'

'Will you be home for lunch?' This from Mrs Hubert, breaking in.

'I thought not,' said Hubert, his grip relaxing and the smile freezing on his face. The hand dropped back to his side. Like the Pumfreys, and the Cresswells, the Huberts obviously lived in a state of armed aggression and took no pains to hide it. The frozen smile was switched to Hackett, but only for as long as courtesy demanded, then

with a nod of his head and another thank you he went on
his way.

'We won't keep you long, Mrs Hubert,' said Roper.

'It's all right,' she said. 'I'm not in a hurry.' The front
door was slammed shut. 'Please…' She had taken a cigarette case from the mantelpiece and signalled towards the
settee with it. Roper and Hackett sat down. Mrs Hubert
plucked a cigarette from the case and lit it, then laid the
case back beside the clock without offering it. Nylon
rasped as she sat down and folded one plump shapely leg
over the other and gave a prim flick to the hem of her
khaki dress. Somewhere outside an engine was turned
over and a car door was slammed shut.

'I'm not sure how I can help you exactly,' she said.
Her voice was deep for a woman, and with a huskiness
that probably came from smoking too many cigarettes.

'I have to ask you a personal question, Mrs Hubert,'
said Roper, preferring to get the indelicacies out of the
way first; although from what he had observed just now
he doubted that either Mrs Hubert or her husband were
all that sensitive. 'You were with Mr Pumfrey on Friday
night, so he tells us. That right, is it?'

'Yes,' she said.

'Until…?'

She shrugged her broad shoulders.   'Difficult to say.'
She fingered the thick rope of costume pearls that hung
over her chest. 'About eleven o'clock, I suppose.'

'And you spent the evening at the Old Mill Country
Club.'

'Yes,' she said.

'Mr Pumfrey didn't leave you at all during the course
of the evening?'

'No.' There was a brief hiatus as she leaned forward to
pick up an ashtray from the coffee table, muffed it,

dropped it, and finally managed to sit it on the arm of her chair.

Makins might, after all, have been disappointed. Now, sitting down, in the better light from the window, it as obvious that her youthful array of hair owed more to her hairdresser than her genes and that her square, plump face, artistically painted though it was, was several years older than her body. She was, nevertheless, a woman of considerable physical attraction and it was easy to understand why Pumfrey had taken up with her. And hidden away in that smoky voice was an undertone far removed from here in Dorset. The Midlands, perhaps.

'You must have been one of the last people to see Mrs Pumfrey alive, Mrs Hubert,' he said. 'Did you know that?'

'Yes,' she said. 'I hadn't really thought about it; but I suppose I was.' She did the business with the legs again, gave the prim flick to her dress, found something, real or imaginary, on her lap, a piece of dust, or a hair, that she lifted off between a finger and a thumb and dropped into the ashtray. Her every movement proclaimed that there was no hurry, her time was Roper's.

'And you left her at half past seven; on Friday evening?'

'Yes,' she said. 'Something like that. I can't be sure of course. Not to the minute.'

'No,' he said. 'Of course not... I presume you and Mrs Pumfrey talked?'

'Chatted,' she said. 'Shoes and ships and sealing wax...nothing important. I'd been up to London the day before. She'd asked me to get her a couple of pairs of tights. I took them over to her, and she paid me for them, and I left.'

And then you went off and met her husband, thought Roper, ye bloody gods.

'She gave no indication that she might be expecting anyone, later on that evening, perhaps?'

She shook her head. 'No,' she said. 'Not as I remember.' Her cigarette was tapped against the ashtray. 'You're thinking of a man, perhaps?' One beautifully pencilled eyebrow lifted; in the half-dark of a bar it might easily have been mistaken for a sexual invitation.

'Got a name in particular have you, Mrs Hubert?'

'A name you can put in your little book, you mean?' she said. 'No. Not exactly. But there *was* gossip... Are you interested in gossip?'

'You told my Sergeant that you'd seen Mrs Pumfrey with Dr Cresswell,' said Roper. 'Anything there, do you think?'

'They looked close,' she said. 'I wouldn't care to say more than that.'

'You never saw her with another man?'

'Yes,' she said. 'A couple of times. But that was business. Her solicitor. I think his name's Foyle. He's got an office up in the town.'

Roper didn't pursue that line. He intended having another chat with Jack Foyle anyway.

'When you drove back from Crow Hill on Friday night, you must have passed Chalk House.'

'Yes,' she agreed. 'I did.'

'You didn't notice anything untoward? Anybody lurking about? Anything unusual?'

No, she had not. On her way from Crow Hill, she had applied her brakes too sharply prior to a curve. The car has skidded on the wet road and sideswiped a tree. Nothing serious, but it had shaken her up a little. She had driven on a little way, then parked in a lay-by and smoked two cigarettes to calm herself before driving the rest of the way home. She had been in no state to observe anything except the road ahead of her.

'Have you spoken to Sarah Cresswell?' she asked helpfully. 'The doctor's wife. Only I remember now that she goes out a lot at night… Walking. She might have seen something. Although you might find her a little vague, you know?'

'Vague?' prompted Roper.

'Oh,' she said. 'It's nothing really. It's just that a couple of times I've been driving home at night and seen Sarah standing in the rain opposite Stella's place. No hat, no umbrella, and practically up to her ankles in mud. On Thursday night I offered her a lift…she was drenched. She pretended she didn't know me. Just walked away.'

And, yes, she had known Seymour. Mrs Wainer had phoned her about an hour ago and told her about the accident last night. He had done some gardening for the Huberts, but only the once.

'…After he'd gone, I found my wristwatch missing; it was only a cheap thing, but I made sure he never worked here again…'

Which was the only thing she told Roper that was new, and it sounded right. Seymour, ever the opportunist.

'Are you and Mr Hubert members of the Country Club, Mrs Hubert?'

She twitched her nose disparagingly. 'No,' she said. 'I've only been inside it twice since we've lived down here. Both times with Bill. They're all horses and green wellies down there. We don't go in for all those country pursuits.'

'So you weren't concerned about being recognised?'

She shrugged. 'No,' she said. 'Not particularly. Bill and I take each other off the shelf from time to time and dust each other down. My husband knows about it, and so does most of the village, I suppose. It's not exactly a secret. I think Bill was more worried than I was. In fact he phoned the club first to see if there was anyone there from Little Crow. At the time, there wasn't. That's why he was peeved to find Lance Wainer there.'

'And when you had, you still stayed.'

'Bill didn't want to. I said what the hell. If we were seen, we were seen.'

It sounded likely. Mrs Hubert, big, bold and only a shade short of being downright brassy, would probably enjoy thumbing her nose at the conventions. Pumfrey wouldn't have.

'You must have driven past Chalk House at about twenty past eleven on Friday night,' said Roper.

'More like half past,' she said. 'Like I said, I had to have a couple of cigarettes while I pulled myself together.'

'And you saw no one?'

'Not that I remember. I—' She broke off suddenly and clicked finger and thumb together. 'I saw a car—parked on the verge—near Bill's place.'

No, she couldn't describe it. Except that it *might* have been pale blue—a saloon. Perhaps a Ford. There were no street-lights nearby, so she couldn't be certain. She had only glimpsed it in passing, and it was unusual only because cars rarely parked there.

She showed them out. Roper and Hackett made a dash for the car. A sudden cold had descended and there were hailstones mixed with the rain. The air was like breathing icy needles.

'Wouldn't surprise me if that had been Seymour's car,' said Roper, as he buckled himself in beside Hackett, but the speculation went no further as the radio clicked to life with their call-sign. It was Price at the other end. Would Roper find the nearest telephone and contact Craig at the laboratory. Price could say little over the air, but he was plainly disappointed about something.

FOURTEEN

IT WAS ONE of the new phone boxes, three glass sides and a top and the other side open to the elements, so that Roper could feel the wind-blown hail drumming against his trouser legs, and could see it rolling around his feet like a miniature cyclone of ball-bearings. It was deafening, too, so that he had to stick a finger in his unused ear and Craig had to shout at him.

'We've run a blood test, Mr Roper.'

'What about it?'

'Odd. We found *some* alcohol—point-0-0-five per cent. So your man wasn't drunk. What we found might even be a residue from the day before. Rather puts the lid on your murder theory, don't you agree?'

Yes, it did. Because if Seymour had been sober, he was hardly likely to have sat calmly in his car while someone else arranged the apparatus of his murder about him. And, if the police doctor had been right, Seymour had borne no marks of violence, or a wound of any kind, so he had not, on the face of it, been bludgeoned unconscious first.

'I understand there's to be a full post-mortem examination, which could prove your theory. I can only say I hope you're right.'

'So do I, Mr Craig,' shouted Roper.

'ANY LUCK with the pub calls?' Roper asked, as he hung up his raincoat.

'No,' said Price. 'Not a lot.'

No publican within ten miles of Little Crow had seen

anyone who fitted Seymour's description in his bar last night. Several knew him as a regular customer.

'How about Cresswell and Foyle?'

'Cresswell was in London on December one, two and three,' said Makins. 'And so was Foyle. But that's all Foyle'd say. He says he'll be in his office at nine o'clock tomorrow morning if you want to talk to him.'

'Phone him back,' said Roper. 'Tell him I do.'

HE LUNCHED ALONE at the Pied Bull, further along the High Street, on a couple of cheese and pickle sandwiches and a half a pint of bitter, and browsed through this month's copy of *The Antique Dealer and Collector's Guide*. By this time next year, with luck and a good wind behind him, he would have slipped into retirement and have become an antique dealer himself, and, as a rule, the magazine he was reading was one that could hold his undivided attention. But not today. On the way here, he had passed the war memorial, and the mahogany front door, wedged between a dress shop and an estate agency, with Jack Foyle's brass professional plate screwed to the strip of wall beside it, and an entryphone on the door frame. Jack Foyle, who had been cagey on the telephone this morning. Jack Foyle, who on December one, two and three, had been up in London, in common with Mrs Pumfrey and Dr Cresswell. That Cresswell had been up there at the same time might have been coincidental. The same could probably not have been said about Foyle, if his reluctance on the telephone this morning was any kind of indication. Mrs Pumfrey had told her sister that she had been in London with a man, and that man had *not* been Bernard Cresswell. That the man in question had not been Jack Foyle was stretching the arm of coincidence a mite too far.

Was Foyle the spare joker in the pack? Had Mrs Pumfrey pushed him into a corner of some sort? It wasn't impossible. He belonged to a profession whose governing body frowned more than disapprovingly on its members' moral peccadilloes; he probably had a wife, children, and certainly a practice that was thriving enough to let him run to hand-tailored suits and that red Scimitar that had been parked outside Pumfrey's on Saturday evening. It was a lifestyle a man would be reluctant to lose, and perhaps would kill to keep.

ROPER WATCHED through the window of the observation cubicle as Brian Seymour's mountainous and cyanose-blotched body, with a label tied to its left big toe, was draped with a sheet preparatory to being wheeled back to the cold room. It was half past three in the afternoon, and Roper had the feeling that the sun would never shine again. He tapped on the glass. Wilson beckoned him in.

'Didn't know you were seeing to that one, too,' said Roper.

'The County Coroner called me in,' said Wilson. And had called him in not solely upon Roper's advice. Two suspicious deaths in four days within a few miles of each other, added to the fact that both the victims were patients of the same doctor, had made the Coroner decidedly edgy. He had wondered if there might have been some kind of domino effect, especially as the two victims had lived within a few hundred yards of each other. In Coroner-think that was tantamount to patients dropping like flies. The next body in Wilson's schedule this afternoon was that of the late Florence Jane Bentley.

'Bentley?' said Roper, because the name did not immediately ring a bell.

'Another lady from Little Crow,' said Wilson, as he

turned away to drop his gloves into a pedal-bin and started to soap his hands and forearms at the stainless steel sink. 'Died on Friday night. Cresswell was her doctor, too.'

Roper remembered. The dying Mrs Bentley, with whom Cresswell and a nurse had spent most of last Friday evening.

'That's not a suspicious, too, is it?'

'Put it this way,' said Wilson, holding his hand under the hot running water. This way was that Mrs Bentley's nephew had spent a couple of hours on Saturday afternoon with his aunt's solicitor, and had travelled all the way down from Suffolk to do so. Although he had seen little of his aunt over the previous ten years, the nephew, Mrs Bentley's sole next of kin, had justifiably held certain expectations. But, on Saturday afternoon, it was explained to him that his aunt had made a new will some eight weeks before her death.

'Don't tell me,' said Roper. 'She left it all to Cresswell.'

'You really do have a nasty mind, Superintendent,' said Wilson. 'But you've got it in one. And after Cresswell's blunder the other night with his sister-in-law…need I say more?'

'Dodgy,' agreed Roper.

'As you say, Mr Roper,' said Wilson, moving a pace sideways to the paper towel dispenser. 'Very dodgy indeed. Mind you, I've taken a little peek at the lady, and at a guess I'd say she merely died of a weight of years. Ninety-one of them.' At the bench, where Wilson had been assembling fragments of Mrs Pumfrey's skull yesterday, his young woman assistant was labelling up plastic bags containing Seymour's more relevant organs and arranging them in a refrigerated box for transport to Wilson's laboratory. With the limited equipment at his disposal here, Wilson had been able to find nothing extraordinary, given the circumstances, about the death of Brian Seymour.

'So you reckon suicide then?'

'Can't really suggest anything else, old chum,' said Wilson. 'No signs of violence, the merest sip of alcohol, and from what few tests I've been able to do here, he wasn't on any of the main-line drugs. So I have to say that he did it from a cold start.'

'It was a bloody convenient suicide,' said Roper. And that convenience, really, was all he had to go on. Of steel-lined, copper-bottomed evidence he had none. Last night, he had felt so certain.

'Agreed,' said Wilson. 'I've still got a few more tests I can do, but I really can't hold out any expectations of anything significant. Sorry.'

And so was Roper.

'Got a job for you, Liz,' he said to Hackett, back in his office. 'I want you to go down and chat up Mrs Broadbent again. Tea and sympathy. Stay as long as you like. See if her vacuum-cleaner's missing a hose.'

Hackett was back a few minutes before five o'clock. A few chirrups of admiration, over several cups of tea, had led to Mrs Broadbent giving her a guided tour of her cottage, including the cupboard under the stairs, where she kept her vacuum-cleaner, a cheap one; and its plastic hose had been coiled behind the cupboard door, on a hook.

So, if Seymour had taken his own life or not last night, somebody, somewhere, was a vacuum-cleaner hose short today.

But, as Hackett said: 'Where the hell do we start looking?'

AT SIX O'CLOCK, in the murky daylight of another drizzling dusk, Roper and DS Rodgers were shown into Wainer's sitting-room by Mrs Wainer.

'I'm sorry about this, Mr Wainer,' said Roper, as Wainer straightened from his armchair and the boxer, perhaps recognising Roper as an old acquaintance, descended wetly upon him with its stump of tail wagging. 'We're clutching at a few straws, sir. Wondered if you might be able to help us.'

Wainer made one of his military flourishes to encompass the settee and two other armchairs. 'Please... You said it was about Brian Seymour.'

'Yes, sir,' said Roper, unbuttoning his raincoat. 'You said you knew him.'

'I said "of him",' said Wainer. 'I knew *of* him. I've had him in a couple of times to help me out in the garden; and he cleared the site for my daughters' tennis-court. I know his landlady somewhat better.' He stretched his long thin legs in front of the imitation glowing logs of his gas fire. The boxer had found a new friend in Rodgers and was amiably chewing his hand. '...I have her in every other Sunday to run a Hoover over the shop and generally tidy up the place. Decent sort. Reliable, you know? You might do better to have a word with her. Come here, Baskerville.'

The boxer reluctantly surrendered Rodgers' hand and flopped down with a sigh on the carpet by Wainer's feet.

'I shouldn't really be telling you this, sir,' said Roper, 'but we found the proceeds of several burglaries in one of Mrs Broadbent's bedrooms; a room Seymour used for a workshop.'

'Really,' said Wainer, his interest plainly sparked and his eyes lighting. 'Any of Pumfrey's stuff there, was it? Or Hubert's?'

'Mostly Mr Hubert's. Unfortunately. If he did have anything of Mr Pumfrey's he'd already got rid of it.'

'Pity,' said Wainer sympathetically. 'Bill Pumfrey lost some bloody nice stuff.'

'You knew it, did you, sir?'

'Yes,' said Wainer. 'I valued it for him. He lost a Cantonese vase. Almost irreplaceable. And not a chip on it anywhere. Bloody shame.'

'We're working on the lines that Seymour must have had a fence,' proposed Roper. 'Or he was a receiver; and perhaps a fence himself. Any thoughts, sir?'

But Wainer was already shaking his head. 'A man like that wouldn't have had the wit,' he said scornfully. 'Only someone who knew antiques would have recognised the worth of some of that stuff.'

'Yes, sir. Quite,' agreed Roper. 'But if we assume that Seymour was the thief, then he seemed to know exactly what to steal, didn't he?'

'Yes,' said Wainer. 'Put like that, I suppose he did.'

'He never came into your shop—asked your advice about something he wanted to sell, say?'

'Hardly,' said Wainer. Then, surprisingly slowly for a man of obvious intelligence, it seemed to occur to him that the question Roper had asked was not the one he had replied to. His lean face stiffened.

'I don't conduct business that way, Superintendent. I don't need to. The shop is only a hobby. I love antiques, and having that gallery is only a way of having as many as possible around me. I don't need to make dirty money fencing for yobs like Seymour.'

Which might have been the truth; or equally might not. Roper, over the years, had met several antique dealers who were dilettantes doing it for love and not the money, but he had not met all that many. He knew of more who were decidedly shady; and a few others upon whose premises the law regularly swarmed after a big-time burglary.

'Did you see Seymour in any of your travels last night, sir? By any chance?'

Wainer spotted that crevasse more quickly. 'Look,' he said crossly, 'just what the hell is all this leading up to, Superintendent?'

'I told you, sir,' said Roper. 'We're clutching at straws. If you only spotted Seymour blowing his nose outside your cottage last night that'd be the most useful bit of information we've had all day.'

Wainer, slightly mollified, but still suspicious, had not seen Seymour last night. And yes, he had been out. At a few minutes before seven, he had driven Pumfrey down to the Country Club to collect Pumfrey's car. At a quarter to eight, Wainer had been back here in Little Crow, in the workshop at the back of his gallery. He cleaned and repaired old clocks. Another hobby.

'Alone, sir?'

'Yes, sir,' retorted Wainer, staring back fixedly at him. 'Quite alone. Until half past ten.'

'When you came back here.'

'Yes,' repeated Wainer. 'To my wife and my younger daughter. Both of whom were sitting in here watching the television.'

Which was all very well and good, but, in Roper's opinion, was scarcely an alibi at all.

MIDNIGHT MIGHT HAVE BEEN an age away, or only minutes. Price, Hackett, Makins and Rodgers had gone their separate ways at eleven o'clock, and in the time since Roper had sat alone in the cramped space between his desk and the window and listened to Crow Hill quieten as it put itself to bed. Roper himself was a night creature.

It was a time when he could clear his mind of all its clutter and bring into sharper focus the things that mattered, draw them, as it were, from the muddle of his cerebral files and put them into some semblance of order.

In front of him was a photocopy of Price's sketch plan of Mrs Pumfrey's bedroom, marked up here and there with a red ballpoint by Roper himself as he had experimented with one or two possible scenarios. A red line across each of the bays represented the closed curtains. A scattering of dots and two small areas of red cross-hatching, in the left bay and on the floor around the left-hand side of the dressing-table, represented the cigarette ends and patches of trodden-in cigarette ash that the SOCO had found. A small circle with CL scribbled beside it, under the dressing-table, was the contact lens discovered by Dave Price.

A prominent X, in the left-hand bay, behind the closed curtains, where the safe was, represented the algebraic symbol for the unknown. Mrs Pumfrey's killer. Because a patch of ash and a cigarette end—trodden on, had been found in the bay by the SOCO. So perhaps some of the action, perhaps even the preliminary bout, had taken place behind the curtains. When Mrs Pumfrey had gone to put the ashtray on the window-ledge for the night. A confrontation. A struggle for the ashtray…

And if it *had* happened that way, the killer—he, or she—must have slipped behind the curtains *after* Mrs Pumfrey had been to the safe for the earrings. But not Brian Seymour. It had not been Brian Seymour; unless he hadn't recognised his own cigarette lighter…

Suicide implied a state of mind bordering on the desperate. When Seymour had received that telephone call yesterday evening, so far as he knew, the only misdeed the law had him lined up for was a comparatively minor traffic offence. Trivia like that would hardly have bothered Seymour with ten years of probation and prison behind him. He had not known, nor ever would now, that he had been about to be questioned regarding two entirely different matters.

And if it wasn't suicide, it had to be murder, didn't it? Seymour had been set up. How? He hadn't been bludgeoned unconscious, that much was certain. Nor had he been drunk. The other scenario, that he had sat willingly in his car while someone else busied themselves with the mechanics of his demise was not even remotely plausible. And if it was murder; *cui bono?*

His fence? Wainer?

The murderer of Stella Pumfrey, who was afraid—or certain—that Seymour had known something?

One by one, under the light of his desk lamp, he looked again through the half-dozen copies of the photographs that the senior fire officer had taken last night. Two flashlit shots showed Seymour sprawled along his back seat, two more showed him lying on the stretcher, two more the Escort with its doors open and its interior dusty with soot...

He didn't spot it at once. Not that he was looking for anything in particular. And even when he did spot it, he could not be certain because the shot of Seymour he was looking at had been taken from Seymour's feet, and obliquely, so that the body was foreshortened, and the legs, too. The shot through the Escort's open driver's door had also been taken from an angle...

That Craig from the Forensic laboratory should have rung just then was, for once, serendipity working on the right side. Even though he had only rung on the off-chance to say that he had found nothing and was shutting up shop for the night.

'Have you got Seymour's jeans there, Mr Craig?'

'I have. Why?'

Roper picked up the photograph of Seymour laid out on the stretcher. 'Any idea of his inside leg measurement?'

'Offhand, no,' said Craig. 'Why do you ask?'

'I've got a photo here. Seymour. Seems to have had very short legs.'

'Yes, he did have, now you come to mention it.'

Roper picked up another photograph. 'And the driving seat of that Escort. It seems to be ratcheted hard back.'

'It is,' said Craig. 'On the last notch.'

'Only—I was wondering if he could have reached his driving pedals,' said Roper.

'Ah,' said Craig. 'Give me ten minutes, will you? I'll buzz you back.'

He was as good as his word. For all his pendulous girth, Brian Seymour's inside leg measurement was a mere twenty-six inches.

'And the only person on our staff here with twenty-six inch legs is one of our young lady technicians. So we sat her in Seymour's driving seat.'

'And?' said Roper, hopefully.

'Her feet wouldn't reach the pedals,' said Craig. 'No way. Whoever drove that car last night must have been at least six inches taller than Seymour. So he couldn't have put it amongst those trees, could he?'

'No, Mr Craig,' agreed Roper. 'He couldn't, could he?'

ROPER DROVE HOME with a restless mind. It was better than a fifty-fifty chance now that Seymour had been murdered, and if he had then he had certainly been murdered more cold-bloodedly than Stella Pumfrey. Seymour's murder—again if it was—had been premeditated. Perhaps even over a period as long as three hours, from some time around seven o'clock last night until some time close to ten. The police doctor had estimated the time of death at ten o'clock, perhaps before but not much later; Wilson had not been able to get much closer. Where had Seymour been for those three hours, who had he met, and was whoever he had met the same man who had made that telephone call? And was that man the same man who had forgotten to ratchet Seymour's driving seat forward after he himself had vacated it? It was only a little mistake, a moment of forgetfulness engendered by haste, perhaps, but it was a stupid thing to have overlooked because it had provided Roper with the most solid piece of evidence that Seymour had not driven that Escort into the bushes last night.

And from that premise, Roper had to ask himself yet again if Seymour's murder was connected with that of Stella Pumfrey. And if it was, what rôle had Seymour played in that murder? Accessory? Witness? As intending burglar, had he been in the house, lurking in the shadows, and seen the murderer come and go? It wasn't impossible.

Which brought Roper back to the Cresswells, because amongst all the conjectures tumbling over themselves to get a hearing, another idea had come to mind as to why Mrs Pumfrey had been kneeling down on Friday night.

She would have to have been on her knees to have opened that safe; wouldn't she?

'YOU GOT A MOMENT, sir?' asked PC Carter.

'Come in, son,' said Roper. He was still hanging up his raincoat. Carter must have followed him up the stairs.

It was eight o'clock on Tuesday morning. The Easter holiday was over and Crow Hill was coming noisily back to life after the break. From the street came a constant hum of traffic. The sun was shining and it felt like spring at last.

'Take a seat.'

Carter plucked at the immaculately pressed knees of his uniform trousers and sat down. Everything about Carter shone, including his face. Roper even wondered if he shaved yet.

'Shoot,' said Roper, sitting himself.

'It's about Seymour, sir,' said Carter. He unbuttoned the top pocket of his tunic and brought out his pocket-book. 'That Escort…he let me give it a test run the other night. The thing is, I took a mileage reading, sir.'

Roper waited.

Carter opened his notebook at the back page. 'It was twenty-six thousand, three hundred and twenty-four point six, sir.'

Realisation suddenly dawned. The pinkly scrubbed PC Carter was clearly a youth of some sagacity. Roper could have completed what the lad had to say—it was so obvious now, and he should have thought of it himself; but everyone deserved their moment of glory, not least a probationary constable doing his best to make his way up the rickety ladder.

'So?' asked Roper. 'What's your idea?'

'Well, sir,' said Carter earnestly. 'I was thinking, if we knew what was on the Escort's odometer *now*, we'd have an idea of where he went the other night, wouldn't we? Assuming, of course, he hadn't used it since I saw it.'

'Good lad.' Roper crabbed a hand for the telephone. 'Let's find out, shall we?… Forensic lab. Mr Craig, if he's in yet.' He drummed a fingernail against the mouthpiece as he waited. It was given to few incidents like this to be in possession of a previous odometer reading recorded so recently.

'Just out of training college, are you, Carter?'

'Yes, sir,' said Carter. 'Six weeks, sir.'

'Going to make a career of it?'

'I hope so, sir,' said Carter.

So did Roper. 'Good morning, Mr Craig. It's Roper. That Escort…don't happen to have its odometer reading to hand, I suppose?'

Craig had. Not quite to hand, but it was in his secretary's office, next door.

Another wait, then the thud of the telephone at the other end striking something as it was picked up again.

'Stylus and tablet ready? The reading we have here is: twenty-six thousand, three hundred and thirty-two point two… Why do you ask? Something else come up, has it?'

Roper held out his hand for Carter's pocket-book, and on a jotter scribbled Craig's figure, and Carter's reading underneath it.

'You've gone very quiet, Mr Roper.'

'Hang about…' Simple subtraction showed that Seymour's Escort had only been driven seven point six miles since Carter had sat in it.

'How far away is Little Crow from Pod Hill, son?' he asked Carter.

'About six or seven miles, sir,' said Carter.

'Check it,' said Roper. 'There's a map in Mr Lambert's office.'

Carter went.

'What is going on there, Mr Roper? I detect a distinct quickening of breath at your end.'

'You do indeed, Mr Craig.' Roper sketched in the fortuitous event that had led to PC Carter recording the Escort's mileage. 'Any luck with that hosepipe, and the newspapers?'

Regrettably there was none. The vacuum-cleaner hose was of the type sold in most electrical goods shops as a replacement part, and the soggy newspapers were all copies of the *Crow Hill Weekly News,* a local advertising tabloid of the sort known in the publishing trade as a 'freebie'. Had they been national newspapers they might, given a little luck, have borne a house number pencilled on by a newsagent.

Carter came back. The road distance from Little Crow to Pod Hill was seven point two miles. Carter, after noting the reading out of sight of Seymour on Saturday, had only driven the Escort two hundred yards at most. So knock off, say, point one of a mile. Which left only point three of a mile to play about with. Which meant—and Roper was almost certain of it—that whoever had telephoned Seymour the other night had lured him directly to Pod Hill—and his death.

At nine thirty, in company with Makins, he was walking briskly along the High Street towards Foyle's office. The sun shone and the windless morning air was laced with petrol fumes that certainly hadn't been there over the weekend. At the pavement's edge street-traders' stalls were already busy and there was a queue waiting for the bank to open. As Makins observed, Crow Hill wasn't quite a cemetery after all.

After a contretemps with the entryphone—neither Roper nor Foyle's receptionist had been able to hear each other over the noise in the street, so that he had to shout his rank and name twice before she pushed the button to let them in—he and Makins ascended the stairs beside the estate agency. What Foyle spent on his suits and his Scimitar, he evidently saved on paint, wallpaper and stair carpet.

His office, however, was as smart as the man himself and designed to impress. A desk like a great mahogany raft, a sumptuous grey carpet, water-colours in black frames of nineteenth-century Crow Hill dotted around the walls.

'No calls for half an hour, Debbie,' Foyle called after his receptionist. 'Please sit down, gentlemen.' A sweep of his hand took in his two visitors' chairs: a pair of mahogany carvers, only reproductions but they would have set him back more than a few pounds. At the back of the building, the office overlooked a small courtyard piled high with black rubbish sacks. One of the windows gave access to an iron fire escape.

Foyle sat down; and half-heartedly offered them tea, or coffee, and seemed relieved that they declined both. He had another appointment at ten o'clock, he explained, so would like to get this wretched business over as quickly as possible.

'But before we begin,' he said, fidgeting with the edges of an A4 pad on his blotter. 'Nothing I can tell you will have any bearing on the death of Stella Pumfrey. I told your man that on the telephone yesterday.'

'You knew Mrs Pumfrey well, sir?' asked Roper.

'I did,' conceded Foyle, still plucking.

'More than professionally?'

'Yes,' said Foyle, lowering his gaze guiltily to the white pad. 'Briefly. An infatuation. It was over almost as soon as it started.'

'From your point of view, sir?' asked Roper. 'Or Mrs Pumfrey's?'

'It was a mutual understanding,' said Foyle. 'We both realised that we were being foolish.'

'Not immediately *mutual* though, was it, sir?' said Roper.

Foyle glanced up querulously. 'And what does that mean exactly?' he said.

'Mrs Pumfrey came here one evening before Christmas, sir,' said Roper. 'You and she had a quarrel.'

Foyle sat back in his chair, and let his hands fall to his lap. And Roper recognised what is known in interview jargon as the buy-signs. Foyle was about to tell the truth, perhaps not all of it, but as much as he had to.

'Who the hell told you that?' he asked wearily, but didn't wait for an answer. 'Yes,' he admitted. 'We had a quarrel. She came here several times afterwards. She wouldn't let go, you see.'

'So it wasn't exactly a mutual understanding then, was it, Mr Foyle?'

Foyle shook his head. 'No,' he said.

At Makins' elbow, at the other end of the desk, stood a silver-framed photograph of a dark-haired woman and two children. Roper wondered if it had been there when Mrs Pumfrey had made her regular evening visits. Somehow he doubted it.

'And you were in London with Mrs Pumfrey early last December?'

'I was,' said Foyle. And Roper thought what a pity it

was that he would never, at least officially, be able to tell Mrs Cresswell that.

'And you were with her most of the time, I take it?'

'Most of it,' said Foyle. 'Look, for God's sake,' he suddenly exploded quietly, 'this can't be relevant, surely.'

'Did you get back on good terms with Mrs Pumfrey, sir?' asked Roper, ignoring the outburst. 'After this quarrel?'

'I never saw her,' said Foyle. 'Except in the street. We never spoke.'

'It must have been a very difficult situation for you, sir,' said Roper.

The irony, for it was, slipped past Foyle unnoticed. 'It was,' he said.

'Your wife never knew?'

'God, no,' said Foyle, a look of horror fleeting across his face. 'Never.'

'Mrs Pumfrey seems to have turned to alcohol around about that time, sir,' said Roper. 'Did you know that?'

'I'd heard,' said Foyle. 'Bill Pumfrey told me. But there wasn't much I could do about it, was there?'

'Mr Pumfrey knew about you and his wife, did he, Mr Foyle?'

'Of course he bloody didn't,' snorted Foyle. 'And I have to say again, Superintendent: all this is quite irrelevant. I admit to having had an affair with a woman who was also a client. And that, so far as I'm concerned, is the end of it. I did not speak a word to her after the quarrel you mentioned.'

'Did she ever threaten you, sir? Perhaps say that she'd tell your wife?'

'Of course not,' said Foyle. 'Stella wasn't that sort. But that's hardly relevant either, is it?'

It was relevant. So far Roper had uncovered nothing

about Mrs Pumfrey that pointed to her being anything but
a generous woman. Mr and Mrs González had thought the
world of her, she had lent Cresswell money without being
asked and, a moment ago, Foyle had almost scoffed at the
idea of Mrs Pumfrey ever being likely to seek revenge on
him for casting her aside. There was many a woman who
would have. But not Stella Pumfrey. Stella Pumfrey had
not been that sort. Apart from her husband and her sister
it seemed that nobody had a bad word to say about Stella
Pumfrey…

'Where were you, on Friday night, Mr Foyle?' asked
Makins. 'It's just for the record.'

The question, coming as it did from another direction,
seemed to catch Foyle unawares.

'I was at home.'

'Alone, sir?' asked Makins.

'Yes, I was alone,' said Foyle irritably. 'My wife had
taken the children along to her mother at Bridport. For
the evening. To collect their Easter eggs.'

'What time did she get back, sir?' asked Makins.

'Oh, for God's sake,' protested Foyle. 'If you think I
killed Stella Pumfrey you're on a hiding to nothing…
About midnight, I suppose.'

Mrs Cresswell, assuming that she was telling the truth,
had last seen Stella Pumfrey alive at eleven thirty on Friday night. Even in his Scimitar, Foyle could never have
killed Mrs Pumfrey, cleared up the mess, then driven the
forty-five miles from here to Portesham in time to greet
his wife on her return home at midnight.

'You're sure about the time, are you, Mr Foyle?' asked
Roper.

'Quite sure,' said Foyle. 'My wife was later than she'd
told me she'd be, she had the children with her, and the

weather was terrible. I looked at my watch a hell of a lot
between eleven o'clock and midnight.'

'Yes, sir,' said Roper. 'I can imagine.' It sounded very
much as if Foyle was telling the truth. He tried another
tack. 'Do you happen to know a gentleman called Brian
Seymour, Mr Foyle?'

Foyle shook his head. He had never heard of him.

Roper led the conversation back to Stella Pumfrey.
Foyle had been her solicitor for three years, and his predecessor, from whom he had bought the practice, for four
or five years before that. William Pumfrey was also a
client. Soon after setting himself up here, Foyle had
helped Pumfrey through his second appearance in the
bankruptcy courts.

'Who settled his debts?' asked Roper.

'Stella did,' said Foyle. 'For the second time.' Something like a curled lip made it fairly evident that Foyle
was not exactly an admirer of Pumfrey.

'When we saw you at Mr Pumfrey's on Saturday evening, Mr Foyle,' said Roper, 'had he called you over
there?'

'Yes,' said Foyle. 'He'd rung me at home, told me that
Stella was dead, and that he'd just come back from the
mortuary—'

'So he rang you in the morning?'

'About a quarter past eleven,' said Foyle.

Hell's bloody teeth, thought Roper. Pumfrey would
scarcely have had time to get his coat off after identifying
his wife's body... 'And, sir?'

'He told me he couldn't find Stella's will; had I got it?
I said I had, and he asked me if I could take it across
there. He invited me to lunch.'

'So he wanted to look at this will before lunch, did he?'
Which sounded to Roper like a most indecent haste; and,

from the expression of distaste on his face, it looked as if
Foyle thought much the same.

'He told me he wanted to get his financial affairs
straightened out as quickly as possible, and since it was
the holiday weekend and neither of us was doing anything... That was his attitude. I told him I couldn't possibly manage it at such short notice, and that I'd call in
to see him round about three o'clock.'

'And how did he respond?'

'Somewhat shortly,' said Foyle. 'He's that kind of
man.'

'Do you think he knew the contents of Mrs Pumfrey's
will before you told him?'

'I think so,' said Foyle. 'Although he certainly never
had it from me. I got the impression that he simply wanted
to see it in black and white in order to reassure himself
that she hadn't made any changes to it that he didn't know
about.'

'And had she?'

Foyle shook his head. 'Mind you,' he said, 'after the
way he treated her, I'm surprised. In fact I'm phoning
around all the other local solicitors this morning to see if
there is another will about somewhere. She might have
prepared one through someone else; I wouldn't have
blamed her.'

So Foyle had a conscience at least. It raised him slightly
in Roper's estimation; but not much. Mrs Pumfrey had
not been all that lucky in her choice of men.

Foyle, at a guess, put the value of Mrs Pumfrey's estate,
excluding her jewellery, at one and a half million, based
on current property and land prices, although it would be
difficult to find a purchaser who could pay that kind of
money, and the house was in need of a great deal of repair. And of course there would be a considerable amount
of inheritance tax; and since Mrs Cresswell and Pumfrey

would only be able to pay that if they sold the house, which they were not in a position to do until the will had been probated, both were caught in the trap in which the modestly rich often found themselves: of being surrounded by money of which they were unable to spend even a penny. Pumfrey was broke. On Saturday, he had come straight out with it and asked Foyle to help him negotiate a loan on the strength of his late wife's will.

'Are you prepared to tell me how much, Mr Foyle?'

'Yes,' said Foyle. 'Two hundred and fifty thousand.'

'And will he get it?'

'Good God, yes,' said Foyle. 'The local bank managers will practically fall over themselves to lend it to him.'

'Did he tell you what he wanted it for?'

'Yes,' said Foyle. 'He was quite frank about it. He was in debt to the tune of fifteen thousand, and the rest he wanted to buy himself into another business. I understood he'd had an offer of some sort—someone from his army days, I think it was.'

'And that,' said Makins, on the way back along the crowded High Street, 'sounds to me like one hell of a motive.'

'It does to me, too, George,' said Roper. 'But he couldn't have done it, could he? He wasn't there, was he?'

They turned up the single well-worn step of the station and pushed through the swing-doors; and walked straight into the little drama going on at the public counter.

A couple of uniformed officers had clearly made a collar. The duty sergeant had lifted the counter flap and was ushering through a PC, a shabbily dressed and bespectacled woman, and a WPC who was bringing up the rear and towing a shopping trolley.

The PC took the woman's elbow and steered her off to the left, towards the interview-rooms, and as he did Roper heard him say grimly: 'This way, please, Mrs Cresswell.'

SIXTEEN

ROPER CAUGHT UP with the WPC as she was about to turn into the interview-room with the shopping trolley. He held her back with one hand and shut the door with the other.

'What's this all about, Constable?'

'Shoplifting, sir,' she said.

'Like what?'

'A tin of sardines, sir.' She lifted her shoulders despairingly. 'Twenty-eight pence worth. Hardly worth all the trouble, was it?'

'A formal complaint, is it?'

No, it was not. Mrs Cresswell had been seen to slip the tin of sardines into her coat pocket by the manager of the local supermarket.

'...She's a regular customer, sir, and he's had some problems with her before, and he says he knows she's got some kind of mental trouble. She nicked a tin last week, too, but he let that one go. He just wants us to scare the pants off her a bit so that she won't do it again. She tells us she's the wife of Dr Cresswell down in the village. And we've got the funny idea that she *wanted* to get caught.'

'She probably did,' said Roper, thoughtfully, and more to himself.

'Sir...?'

'It's a private war she's waging, Constable... I'll do the talking and you can stand by the door. All right?'

'Yes, sir.' The WPC looked relieved that the unpleasant duty was taken into more senior hands. And so did the

PC waiting in the interview-room with Mrs Cresswell. On the table between them was Mrs Cresswell's handbag; and the tin of sardines. The constable rose, and Roper took his place.

'Do you mind emptying out your handbag, Mrs Cresswell?'

Wordlessly, she unfastened the flap and tipped the contents of the bag on to the table.

Roper picked up a wallet and passed it across to her.

'Now that, please, Mrs Cresswell.'

That was emptied too. Three twenty-pound notes, two tens, and a five, two credit cards and a cheque guarantee card for the sum of one hundred pounds, and four postage stamps.

'Now you can put it all back again.'

Roper watched as, still without a word, she stuffed the notes and cards back into her wallet and repacked her handbag. Behind her thick, pebble-lensed spectacles, he could easily have passed her in the street and never recognised her. This morning, she was dowdier than ever in a scruffy tweed suit that looked as if she did her gardening in it.

'What's in the trolley, Mrs Cresswell?'

'Nothing,' she said.

Roper glanced across at the WPC. She nodded. He transferred his gaze back to Mrs Cresswell.

They eyed each other across the table.

'I'd like you to let my husband know I've been arrested,' she said.

Roper had already guessed that. He sat back in the hard uncomfortable chair. 'Do that will you, Constable,' he said to the PC. He glanced at his watch. 'And then ring upstairs and tell Sergeant Makins I'd like him down here in five minutes' time.'

'Yes, sir.'

The WPC stood aside with the door as she opened it. The constable went out. The door catch clicked shut again.

Roper and Mrs Cresswell sat eye to eye again. Giving her a paternal lecture on thieving would be about as much use as trying to breathe life back into Brian Seymour. Behind the pebble lenses, her pupils were like two bright buttons.

'Enjoying this little game, aren't you, Mrs Cresswell?' he said, when the silence had dragged on long enough.

She tilted her head quizzically. 'Game?' she said. 'What game?'

'Playing silly-buggers,' said Roper.

'You're very rude,' she said. 'I'm sure I could report you for that.'

'You haven't heard the half of it yet, Mrs Cresswell. I could make your ears light up.'

'Yes,' she said equably. 'You probably could.'

Roper pushed the tin of sardines in front of her. She gave them not a glance.

'I stole them,' she said. 'And I want you to charge me.'

'Or you can take them back to the shop and pay for them.'

'I hate sardines,' she said. 'And so does Bernard.'

'So you are just playing silly-buggers. Right?'

Her smile dissolved and her face stiffened. 'Are you going to charge me or not?'

'You'd like that, wouldn't you, Mrs Cresswell? Big headlines in the local rag: Doctor's wife on shoplifting charge. Do wonders for his practice that would, wouldn't it?'

She turned her face away disdainfully.

Roper shot his cuff and looked at his watch. 'I'll bet

right now he's in his surgery, with twenty patients outside, and wondering how he's going to explain to them that he's got to leave them for a while because he's got to collect his wife from the local nick.'

'He'll manage,' she said. 'He always does. He has great charm, does Bernard.'

'Really dislike him, don't you, Mrs Cresswell?'

She didn't answer. A minute or two passed. She began to fidget.

'What the hell are we waiting for?' she said.

'We're waiting for your husband to take you home,' said Roper.

'After you've charged me. I presume you *are* going to charge me.'

'I wouldn't give you the pleasure,' said Roper. 'Besides, it isn't worth the paperwork.'

The two bright buttons regarded him balefully. Silence again. Roper decided it might be worth bending the rules a little.

'You're wrong, Mrs Cresswell,' said Roper. 'Do you know that?'

'About what?'

'Your husband and your sister. I can't say you're wrong all ways, mind, but you're certainly wrong about that trip to London.'

'You would say that, wouldn't you?' she sneered. 'You're all bloody men together, aren't you?'

'I've got proof.'

'And so have I,' she said.

Roper shook his head. 'You've only got what we call circumstantial evidence, Mrs Cresswell. Very dodgy, is circumstantial evidence. What I'm talking about is verbal evidence from a third party. A clear admission. The man your sister spent three days in London with.'

'You've probably made it up,' she said. 'The police do that when it suits them, don't they?'

But she wasn't entirely certain. Her interest had quickened, hard though she tried to disguise it.

'You watch too many TV coppers, Mrs Cresswell.'

He hunched over the table, his hands clasped. 'Your husband gave you a telephone number, and so did Mrs Pumfrey. D'you think they'd have done that—given you the same hotel telephone number—if they'd been having a crafty few days together?' He could also have suggested to her that, with her obviously poor eyesight, her husband's racy Toyota and Foyle's red Scimitar might look remarkably similar from the back. But he couldn't without identifying Foyle more closely.

'They gave me the numbers separately,' she countered. 'Neither knew the other one had.'

'No,' said Roper. 'And they wouldn't have, would they, Mrs Cresswell?'

She opened her mouth, but shut it again as a knock came at the door. The WPC opened it, and Makins came in.

Roper rose. 'This is Detective Sergeant Makins, Mrs Cresswell. Got your pocket-book, Sergeant?'

'Yes, sir,' said Makins.

'I was just telling Mrs Cresswell about the interview we've just had with a certain gentleman. Regarding the visit he made to London with Mrs Cresswell's late sister. Sit here, will you, Sergeant, and read out to Mrs Cresswell the relevant passages from your notes. Call him Mr X. Then when Dr Cresswell turns up you can hand Mrs Cresswell over to him and tell him we're not preferring any charges. I'll be upstairs, if you want me.'

Roper left the interview-room, glad to be out of it. Marriage counselling was not exactly his forte. A lifetime bachelor himself, he was getting married in Bournemouth registry office this coming Saturday morning, and from what he had seen of married life in Little Crow he was beginning to entertain serious doubts that wedded bliss was all it was cracked up to be.

Upstairs, Price was on the phone. Three messages on Roper's desk: the safemakers' engineer would be here by lunchtime. Cresswell's elderly lady patient, Mrs Bentley, had died, in Wilson's considered opinion, of several carcinomas and a cerebral blood clot. And would Roper please contact Craig at the laboratory.

'And we've got to be out of here for a couple of hours this afternoon,' said Price, as he put the phone down, then lifted it across to Roper's desk. 'The decorators are coming in to put the venetian blinds back.'

'Couple of hours?' grumbled Roper. Four screws and a bit of elbow grease… 'I could do it m'self in ten minutes. What did Craig want?'

'He didn't say. Just that he's run some more alcohol tests on Seymour and thinks he might be on to something.'

'Like what, Mr Craig?' asked Roper, when he finally got through to the Forensic laboratory. The rhythmic tinkle of a teaspoon stirring in a cup came from the other end.

'You don't have to *drink* alcohol. I was lying in my bath this morning—and I thought: by gum, he didn't have to drink the stuff at all, did he?'

'Poured it into his ear, did he, Mr Craig?'

'Close, Mr Roper, very close. But I was thinking more of his nostrils, or rather his breathing passages generally.' Craig paused to sip noisily at his mid-morning beverage. 'And my man here has just isolated traces of inhaled diethyl ether in Seymour's lung tissues. I thought you'd like to know that.'

Roper drew a jotter closer and uncapped a ballpoint between his teeth. He knew he'd smelt another odour the other night...

'This diethyl ether, Mr Craig,' he said. 'Is that the anaesthetic ether or some other sort?'

'The anaesthetic,' said Craig, after another noisy sip. 'You didn't perhaps find a bottle or perhaps a pad of some sort lying about anywhere?'

'If I had, sir,' said Roper weightily, 'I could have saved a lot of people a lot of trouble.'

'Yes,' agreed Craig. 'Quite. Then we have to conclude that Mr Seymour, God rest him, was helped on his way by a second party.'

'What else is ether used for—apart from knockout drops?'

'Internally for colic,' said Craig. 'Externally for swabbing over the site for a surgical operation—'

An image of Cresswell came and went.

'—and you might be given a dab of it before an injection.'

The image of Cresswell floated back again.

'It's the sort of stuff a doctor would always keep handy, is it?'

'Definitely,' said Craig. 'He wouldn't be without it.'

'And it's only used medicinally, is it?' Because, if it was...'

'No,' said Craig cautiously, dashing Roper's rising hope at a stroke. 'Not exclusively. It's sometimes used as an industrial solvent. A degreasing agent. Mind you, you'd need plenty of fresh air about while you did the dunking.'

'I don't doubt it,' said Roper. 'How about Seymour's car?'

'Nothing new at all, I'm afraid.'

'How about dabs?'

The prints on the steering-wheel and the door catches had been only Seymour's. If anyone else had driven the car, then he, or she, had probably worn gloves. There had been no immediately identifiable fibres caught up anywhere which might provide a lead.

Craig's findings were not the great leap forward that Roper needed. That Seymour had been murdered was no longer in doubt. The only question now was why. If he hadn't killed Stella Pumfrey, and Roper was certain that he hadn't, it was possible that he had been killed by the same person, or persons, who had; and even likely because, statistically at least, the chances of two people from the same village being murdered in less than a week, by killers operating independently of each other, had to be remote. Brian Seymour himself was an unlikely killer. Even given that he was a habitual villain, nowhere on the sheet from the CRO was there any hint of violence on Seymour's part.

But for someone, somewhere, the only way out had been to kill him.

Why?

'Perhaps he knew something about the Pumfrey business,' said Price.

'If he did,' said Roper, 'then we're looking for a man on that one too.' And a hefty man at that. Seymour would not have gone down without a struggle. And perhaps it was the same man who had made that phone call that lured Seymour out on Sunday night.

'Someone with access to ether,' said Price. 'Shouldn't be difficult. Dr Cresswell, for starters.'

Roper bearded Cresswell when he came to collect his wife. He told Roper he bought his ether in half-litre bottles, of which he presently had three, all of which were unopened and were stored in the refrigerator in his surgery. The last time he had used ether had been over a week ago, when he had finished the contents of a bottle.

'Keep it locked up, sir?'

'No,' said Cresswell. 'Not exactly.' The man seemed to grow older every time Roper saw him. 'There's no lock on the refrigerator.'

'But the surgery's kept locked?'

'Yes,' said Cresswell. 'When I'm out of it, of course.'

His answers seemed honest enough, and when Roper had brought up the subject of ether, Cresswell had evinced neither alarm, nor surprise; nor even interest.

'May I collect my wife now, Superintendent?' he said wearily, after a despairing glance at his watch. 'I really do have a lot of work to catch up with.'

'Sure you have, sir,' said Roper, standing aside.

'And I'm sorry,' said Cresswell. 'Desperately and sincerely sorry.' He put out his hand. 'You've been very understanding. Thank you.'

'All part of the service, sir,' said Roper. But he did not, in this instance, extend his own hand.

HE STOOD at the office window and watched them leave. Nothing had changed. Mrs Cresswell flung herself into the front seat of the Toyota and slammed the door behind her; and Cresswell joined her as sullenly after tossing—or perhaps hurling—the shopping trolley into the boot and crashing down the lid on it. He drove away from the kerb with a squeal of rubber.

'Mrs Cresswell wears spectacles,' he mused, still at the window.

'What about it?' said Price.

'The last time I saw her she was wearing contact lenses,' said Roper, recalling the glitter in Mrs Cresswell's eyes as she had sat in her firelight. 'I'm bloody sure of it.'

'It often runs in families,' said Price.

'What does?' said Roper, whose mind had now wandered off in a different direction entirely.

'Myopia,' said Price.

But Roper hadn't heard that either. He had sat down, licked a thumb and was riffling through his pocket-book. Then he found the page he was looking for.

'Klein,' he said. 'Elizabeth Klein. Mrs Pumfrey's optician. Seventy-one, Crow Hill High Street. Where's the contact lens you found in Mrs Pumfrey's bedroom?'

'Lambert's safe,' said Price.

'Might be worth having it checked out.'

'Why?' said Price. 'We know it was one of Mrs Pumfrey's, don't we?'

'That's just the point, Dave,' said Roper, tucking his notebook back in his pocket. 'If you think about it, we don't know anything of the kind. We assumed. Supposing it wasn't?'

MRS KLEIN was tall and lean and white-overalled, and bespectacled herself, and not quite sure where she stood, ethically speaking. Yes she had heard about the unfortunate death of Stella Pumfrey, an exceptionally nice woman, such a tragedy. And yes, she had conducted Mrs Pumfrey's last eye-test herself, about a year ago, and written out the prescription for her contact lenses, two pairs, and, when they had finally arrived, made sure that they fitted properly.

'...but I couldn't possibly show you her records...if you had a warrant, or something of that sort...'

'One set of contact lenses is very like another, is it, Mrs Klein?'

'Well, no,' she said. 'Not necessarily. There are several types. Soft, hard, tinted...gas permeable...'

'How about this one?' said Roper.

Mrs Klein took the plastic envelope from him and held it up to the daylight through her shop window.

'It's a gel type,' she said. 'I don't do many of those.'

'But is that the sort you prescribed for Mrs Pumfrey?'

She regarded him gravely through her spectacles, plainly still pondering her problem of professional ethics. 'This one was taken from Mrs Pumfrey's body, was it?' she said. She was weakening; Roper could feel it.

'Beside where she was killed,' said Roper, piling it on a little. 'A couple of feet. The shock of the blow knocked it out, most likely. Nasty business.'

Mrs Klein grimaced. 'Terrible,' she agreed. She handed the envelope back again. 'Local gossip says it was probably a burglar.'

'Yes,' agreed Roper. 'Probably.'

She looked at him. He looked at her. Time passed. It felt like minutes.

'All right,' she said at last, to Roper's immense relief. 'I'll take a look for you, shall I?'

'Bless you,' said Roper.

Mercifully, Mrs Klein's receptionist ran her card-indexing system with a military precision. Mrs Pumfrey's card was in the first drawer she opened. She handed the card to Mrs Klein. Had Roper been superstitious he would have crossed his fingers, because Mrs Klein was frowning and giving the card a second look, front and back, and then a third and even closer look.

'Something up, Mrs Klein?' asked Roper.

'Yes,' she said. 'There is.' She came back to where Roper and Hackett were waiting at the counter, still puzzling over the card she was holding.

'Like what, Mrs Klein?'

'That lens you showed me was a gel,' she said, her forehead still puckered. 'And the lenses I prescribed for Mrs Pumfrey were hard. So that lens *couldn't* have been Mrs Pumfrey's, could it—unless she's been to another optician since.'

MRS KLEIN, however, was not prepared to proceed further without an authorised warrant. By midday, Roper had persuaded a magistrate to provide one. And by half-past midday Mrs Klein had undertaken to assess the precise focal length of the lens in question, and WDS Hackett, with the assistance of Mrs Klein's receptionist, was presently engaged in sorting through the five or six thousand index cards and abstracting all those of patients who had been prescribed soft contact lenses. Mrs Klein had warned that one lens would not point necessarily to a specific patient, whereas a pair would have done. But, so far as Roper was concerned, if the suspect lens pointed at as many as half a dozen people, it would certainly diminish the diameter of the circle that he was presently running around in.

Whether or not the lens would also provide positive identification of the murderer of Brian Seymour was a matter of wider conjecture, unless, of course, the contact lens had belonged to someone who also had ready access to diethyl ether.

Like Sarah Cresswell. Or her husband. Or even both, however unlikely that seemed. Roper had had a few words over the telephone with Wilson. Pure and undiluted ether was not easily purchased by the general public. Wilson had also told Roper that diethyl ether was not the swiftest of anaesthetics. For someone of Seymour's size, it would have to have been administered for at least ten seconds before Seymour had even begun to lose consciousness. And he would have struggled.

'So we might be looking for two people, then?'

'Yes,' agreed Wilson. 'You might at that.' In other circumstances, Wilson would have expected to see ether burns around Seymour's lips. But Seymour's thick beard had probably protected him from those. Which, if it had not been for that driving seat being in the wrong position, would have made for an almost perfect murder.

'Whoever killed Seymour had to be a man,' said Price, as he and Roper forked up their steak pie and chips along at the Pied Bull.

'Or two men,' said Roper. And whoever they were their trust in each other was such that each had to rely absolutely upon the other to keep his mouth shut.

At half past one, they were negotiating the tarpaulin sheets that the decorators had draped over the stairs while they painted the staircase ceiling.

Makins and Rodgers were back after overseeing, with Pumfrey, the opening of the safe in Mrs Pumfrey's bedroom.

'Any luck?' asked Roper.

Makins opened his pocket-book and took out a folded sheet of paper ripped from a cheap jotting pad. It was a receipt, or rather two receipts scribbled one after the other on the same sheet of paper. The top one was for a pair of gold and garnet earrings, signed by Sarah Cresswell. The lower one was for a diamond pendant on a gold chain. That had been signed by Stella Pumfrey. The date at the top of the sheet was that of Good Friday. It looked as if Mrs Pumfrey had written out the top receipt and Mrs

Cresswell the bottom one, probably hastily and, who knew, in the face of Mrs Pumfrey's protestations.

'How about the safe combination?' asked Roper.

'Mrs Pumfrey's birth date,' said Makins. 'Simple.'

'Pumfrey ought to have known that,' observed Roper.

'I think he did,' said Makins. And for all his baby face and blond hair, he was a very shrewd copper, was Makins.

'Anything else missing?'

'Not according to Pumfrey.'

And who knew if he was telling the truth, either.

Makins held out his hand for the receipts. 'Pumfrey wants that back.'

'Get a photocopy, George,' said Roper, still holding on to one end. 'I'll take the original back myself.'

THE DESCENT from Crow Hill was fast becoming familiar, although this was the first time Roper had driven down it in sunshine.

'What are you going to ask him about?' asked Price.

'Insurance,' said Roper.

'Fiddle?'

'I reckon. Something between him and Wainer.' Roper didn't know what the link was yet, but he was fairly sure there was one. And somewhere along the line Seymour fitted in, and that was why Seymour had been murdered, and perhaps Mrs Pumfrey too, however indirectly.

Little Crow, glimpsed through the treetops and bathed in sunshine, looked like a painstakingly detailed model. Like the town up the hill, the village had sprung to life today. He turned right beside the crumbling wall of the graveyard. And a second later slammed on his brakes so hard that Price shot forward against his seat-belt.

'Sorry,' said Roper, ramming into reverse even before he had spoken, and backing a few yards until he could

look through the open gateway of the erstwhile village
school. Fluorescent lights glowed through the barred windows and the gallery doors were open. A grey Mercedes
was parked in the yard.

'I thought Wainer was away on holiday,' said Price.

'So did I,' said Roper.

SEVENTEEN

INSIDE THE SCHOOL, the smell of old plimsolls and wet navy-blue raincoats was long gone. What had once been two classrooms had been knocked into one large showroom with islands of antique furniture separated by walkways of green carpet. The roof beams were hung with a dozen or more crystal chandeliers with price-tags dangling from them, and over on the right an illuminated glass display case was crammed with a collection of porcelain. At a desk next to it a smartly suited man with grey hair, probably the owner of the Mercedes, was hunched over an open cheque book. The woman standing over him looked like his wife. There was no sign of Wainer.

'I'd forgotten that,' muttered Roper. He pointed to a printed sign standing on a carved Jacobean sideboard. Quality and antique clock mechanisms cleaned and repaired. Twenty-eight-day service.

'What about it?' said Price.

But before Roper could reply, a brisk tattoo of heels sounded on bare wooden boards, and through a doorway at the back of the gallery, and down three wooden steps, and carrying against her heroic bosom a large cardboard box, stepped a businesslike Mrs Hubert. Half hidden behind a Victorian whatnot, Roper watched the man rise with his cheque in his hand. Mrs Hubert stood the cardboard box on a mess of papers on the desk, then reached down for a pair of spectacles to examine the cheque; while the Mercedes driver lifted the flaps of the carton, perhaps to be certain that he'd got exactly what he'd paid for.

Satisfied with her scrutiny of the cheque, Mrs Hubert smiled brightly as she removed her spectacles.

Roper drew Price out of sight of the desk.

'Mrs Hubert,' he whispered, lifting a warning finger as Price's eyebrows lifted appreciatively. 'You haven't seen her before?'

Price shook his head.

'I don't want her to see me,' Roper said softly. 'You've got a clock—a longcase, made by Knibb. Family heirloom. It's got an iron and brass mechanism and you think it's dirty and you want it cleaned. But you don't want the mechanism stripped down because you're a very fussy customer. You want to know where the work's going to be done and how, and you want to see it all for yourself. Especially you want to know what kind of solvent the mechanism's going to be dunked in. You got all that?'

'Right.'

'I'll be outside.'

Price nodded, and as he drifted out into the main body of the gallery Roper, ducking occasionally, stole quietly back towards the sunlit doorway where Mrs Hubert was seeing out her two clients.

At the other end of the gallery Price coughed loudly, and as Mrs Hubert turned about to attend to his needs, so did Roper move quickly and silently behind her and return to the car.

Some ten minutes passed. The Mercedes had gone and a glittering grey Rolls-Royce took its place beside Roper's Sierra. Wainer's gallery might be tucked away in the wilds, but it clearly didn't lack a classy clientèle. So much so, that Wainer couldn't afford to shut up shop when he went on holiday. And left Mrs Hubert in charge. And he wouldn't have done that unless Mrs Hubert knew what she was about when it came to a bit of wheeling and dealing. You got to know a fair few villains in the antiques business. Roper knew a few himself. Wainer probably did. Supposing Mrs Hubert also did? Because—on too many occasions lately—just before Wainer went on holiday somebody got burgled and lost a valuable artefact or two. What better place to stash them than an antiques shop full of similar artefacts—while its owner was away on holiday? Somebody sees a van drawn up outside a private house and being loaded with, say, a huge *famille rose* vase, that might be suspicious. The same van drawn up outside an antiques shop—that was business. A cash deal. Wainer wouldn't ever know about it. And to make things look right, you had your own house robbed too. Except you didn't sell the proceeds. You left them with your partner in crime, namely Brian Seymour, to look after until the heat was off—and you'd claimed the insurance money...

He leaned over to open the passenger door as Price reappeared.

'What did she say?'

'Fifty quid,' said Price. 'Including the insurance. He puts the mechanism in a fume bottle, a sort of bell-jar gadget, with a dish of ether in the bottom. And when the grime softens he gives them a final dunk or two in carbon tet.'

'And you said...?'

'Dangerous stuff, ether. I suppose you have to keep it outside?'

'And she said...?'

'Oh, yes. We keep it in an old refrigerator in what used to be the school coke shed. Mind you, we only keep a little at a time.' Price, after a passable impression of Mrs Hubert's smoky voice, dropped back into his own. 'And bloody Wainer's in Portugal, isn't he,' he added pithily.

'It isn't Wainer,' said Roper. 'It's Mrs Hubert. She was Seymour's fence. And Pumfrey's in on it too. Up to his neck. Bet your life.'

'How about proof?'

'I think we've got some,' said Roper. Mrs Hubert had not noticed the engraving on Seymour's lighter until it had been pointed out to her, and Roper himself had seen her pick up an ashtray so awkwardly and clumsily that she had dropped it on to the surface of her very expensive coffee table. Neither incident of itself had seemed particularly relevant at the time. Now, belatedly, it led to an inescapable conclusion. Mrs Hubert desperately needed spectacles. She had spectacles; so why didn't she wear them all the time?

'All right,' said Price. 'I'll buy it. Why?'

'Because everybody who knows her thinks she wears contact lenses,' said Roper. 'And she doesn't want 'em to know she's lost 'em. How about that?'

At the yard entrance, instead of turning right, towards Chalk House, Roper turned left towards Crow Hill.

'I thought we were going to see Pumfrey,' said Price.

'I'm going back to hustle Hackett,' said Roper.

THE VENETIAN BLINDS were back at the windows, Makins was just attending to the ringing telephone and DC Mills broke off the deedy conversation he was having with Rodgers.

'It's for you,' said Makins, holding the telephone receiver across the desk to Roper. 'It's Liz Hackett. She reckons she'll be another couple of hours.'

Roper took the handset from him.

Mrs Klein had assessed the focal length of the contact lens. It was now down to Hackett and Mrs Klein's receptionist to find a matching index card. Hackett had only rung in to say that she had just finished looking through the C cards; and Mrs Cresswell *did* wear soft contact lenses; but nothing like the one Mrs Klein had just tested.

'We're just going to make a start on the ''D''s.'

'Skip the ''D''s,' said Roper. 'Go straight on to the ''H''s. Specifically Mrs Hubert. If she's a client of Mrs Klein's, too, I want to know.'

There was a pause. 'But wasn't Mrs Hubert out with Pumfrey, sir...on Friday night?'

'Not when Mrs Pumfrey was killed, she wasn't,' said Roper. 'And I've got a sneaky feeling that she might have been fencing for Seymour—might even have been his professional adviser. Ring me back.'

'And what do you want, Mills?' asked Roper, as he passed the phone back to Makins.

Mills was shuffling his feet and generally looking as if he wanted the floor to swallow him up.

'I'd like a word, sir,' he mumbled. 'It's sort of private, sir.'

'I'm busy, lad. Unless it's about Seymour or Mrs Pumfrey.'

'It is, sir,' mumbled Mills. 'But if we could go outside, sir. Please. It's important, sir.'

Mills clearly had something on his conscience.

Roper went back outside. Mills followed him and drew the door to. Further along the passage an electrician on a ladder was putting back a light fitting.

'There's a girl downstairs, sir,' said Mills. 'She wants to see the officer in charge of the Pumfrey investigation. She's got information, sir, so she says.'

'Why didn't you wheel her up?'

'It's not that simple, sir,' said Mills. 'I've been trying to chat her up for weeks. And the other afternoon, I sort of cornered her in the Wimpy and gave her a bit of the

old madam. I told her I was a sergeant…and I was sort
of your right-hand man, sir, and that you and me were
working on the Pumfrey case together. And just now I
met her in the street…and now she wants to talk to you,
sir.'

'Your love life's your own business, Mills,' said Roper.
'Where's Mr Lambert?'

'Court, sir.'

'I'll see her in his office. What's her name?'

'Moffat, sir,' said Mills, obviously relieved to have got
off so lightly. 'Sharon Moffat.'

ROPER PUSHED LAMBERT'S visitor's chair closer to the
desk. 'Can we get you something, Miss Moffat…tea? coffee?'

She shook her head to both as she lowered herself to
sit on the very edge of the chair, the fabric of her black
gloves stretched tightly over her knuckles as she clutched
the frame of her handbag. She was nineteen, perhaps
twenty and exceptionally tall. Her black suit was cheap
but stylish, her perfume pervasive and expensive.

'Sergeant Makins here will be taking a few notes,' said
Roper, as he sat down and drew Lambert's chair nearer
to the desk. 'I take it you don't mind that?'

She shook her head again. If you didn't look too hard,
and took her face as the sum of its part, she was an attractive young woman. But if the parts were taken separately, there lurked behind them a hint of wilfulness. Her
chin was sharply pointed, her eyes too shrewd, her mouth
a tight little painted purse. Although Roper did not doubt
that Miss Moffat had the young lads of Crow Hill practically falling over themselves to get at her. Around these
parts, Miss Moffat had to be very nearly unique.

'You're a friend of Derek Mills, Miss Moffat,' he said, to break the ice.

'Yes,' she said. 'Sort of.'

'And you told him that you might be able to help us…about the death of Mrs Pumfrey.'

'Yes,' she said. She was still sitting stiffly, gripping her bag. Like a firework, Roper thought, with touch-paper quietly smouldering.

'Derek said you'd found a lighter,' she said.

'We did,' said Roper.

'A gold one with S and B engraved on it.'

'Yes,' agreed Roper. 'That's right.'

'Only I gave Brian Seymour one like that,' she said. 'And I wondered if it was him. Killed Mrs Pumfrey.'

But that was not all she had come to say. She continued to smoulder. Roper tented his fingertips under his chin. And waited.

Then she erupted. 'He cost me a bloody job,' she said.

Roper's mind darted at once to Mills, and he wondered if she had called in here to make trouble for Mills. She looked that sort. The tight little bud of a mouth had budded tighter still.

'Who did, Miss Moffat?' he asked quietly.

'Bill Pumfrey.' She spat it out like a dirty word. 'Cost me my bloody job, didn't he? I told them at the paper shop I wouldn't be coming in any more and now they've got somebody else, haven't they, and now I'm out of work, aren't I?'

Roper's pulse had quickened perceptibly, and Hackett's phrase about a woman scorned came back to mind. This one was an avenging fury. And *Bill* Pumfrey? Nobody outside of a select few cronies, and certainly not a chit of a girl who worked in a newspaper shop, would ever call Pumfrey Bill.

'You're leaving me behind, Miss Moffat,' he said cautiously, fighting off the terrible temptation to prompt her.

'She was murdered, wasn't she? His wife?'

'So far as we know,' agreed Roper. 'Yes.'

'About half past eleven Friday night. That's what Derek said.'

'Yes,' said Roper.

'And he said he was out with some *other* woman, didn't he?' she went on venomously. 'And he wasn't, and he couldn't have been.'

'Why not, Miss Moffat?' asked Roper.

'Because he was with me,' she said.

And Roper did not doubt her for a moment, because young Miss Moffat's luxurious crowning glory was the colour of polished mahogany. Only, unlike Mrs Hubert's, it was genuine.

SHE LIVED UP HERE in Crow Hill. And it was in the High Street, by the war memorial, that Pumfrey had picked her up in his car on Friday evening. About seven o'clock. Late. He'd said quarter to seven. She'd had to stand in a shop doorway out of the rain. And she'd been wearing her mother's fur coat, too, a new dress and new shoes, and standing in a shop doorway for twenty minutes dressed like that made her feel like a tart, didn't it? Anyway, then he turned up, and said he was sorry, he'd been held up by a spot of business and he'd got something for her. A wristwatch. This one. He'd bought it the day before, up in London, at least that's what he told her.

He was going to take her down to the Country Club; which came as a pleasant surprise. Whenever she'd been out with him before, it was always out in the sticks, never anywhere round here where somebody was likely to recognise him, of course it wasn't, was it.

Anyway, they'd arrived at eight o'clock, parked in the darkest corner of the car park. Which she thought was a bit funny, because there were plenty of parking places and several under floodlights which would have been safer. He told her to stay in the car. She watched him go into the club through the restaurant entrance—she realised now to see if there was any one in there who knew him. Then he came back for her. The table he had booked was in the darkest corner. Well, she didn't really mind that. Then he went to the gents'. When he came back he was upset about something. He'd seen somebody he knew. Put him in a mood for the rest of the night, that did, kept looking over his shoulder. She'd noticed that particularly—

'What time did you and Mr Pumfrey leave the Country Club on Friday night, Miss Moffat?' asked Roper, breaking in.

She could not be certain, but thought it might have been around half past ten. Her father insisted that she was always home by eleven o'clock. Pumfrey had always seen that she was; except on Friday. On Friday he had tried to prevail upon her to stay another hour at the club. And it was coming back in the car that he promised to tell his wife that he was going to leave her—of course she knew now that that was so much pie in the sky, but after a couple of hours in the club—she'd been drinking Martinis—well, she'd got a bit, you know...

'Exactly when did he drop you off? D'you remember?'

'I was indoors at eleven o'clock,' she said. 'Perhaps a bit afterwards.'

Which still meant that Pumfrey could not have been around when his wife had been killed. Mrs Cresswell had left Mrs Pumfrey alive at eleven thirty. Pumfrey had reappeared at the Country Club at eleven fifteen. So why had he lied?

Something else that had been niggling at Roper over the last few days was why Pumfrey had driven back to the Country Club—at some speed and in foul weather—on Friday night for what only amounted to another hour's drinking. Now it was obvious. He had needed to be seen, at a place where he was known—and his companion was not—well away from the vicinity of Chalk House. Because he knew the house was going to be burgled, perhaps he had even known at what time. And that was why, for once, he would want to keep Sharon Moffat out later than usual. Sharon Moffat who, at a glance and through half-closed eyes, bore a passing resemblance to Samantha Hubert; and perhaps that resemblance was no mere co-incidence. Most men, and probably a lot of women, asked to describe either of them, would say, well, she's a tall redhead, and consider that to be a sufficient description.

So perhaps, in the first instance, Pumfrey had been setting up an alibi for Mrs Hubert as well. Samantha Hubert was not a member of the Country Club. They wouldn't have known her down there, and provided Pumfrey had scouted the restaurant first, and kept Sharon Moffat in a dark corner, he might have got away with it—in fact he had, except that Sharon Moffat had insisted on being taken back home by eleven o'clock. What Pumfrey had not anticipated was that his wife would be murdered while he was winging his way back to the Country Club, and that his sister-in-law would call at the house for the first time since Christmas. And that Sharon Moffat was not the sort of young woman, unlike Mrs Pumfrey, who could be cast aside with impunity.

Anyway, he'd offered her this job—he was going into the burglar and fire alarm business which, in Roper's

opinion, had to be some kind of joke—a sort of receptionist she'd be, so that they could see a bit more of each
other, and on Monday evening, so he'd told her, he'd pick
her up in the car park by the public library and they'd
talk some more about it. Anyway, she'd waited, and he
hadn't turned up, had he?

And then, about seven o'clock, soon after she'd got
home after meeting Derek in the Wimpy, he'd phoned her,
hadn't he? Spun her some yarn about how he'd been de-
layed and he was sorry but now something else had
cropped up, and how it would be better, in the circumstances, if he and she weren't seen together for a couple
of weeks. And he'd rather she didn't talk to anybody
about the two of them as well. Just for a while. It wouldn't
be quite the thing. Bad form, he called it. Can I phone?
she had said. No, he had replied. I'd rather you didn't.
He would be in touch. And then he had put the phone
down on her. Just like that!

'How did you come to meet Mr Pumfrey in the first
place, Miss Moffat?' asked Roper, as a matter of private
interest.

'I worked there,' she said. 'The Pumfreys' place. When
we first came down here, when my dad's firm offered him
this better job.' Her father was a security guard, an area
supervisor. Night work mostly and—

'When, Miss Moffat? When did you work there?'

Last summer it had been. Only a few weeks. Domestic
work. She'd hated it. Pumfrey had come on a bit strong—
fancied her, you know. But nothing came of it then; but
a couple of weeks ago she'd been waiting at a bus stop
in Blandford, in the rain, and this car had pulled into the
kerb. Pumfrey had been driving it. He'd offered her a
lift...and well, you know...one thing had led to another
after that.

As ROPER SAW HER down the stairs, so was DC Mills waiting at the bottom with another visitor. Roper waited for them to come up.

'Mr Oldershaw, sir,' said Mills. 'He'd like a word.'

Mr Oldershaw was about thirty, with an old man's stoop, a thatch of wayward dark hair and a suit that had seen far better days. Under his arm was tucked a cardboard envelope file, which he almost dropped as he extended a hand. His grip was earnest.

He explained diffidently that he was a solicitor and that he had come along in response to a message left on his answering machine by Mr Foyle.

In the file under his arm was Mrs Pumfrey's last will and testament, and it had to be the last because she had only signed it last Wednesday afternoon, in Mr Oldershaw's own office. As he understood it, Mrs Pumfrey had made some very substantial changes from her previous will…

EIGHTEEN

ROPER MUCH PREFERRED his villains to be male. He had been born, and bred, during the last generation when men were schooled to give an extra respect to women merely because of their gender. It was a habit difficult to break, more so when the woman sitting at the other side of the table from him in the interview-room was, externally, at least, as quintessentially female as Samantha Hubert.

Between them, on the table, was the contact lens and the index card that Hackett, an hour ago, had brought back from Mrs Klein's. And at the end of the table, next to Mrs Hubert, sat Jack Foyle, here on the instructions of Mrs Hubert's husband and despite Mrs Hubert's protestations. Hackett sat at the other end of the table, bent over an A4 pad and writing down every word that passed. In the occasional passages of silence a tape recorder hummed softly. Price and Rodgers were down in Little Crow picking up William Pumfrey. If Mrs Hubert was going down, she intended to do so in company.

'And Seymour was outside keeping lookout,' said Roper.

'Yes,' said the bespectacled Mrs Hubert, with evident pride. 'It was always me who went in. I knew the geography better.' She reached for her cigarette packet and negligently lit another cigarette from the stub of the last.

'You say you saw Mrs Pumfrey's bathroom light go on. What did you do then?'

'I let myself in through the kitchen door.'

'With a key?'

'Yes,' she said. 'Of course with a key.'

'A key made by Seymour?'

'Yes,' she said. 'From one Bill Pumfrey lent us.'

'Supposing the burglar alarm had been switched on?'

'I knew I had a minute before the bell started clanging. I could have switched it off by then.'

'Mr Pumfrey had shown you how to operate it, had he?'

'Had to, didn't he?' she said. 'We couldn't have worked it all otherwise, could we?'

'And that's how you got in the house at Christmas?'

'Yes,' she said.

'But the alarm did ring on one occasion,' Roper reminded her.

'Oh, that,' she said, with a little throwaway gesture. 'That was Seymour. We'd switched the alarm on again on the way out. And the damned key he'd made got stuck in the lock. Getting it out set the alarms off. We had to run like hell.'

Roper had to take his hat off to Mrs Hubert. Of all his many customers, few had come cooler.

'Then?'

'I waited under the stairs.'

'How long?'

She shrugged. 'Five—six minutes.'

'Until you thought Mrs Pumfrey was in her bath?'

'Yes,' she said. 'I heard her shoot the bolt on the door.'

'And then you crept upstairs.'

'Yes,' she said.

'What were you after, exactly?'

'The stuff in Stella's safe,' she said.

'Which you knew how to open.'

'Yes,' she said. She shrugged her broad shoulders again. 'Bill had lent us the key to copy, and told me the combination. It should have been a doddle.'

'Mrs Hubert,' cautioned Foyle. 'If you'll take my advice, you'd do better to keep to the facts and leave out the comments.'

She turned her head and smiled blandly at him. 'I don't give a shit, actually.'

'You were in Mrs Pumfrey's bedroom. Then what?'

'Somebody leaned on the bloody doorbell.'

'Leaned?'

'Leaned,' she said again. 'It seemed to ring for ever and bloody ever. Didn't bloody stop.'

Roper waited for her to go on; but she didn't and he had to prompt her again.

'Did Mrs Pumfrey answer it, this ringing doorbell?'

'She couldn't have been in the bath,' retorted Mrs Hubert. 'Another second and she might have been.'

'How do you know that?'

'I heard the bolt on the bathroom door again; and saw her march along the landing still tying her robe. She wasn't wet.'

'And who was the caller?'

She smiled wryly. 'Bloody Sal Cresswell. Her bloody sister.'

The rest of Mrs Hubert's story came piecemeal, but with growing inevitability. She had heard the two sisters downstairs in the hall, Mrs Cresswell's voice raised, Mrs Pumfrey's barely audible as she tried to placate her. It was at this juncture that Mrs Hubert's plans began to go awfully wrong. Mrs Pumfrey, with Mrs Cresswell following her, came back upstairs. Mrs Hubert, having heard the substance of their conversation, realised that they were coming straight to the bedroom, and to the safe. Luckily, she knew where the safe was, and so knew which of the drawn curtains it was safest to hide behind.

Roper pushed Price's sketch closer to her. 'Which one, Mrs Hubert?'

A pink-lacquered fingernail pointed to the bayed recess to the right of the dressing-table. 'That one,' she said.

She had heard everything after that, and witnessed Mrs Pumfrey part the curtains over the other bay, and drop to her knees to open the safe.

'I want the bloody box, too,' had demanded Sarah Cresswell.

'Tomorrow,' had said Stella Pumfrey. 'I'll look for it tomorrow. I promise. Please, Sal. I'm tired. I promise I'll look it out tomorrow.'

And still Sarah Cresswell wouldn't go. She wanted to sign a receipt. Now. Tonight. 'I know you,' she'd sneered. 'You'll only accuse me of stealing the bloody things when it suits you.'

So back they had gone downstairs. After a few minutes, she had heard Sarah Cresswell call out: 'There's some paper here—by the telephone.'

Another altercation followed. Then silence. Then, after a few minutes more, the front door had closed. Stella Pumfrey had come back upstairs. Her first call was to the bedroom, to close the safe. To Mrs Hubert's chagrin, Mrs Pumfrey did not then return to the bathroom. She lit a cigarette, and started hunting through drawers. She eventually found what she was looking for, a small blue box, in the cabinet beside her bed. She put it on the dressing-table, then turned to the ashtray lying on the bed and stubbed out the cigarette. Then, to Mrs Hubert's relief, she did, finally, return to the bathroom. Thinking that she would be in there for at least a quarter of an hour, Mrs Hubert darted into the other bay, where the safe was. All she then had to do was to wait for the bathroom door-bolt to be shot again. Then she could get to work.

But she never heard the door-bolt. It had not occurred to her that nearly twenty minutes had passed since she first had entered the house and that Mrs Pumfrey's bath water was tepid by now and that she might only have gone back to the bathroom to pull the plug on it. Which she did. She was back in literally seconds, clearly in a mood for nothing but her bed. She picked up the ashtray, as she did every night...

And came face to face with Mrs Hubert behind the curtains.

'God, she was quick,' said Mrs Hubert with honest admiration. 'I don't think she'd even realised who I was. She caught me here...' She lifted aside a wing of her dyed red hair to show a dried scab an inch or so above her left ear. There was a brief and furious struggle for the ashtray. Mrs Hubert remembered swinging it twice. The first time driving Mrs Pumfrey to her knees. The second time fatally although she had not known that at once because she was dazed and couldn't see properly because she had lost a contact lens.

AN ACCIDENT. She could make it look like an accident. She recalled that a few weeks back Stella Pumfrey had tripped and fallen at the foot of the stairs. So why not again? And quickly, because the green rug was rapidly becoming saturated with blood and if it soaked right through to the carpet beneath it would be too late. She had lashed the body into the rug with two belts from Stella Pumfrey's wardrobe and dragged it down the stairs, then brought the matching rug back with her. With her vision impaired she knew that she could afford to take no chances. She lost count of the number of trips she made to the bathroom with alternate handfuls of wet and dry toilet paper. She had washed everything that could possibly have been splashed with blood.

But still she had not found her missing contact lens, and that, she had known, was as good as leaving her signature behind. That had been when the idea of taking Stella Pumfrey's lenses—both of them, had come to her. If both of Stella Pumfrey's lenses were missing, and the police eventually found two lenses, they would surely assume that they were hers.

'You did this on your way out, I take it?' said Roper.

'Yes,' she said.

'You must have been very calm.'

'Don't answer that,' said Foyle.

'Yes,' she said, ignoring him. 'I was by then.'

Roper had a momentary ghoulish picture of the glamorous Mrs Hubert, icy cool and purblind herself, crouched over Mrs Pumfrey's dead body while she plucked out her victim's contact lenses.

'What about your other lens?'

'I took it out and ground it into the carpet.'

'I'm surprised you could see to do that.'

'I couldn't,' she said. 'I had to get down on my hands and knees and bash it with my shoe.'

'Seymour didn't help you at all?'

'God, no,' she retorted scornfully. 'I didn't tell him anything. He hadn't got the guts for that sort of thing. As it was, he nearly wet himself wondering where I was.'

The mule on the landing, the blood on the newel post, the lighter that she had noticed earlier on the hall table, and the cigarette, had all been afterthoughts. The cigarette had come from the casket on the coffee table in the sitting-room.

'Did you know the lighter was Brian Seymour's, Mrs Hubert?'

For the first time she showed some emotion, but even then it was only surprise. 'No,' she said. 'I didn't, dammit.'

She had taken all the incriminating evidence, the rubber gloves, the ashtray—in case there was a trace of her own blood on it, and the scraps of toilet paper, away with her. In the plastic bag in which earlier that same evening she had brought over Stella Pumfrey's new tights. She had disposed of them, somewhat unimaginatively, in the light of her previous track record, in the bottom of her own dustbin.

'Did Seymour ask you what was in the bag?'

'Yes.'

'And what did you tell him?'

'I told him I couldn't get the safe open. So I'd picked up a few things that were lying about handy.'

'And he didn't question that?'

'No,' she said. It was pretty clear now who the boss had been.

'And these house breaking expeditions with Seymour. How did you get started on those?'

'Kicks,' she said dispassionately. 'A bit of excitement. Crow's a pretty boring hole; but I suppose you haven't been around here long enough to notice that yet.'

'What did you do with the proceeds?'

'Sold them,' she said.

'Dealers?'

'Yes,' she said. 'Mostly.'

'Dealers who wouldn't ask questions?'

She smiled.

'It would help if you answered, Mrs Hubert,' said Foyle.

'Look,' she said, turning on him. 'My husband dragged

you in on this; I didn't. So far as I'm concerned, you can push off whenever you like.'

Roper waited for the hiatus to subside.

'What was the arrangement with Mr Pumfrey, Mrs Hubert?'

'A split,' she said. 'Fifty-fifty. He got half of what I sold for, and he gave me ten per cent of the insurance money.'

'And your husband's snuffboxes?'

'I had a market for those,' she said. 'A dealer from Jersey. He was flying over on Thursday to pick them up. He was going to pay cash, too.' She twitched her mouth wryly at the unfair hand that fate had dealt her.

'You told us you'd cracked your car into a tree on the way home,' said Roper. 'I presume that was because you couldn't see.'

'Yes,' she said. They had used Seymour's car on Friday night, the one she had told Roper, truthfully, that she had seen parked on the darkened verge near Chalk House. The other small grain of truth had been that her own car really had been parked up at Crow Hill that night. Without her contact lenses or spectacles it had taken her a quarter of an hour to drive back down to Little Crow. She had skid-ded at a corner in the rain, and sideswiped a tree. She had told her husband the story about the dog to account for the fact that she'd got the shakes by then. She had only beaten him into the house by a short head.

'Your husband didn't notice you weren't wearing your contact lenses?'

She smiled, amused. 'He doesn't get that close, pet. Not these days.'

The tape behind her clicked to a stop. Hackett rose from her chair to turn the cassette over. Voices echoed in the passage outside. One of them sounded like William Pumfrey's. If Mrs Hubert recognised it she gave no sign.

'WHEN DID MR PUMFREY know you'd killed his wife?'

'I rang him on Saturday morning. Before he went to the mortuary.'

'And what was his reaction?'

'He said we'd done him a favour. And it was okay because the police had been last night and said it was an accident. And nobody seemed to be quite sure when it had happened, so the alibi we'd set up for the break-in might still work. Even though that silly little cow he'd taken to the club had insisted on being home at eleven o'clock.'

The demise of Seymour had been planned over the telephone on Saturday night, after Roper had warned Pumfrey of that second autopsy on his wife. Seymour was going to be the weak link in the chain if the result of the autopsy went the wrong way.

'Whose idea was it?' asked Roper.

'Bill's,' she said. 'He had a brother who killed himself like that. The ether was my contribution, though.' She added the last with evident pride.

'You know about ether?'

'Only that it was an anaesthetic and I knew where to lay my hands on some. The seal on that gadget Lance Wainer uses for his clocks leaked once; I found him stretched out on the floor. I thought he'd had a heart attack. We reckoned we'd have to knock Seymour out for at least fifteen minutes.'

The vacuum-cleaner hose, like the ether, had come from the antiques gallery, whence Mrs Hubert knew that it would not be missed until next weekend when Mrs Broadbent came in to clean. In the meantime she had in-

tended to purchase another to replace it. Wainer would
never notice the difference.

'You had your own keys to the gallery, I take it?'

'Yes.' And legimately, too. Wainer had given them to
her. Wainer travelled about to sales a lot. It wasn't just
during his holidays that she looked after the business for
him.

'Who made the phone call to Seymour?'

'Me,' she said; but Roper had already guessed that.
With her voice dropped another pitch or two, it would
have been an easy mistake for Mrs Broadbent to have
made. Seymour would never have gone out on Sunday
night in response to Pumfrey's voice.

'What reason did you give him?'

'I said we had to talk. He'd got wind that Stella was
dead by then, and guessed I'd done it. I told him I thought
the police were on to me and if he didn't turn up, if I got
caught, I'd make sure they caught him too.'

She had arranged to meet Seymour in a lay-by at the
top of Pod Hill at seven thirty. She herself had arrived
later, at seven forty-five, because she had had to wait further back along the road for Pumfrey who had taken
longer than expected to pick up his car from the Country
Club. Pumfrey had then transferred to her car where, after
taking the bulb out of the courtesy light, he had wedged
himself out of sight on the floor between the back and
front seats.

'Where the hell have you been?' raged Seymour, when
she had wound down her window in the dark lay-by.

'Get in,' said Mrs Hubert. 'We don't have a lot of
time.'

Seymour had climbed into the Metro beside her.

'Fasten your seat-belt.'

'Why? Where are we going?'

'Just fasten the bloody thing!'

Caught up in Mrs Hubert's simulated panic, Seymour buckled himself in—which was crucial to the whole operation.

'What's that funny smell?' had asked Seymour; which was the last coherent sentence he ever uttered, because by now the pad soaked with ether was coming over his right shoulder and Pumfrey's left arm was going around his neck and locking him against the headrest. All Mrs Hubert had to do was to hang on to Seymour's right arm and make sure he didn't press the release button on his seatbelt.

It took a long time; in the close confines of the Metro she and Pumfrey were almost knocked out themselves before Seymour went under. The dead weight of Seymour was then rolled out on to Pumfrey's raincoat laid out on the grass verge and then dragged the few yards to the Escort. Seymour was then hefted on to the back seat.

While Pumfrey transferred the vacuum-cleaner hose and the plastic bag of wet newspapers from the back of the Metro, Mrs Hubert sat over Seymour with the ether bottle in case he started to come round. Then Pumfrey got into the driving seat of Seymour's car and Mrs Hubert returned to hers, following him the mile or so down the hill until he found a dark spot where he could get the Escort off the road and behind a reasonable amount of cover. There, having had the rest of the ether poured over his jacket, Seymour was left in the Escort, with the doors shut and the heater running and the choke set to idle, to breathe his last. Pumfrey and Mrs Hubert sat out twenty minutes in the Metro before driving back up the hill to where Pumfrey's car still was. Pumfrey, in his own car, then drove back down the hill, where he waited another twenty minutes to be certain Seymour did not come out of the Escort.

'What did we do wrong?' she asked. She seemed genuinely curious.

'Not much,' said Roper. 'Pumfrey forgot to ratchet Seymour's seat forward again before he got out of the car. That's all.'

She rolled her eyes contemptuously upward. 'My God,' she scoffed. 'Men. Can't rely on them for anything, can you?'

'HOW ARE YOU getting on in there?' asked Roper.

'He's writing a statement,' said Price. 'We can't feed him with paper fast enough.' They stood in the passage between the interview-rooms. 'How about you? All tears and paper handkerchiefs, is it?'

'I'm not even sure she knows she's committed a crime,' said Roper. 'She's in there now telling Hackett what she and Seymour got up to in their spare moments. I'm not surprised he didn't have any energy left for Mrs Broadbent.'

'Liked a bit of rough trade, did she?'

'Apparently.'

'She told you what her husband does for a living yet?'

'I haven't asked,' said Roper.

'He's an insurance underwriter, so Pumfrey tells me. It's him who's had to fork out after Pumfrey's burglaries. She was robbing Peter to pay bloody Paul, wasn't she?'

Roper was not even mildly astonished. Nothing about Mrs Hubert had the power to surprise him any more.

NINETEEN

FURTHER ALONG the crowded restaurant bar of the Pied Bull, half-hidden by a pier, Derek Mills slid back his cuff for the fourth time in as many minutes and looked at his wristwatch. Roper watched him over his beer jug.

'Who d'you reckon he's waiting for?' asked Price.

'The Moffat girl,' said Roper. He sipped at his beer. 'She won't turn up.'

'You reckon?'

'I know,' said Roper, burying his nose in his jug again.

Mills drained his glass. He had at last discarded his urban terrorist's uniform and put on a smart grey suit. He looked better for it. Closer to hand, the two Cresswells faced each other across a white tablecloth like two wary fencers with their guards up; but that they were here at all, and together, surely signified something.

Not here this evening, however, were two people who perhaps for the first time in their lives could very well afford to be. Mr and Mrs González. 'For their many kindnesses', Mrs Pumfrey had had Mr Oldershaw write into her last will. William Pumfrey had been left nothing. Which, in Roper's opinion, was bush justice made flesh. During a chat in the corridor of the magistrates' court this afternoon they had told Roper that, after their spell of caretaking at Chalk House, they were going back to Spain to fulfil a lifelong ambition. And that was to buy a little boarding-house somewhere down on the Mediterranean seaboard. Roper had wished them good luck, and meant it. Both Mrs Hubert and Pumfrey had been remanded in custody pending their appearance at the Assizes next week. Mrs Hubert has stayed blasé until the very end.

He watched Mills give another anxious pluck of his grey cuff.

'What are you and your missus doing on Saturday morning, Dave?' he asked, trying to sound casual, pulling a fistful of coins from his pocket and letting a couple fall noisily on the counter to attract the barman.

'Not a lot,' said Price into his glass. 'Why?'

'I need a couple of witnesses,' said Roper, picking up his jug again. 'I'm getting married.'

'You're kidding,' said Price.

'Too serious to joke about, old son,' said Roper gravely. 'You on or not?'

'On,' said Price. 'Where?'

'Bournemouth Register Office,' said Roper, dropping another pound coin to join the two already on the counter as the barman came up. 'Ten forty-five—' He broke off and crooked a finger as he finally caught Mills' unwilling eye. '—Same again, old lad,' he said. 'And whatever the lad in the grey suit along there's drinking.'

'I thought you didn't like Mills,' said Price, as the barman went away again.

'Salving my conscience,' said Roper. 'I choked the lad off for jumping to conclusions, then went away and jumped to a few myself.'

'We *all* thought that lens was Mrs Pumfrey's,' said Price.

'That's what I mean,' said Roper. 'We shouldn't have, should we?'

'No, I suppose not,' agreed Price.

Mills came up reluctantly beside them.

'Came clean and told her you weren't a DS, did you, son?'

'Yes, sir,' said Mills. He shot his cuff again. 'I reckon she's stood me up.'

'That's life, son,' said Roper. 'Just when you think you've cracked it, back it gets on its hind legs and gives you an even bigger smack in the mouth. You eaten yet?'

'No, sir,' said Mills.

'Good.' Roper passed him a menu, then the newly arrived single whisky.

'Cheers, son,' he said, lifting his own glass.

'Cheers, sir,' said Mills.

A few yards away, suddenly and quite vividly, Mrs Cresswell smiled at her husband.

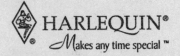

Available in November 1998 from

Never Let Her Go

by award-winning author

Gayle Wilson

The New Orleans Police Department needs to
protect injured undercover agent Nick Deandro
until he recovers his memory, so they assign
Detective Abby Sterling to be his bodyguard. Abby
has her own reasons for wanting Nick to remember.
The most important is that she is carrying his baby....

Available at your favorite retail outlet.

Lost & Found

All new...and filled with the mystery and romance you love!

SOMEBODY'S BABY
by Amanda Stevens in November 1998

A FATHER FOR HER BABY
by B. J. Daniels in December 1998

A FATHER'S LOVE
by Carla Cassidy in January 1999

It all begins one night when three women go into labor in the same Galveston, Texas, hospital. Shortly after the babies are born, fire erupts, and though each child and mother make it to safety, there's more than just the mystery of birth to solve now....

Don't miss this *all new* LOST & FOUND trilogy!

Available at your favorite retail outlet.

HARLEQUIN®
Makes any time special ™